'Arabella… Any minute now I may forget that I shouldn't be here, alone with you.'

'Please don't go.'

At that unequivocal invitation, without restraint he closed the distance between them. His arms curled around her and once again she felt the immense thrill of being held against him. She was overcome by a passionate desire to surrender herself to him.

As his lips touched hers, despite the roughness of his beard which brushed her face, a sharp intake of breath betrayed her longing for him. The force between them had grown powerful and impatient, and the longing could no longer be denied.

Author Note

The English Civil War in the seventeenth century, which saw almost ten years of conflict, upset the lives of people in England profoundly—and in ways they could not have envisaged. There were strong differences of opinion, and those loyal to the King found the concept of a country without a monarch at the head of its social order virtually unimaginable.

The war saw the execution of a king, followed by the establishment of a military dictatorship under Oliver Cromwell. It gave rise to new ideas, political and religious, but following years of repression and the death of Cromwell the people called for the monarchy to be restored.

I have always been fascinated by this time, and have chosen to focus this story on the Royalist cause, with my hero and heroine on the same side.

ROYALIST
ON THE RUN

Helen Dickson

MILLS & BOON

Published in Great Britain 2016
by Mills & Boon, an imprint of HarperCollins*Publishers*
1 London Bridge Street, London, SE1 9GF

© 2016 Helen Dickson

ISBN: 978-0-263-91718-5

Our policy is to use papers that are natural, renewable and
recyclable products and made from wood grown in sustainable
forests. The logging and manufacturing processes conform to the
legal environmental regulations of the country of origin.

Printed and bound in Spain
by CPI, Barcelona

Helen Dickson was born and still lives in South Yorkshire, with her retired farm manager husband. Having moved out of the busy farmhouse where she raised their two sons, she has more time to indulge in her favourite pastimes. She enjoys being outdoors, travelling, reading and music. An incurable romantic, she writes for pleasure. It was a love of history that drove her to writing historical fiction.

Visit the Author Profile page
at millsandboon.co.uk for more titles.

Chapter One

Arabella couldn't say if it was the children crying in the room next to hers that woke her, the hard-edged rain pelting the windowpanes that sounded like stones, or a shutter banging against a wall in the far reaches of the house.

Opening her eyes, she listened to the wind blowing and moaning like a tortured soul over the land. She prayed the shutter wouldn't blow off. And then she realised what it was that had disturbed her—the rhythmic beat of horses' hooves approaching the house.

Soldiers. Who else could it be?

Closing her eyes, with foreboding in her heart she prayed they weren't about to have a repeat of what had happened in the past, when Parliamentary soldiers had sacked the house.

'Are the vultures about to gather again?' she muttered, knowing she should pray hard and fast that it was not so, but she was too weary to do what had proved useless in the past. With her heart racing and shivering with cold, she got out of bed and went to the window and looked out. Rain was falling hard, but the moon between the swirling clouds was full and bright, illuminating the sturdy walls of this fourteenth-century manor house in the county of Gloucestershire. Four riders, Royalist soldiers—the wide-brimmed hats with swirling plumes worn by two of the men indicating this—were riding through the gatehouse. They halted in the courtyard, but for King or Parliament it made little difference. They would want feeding and there was little food at Bircot Hall to be had. The soldiers were dismounting, staring about them with a confident air.

Pulling on her dress of deep blue which she had shed earlier, one of the few dresses left to her after the Roundheads' purge of the house in search of anything worth stealing, she heard a loud persistent hammering on the stout oak doors. Wind shook the house as she hurried from her room and the darkness seemed charged with energy. Every fibre of her being was on alert. She had a throbbing in the base of her skull all the while, for there is nothing as contagious as panic.

The atmosphere of acute anxiety was rife when she arrived in the hall, with the few servants—Sam Harding, his wife, Bertha, and their son, Tom, who remained loyal—and family standing close together, all with strained eyes and drawn faces, not knowing what to expect. Even Alice's children, aware of the tension, were fretful and clinging to their mother's skirts.

Arabella looked at them, at Alice, her sister, aged beyond her thirty years by the trials and tribulations the Civil War had wrought. In the absence of Robert, Alice's husband, who had fought for the King and was now in exile in France, Alice had withstood the invasion of the Parliamentarians into her home and shown herself capable of gallantry at least equal to that of her husband. But she was weary with all that had befallen them and trying to keep her children fed.

Then there was Margaret, even tempered, calm and rational. She was Alice's twenty-year-old sister-in-law. Holding deeply religious convictions, Margaret had no desire to complicate her life with a husband and children, preferring to devote herself to her family and to prayer. It would take more than the Civil War to break Margaret's composure and her faith in God. But Alice had told Arabella that she was not totally convinced by her sister-in-law's convictions. Margaret had led a sheltered existence for most of her life and Alice held a firm belief that Margaret would eventually succumb to the male sex when the war was over and the world was opened up to her.

Sam, an old and faithful retainer, glanced anxiously at Arabella.

'Shall I open the door?'

Arabella looked at Alice, who nodded, trying to calm her three children. 'I think you should, Sam,' Arabella said, 'and then maybe you should build up the fire. We cannot begin by offending them. Better to placate them—although being Royalist troops, they are not our enemy.'

When Sam had drawn back the bolts and opened the door, an officer strode briskly into the hall with his high, leather, silver-spurred boots ringing on the stone flags. The gust of frigid air was not much of a shock compared to the man standing there. Arabella stared at him, feeling something dark pass through her, like a cloud heralding a storm. Beads of rain clung to his eyebrows. Having removed the wide-brimmed hat from his head, with his long riding cloak hanging from his shoulders, a sword at his hip and the long dark hair curling about his ears, he had a dark, satanic look.

He was tall, his hair catching the glow from the few beeswax candles in wall sconces, which did little to lighten the gloom of the hall with its walls of dark-oak panelling. He was clean shaven, his skin swarthy, his face with its sharp cheekbones slashed with eyebrows more accustomed to frowning than smiling, which he was doing now. His mouth was hard and firm, the chin beneath it square, tense and with an arrogant thrust.

He was totally unconscious of himself or the effect he might produce on those gathered in the hall. Behind him came two of his men. His gaze passed over the inhabitants, as if searching for something—someone.

Arabella's shock at the sight of him showed in sudden startling contrast, as her skin blanched, her eyes darkened and she put a hand to her throat as though it had become constricted. The room seemed to shrink around her.

Unaware of the stir he was causing in the young woman's breast, he halted in front of the small group of habitants. He inclined his head slightly, not with anything which might be called humility, and his voice rang out in the vaulted hall.

'I am Colonel Sir Edward Grey of His Majesty's army.'

All Arabella could do was stare at Edward Grey, a man to whom she had been pledged when she was nine years old by their respective parents. At seventeen years of age, Edward had agreed to the contract, but as a man of five and twenty he'd been less interested to consider courtship and marriage to seventeen-year-old Arabella. After three years of war and the onset of fresh hostilities between King and Parliament, and Edward Grey's infatuation with another woman, he renounced the requirements of the contract he had made with her father. Arabella would have found his breaking of their betrothal less painful had he not been so handsome—and in maturity, leaner, taller and more virile, he was far more so.

As a child she had adored him. He had been the hero of her girlish fantasies, in every way her shining knight. He had made her child's heart pine for want of him, and on reaching seventeen she was sure she was in love with him. She recalled the nights she had lain in her bed unable to believe how lucky she was and, when the war came and he went to fight, she had been unable to endure the thought of his being wounded in battle.

When he cast her over the world had become a darker place. It had been five years since she had last seen him. Despite the war and all its hardships he was little changed. There was still the same masterful face and he had not lost his aura of pride. It was in his stance, in his bearing and in his eyes as they passed over those gathered. Neither time nor war, it seemed, had any power over Edward Grey.

Arabella had followed his exploits over the years, of how as a quick-thinking and energetic cavalry officer his bravery and confident attitude kept up the morale of his troops. His victories were much talked about and tales of his exploits, true or false, believed by all who listened to them.

She had thought of him often in the past and now he had thrust himself, a solid, real presence, into her future. She felt the trembling in her knees quivering up her thighs and into her stomach. She would faint in a minute if she didn't get a hold of herself, but still she stood, enduring a cold and sickening shock. She experienced anger, outrage, bitterness, all the strong emotions which stiffened her spine. How dare he come here? How dare he insinuate himself into her presence after the callous manner in which he had treated her in the past?

Colonel! So, he had been promoted. He wore his new position well.

Taking a deep breath, she tried to think clearly. 'I know who you are,' she said quietly but firmly, moving slowly out of the shadows towards him. 'Do you not recognise me, Edward?'

He stiffened, brought up sharp by her words. He suddenly swung his gaze to her and held her in the dark-blue depths, his eyes narrowing in masculine predatory appreciation. Suddenly she was the captive of those fathomless dark-blue eyes and, while doubtless those around them went on breathing, Arabella felt as if she and this man were alone in the world. She felt as if something inside her had moved, subtly but emphatically.

Recognition dawned and he took a step forward, a puzzled frown creasing his brow. 'Arabella?'

Staring into those enigmatic blue eyes that had ensnared her own, Arabella felt as if she were being swept back in time. 'Have I changed so much?'

The tantalising lines in his cheeks deepened as he offered her a smile that seemed every bit as welcoming and persuasive as it had once been. 'You are—changed. Forgive me. It is you I seek. I was told I would find you here.'

Arabella stared at him. After all they had once meant to each other, when he had come to her home and they had walked and talked together, she had thought she was the most important thing in the world to him. When he had talked about the future they would have, how rosy that future had seemed to them both. And now, didn't that past camaraderie allow them more than the stilted decorum of strangers?

For years she had imagined what it would be like if they should meet again, how she would spurn him as he had spurned her, yet now her heart beat a gentle tattoo in her breast like a besotted maid. She did not know whether to be angry, relieved or disappointed that he had sought her out, after all this time, but she suspected that whatever it was that had brought him did not bode well for the future.

A wry smile curled her lips and when she spoke her voice was noticeably lacking in warmth, conveying to him that she still bore a grudge, that she had not forgotten what he had done to her.

'But you did not recognise me. It's hardly flattering, though not surprising. Five years is a long time and much has changed. You have seen Stephen?' she asked, eager for news of her brother, who had fought side by side with Edward Grey throughout the years of war.

He nodded. Tossing his hat and cloak on to a

chair, he came to where she stood apart from the rest. He towered over her, but she was fearless.

'He told me where I would find you. He is to join me—within hours, if everything goes well.'

Arabella's heart lifted with joy. 'Stephen is to come here?' She looked at Alice. 'That is good news, is it not, Alice?'

Trying to soothe her four-year-old daughter Nanette, Alice nodded, her eyes filled with gladness.

Edward's gaze swept Arabella from top to toe. He lifted a dark winged brow and a faint smile touched his lips.

'Look at you. You've no flesh on you.'

Turning from her, he went to the hearth where he stood, warming his hands. The logs Sam had fed into the fire sizzled as the flames ate into them.

'Times are hard,' she returned coldly, offended by his glib comment, but determined not to show it. 'Rations are scarce and have been for many months. Look around you. You see how things are here. You are looking at a sacked house and starvation.'

He frowned, his expression showing his concern. 'You have had trouble?'

'We did have some uninvited guests, yes,' she replied drily.

'You have no men to protect you?'

'Only a handful of servants—however ill equipped—and you have seen the house. It offers no defence against a hostile army.'

He looked at her hard. 'And you? Did they harm you?' She bit her lip. 'Come now. This is war, Arabella, and I know well the atrocities done to women by the hands of a triumphant enemy.'

'No—they left us alone. You were a captain when we parted company and now you are a colonel. I have nothing to say against your appointment, but if you have come here to commandeer livestock and foodstuffs with which to feed your army, insisting that military necessities come first, then you are going to be disappointed.'

'That is not why I am here, and there are only four of us—five when your brother gets here. What happened here?'

'Some months ago the Roundheads took over the house. Their behaviour was indefensible. The soldiers were quite out of control. Despite their puritan tendencies and without the steadying presence of proper leadership, the majority of them were drunk from dawn to dusk. Our Parliamentary brethren are not all as pious as they would have us believe.'

'Were any of you molested in any way?'

Arabella shook her head. This was a conversation he should be having with Alice, but her sister was still trying to console Nanette, who was crying and clearly afraid of the fearsome-looking men who had burst into her home.

'We were unharmed, but the war goes on and we live in constant dread that it will happen again. The Roundheads were here for four weeks. As you see they did not treat us or the house well. Doors were broken down, panelling ripped from the walls as they searched for places of concealment, hoping to find Royalists evading capture. Horses, sheep and cattle and all other livestock were rounded up along with the deer in the park. The granaries were emptied—along with cellars of ale and wine. It will be a long time before the land gives a return.'

Arabella looked beyond him to the door where a young woman had entered and, perched on her hip, she held a child. The infant, a boy, was about two years old. He hid his face in the woman's shoulder, his thumb firmly in his mouth, seemingly afraid to look about him, to be curious as small children are. Puzzled, she looked from the child to Edward.

'Who is this? Whose child is he?'

Edward beckoned the young woman forward.

'Dickon is my son, Arabella. This is Joan, his nurse.'

Arabella dragged the air into her tortured lungs, fighting for control, and as she did so the boy lifted his head and his thumb plopped from his mouth. Turning his head, he looked directly at her. She was unprepared for the pain that twisted her heart. It was like looking at Edward. The boy had the same startling blue eyes framed with long black lashes. His hair was dark, the curls framing his exquisite face. She could not tear her eyes away from him. Even at so young an age he had the same arrogant way of holding his head as his father, the same jut of his chin. Yet there was a distress in him, an anxiety that was unusual for one so young.

Tearing her eyes away from the boy, she fixed them on his father. 'I heard that your wife died, Edward.' So deeply had Arabella loathed the woman Edward had married that even though she had died the bitterness Arabella held still remained and she would choke if she allowed her name to pass her lips.

'Yes. Anne died shortly after giving birth to Dickon,' Edward uttered, his voice flat.

She stared at him, searching for an emotion that would tell her how he grieved the loss of his wife. But there was nothing. 'I am sorry for your loss.' Her voice was as emotionless as his had been, but she could not pretend to emotions she did not feel.

'And I for yours. Your husband was killed during the battle at St Fagans, I believe.'

Her expression tightened on being reminded of John Fairburn. His body had been brought back home in a coffin for burial. Having no wish to look on John's dead body and being told he had been so badly wounded she wouldn't recognise him anyway, she had buried him with the rest of his ancestors in the churchyard.

'Yes. I am a widow—but that is none of your concern. Whatever the reason for your being here, I want you to know you are not welcome. You and I have lived our separate lives for a long time now and I would like it to remain that way. When you married Anne Lister you severed all ties between us.' The expression on his face seemed to tell her that nothing she might do or say could reach him.

'I will, of course, do as you wish, Arabella, and leave when Stephen gets here, but it is also imperative that I find a temporary home for my child.'

Arabella began to shake her head from side to side, for it was beginning to penetrate into her dazed mind what he had in his.

'You cannot mean that you expect me to…' Her expression was appalled. 'No—no, I will not. How can you ask this of me? Have you not done enough to…humiliate me in the past? You cannot, in all conscience expect me to—to take him in.'

'There is nowhere else, Bella—nowhere that is safe—no one else I can trust.'

Bella! He had called her Bella! No one else had called her that since he… Angrily she thrust such sentimental thoughts from her. 'There has to be. You have a sister—Verity. Surely…'

'With England under the rule of Parliament, Verity and her family have sought exile in France.'

'Then why didn't they take your son with them?'

'I was too late.'

'But why me? Why bring him to me?'

'I have need of an ally in whom I can place complete trust. I sought you out because I thought that person might be you. There is a heavy price on my head. To lay their hands on my son would be a coup indeed for the Parliamentarians. Already the homes of my family and my estate in Oxfordshire have been invaded and torn apart by Parliament's search for me and my son.'

'And what of *our* safety?' she demanded, her eyes burning with righteous anger that he could demand this of her. 'By coming to this house you have endangered us all. To give succour to your son would count as treason to Parliament. They would hang us all.'

'Not if you were to pass him off as your own should the need arise.'

Appalled, Arabella stared at him. 'You ask this of me?' she gasped. 'Have you no heart? I had a child, too, Edward—a daughter.' Tears pricked her eyes and her throat drew tight as she thought of her own dead daughter. 'She was called Elizabeth. She died of a fever just one year after I received news of my husband's death.'

'I am truly grieved to hear that,' Edward said, compassion tearing through him. 'Stephen told me about your daughter.'

'Did he indeed? I am only surprised you remembered I existed at all. And now you come here and dare to ask me—a woman you have not seen in five years, a woman you had so little care for you broke our betrothal—to pass your son off as my own?' Her words carried with them all the raw emotion she felt over the death of her child.

Her words brought a look of pain to his eyes.

'You are wrong, Arabella. I did care for you—deeply. I must confess that my conduct towards you at the time has been a cause of enormous regret for me and I hope that my manners have improved over the years.'

Arabella was outraged, her eyes burning. 'I wouldn't know anything about that, but I suppose because you believe you have acquired some manners, you thought it would be all right to come here when my brother suggested it. How dare you presume! How dare you think you could do that to me—to place me in such an impossible position?'

'I do realise the gravity of the situation. It was not my intention to cause you hurt, Arabella.'

Arabella's emotions came rushing to the surface and the anguish of the last few unhappy years were released in one sweeping moment. 'I don't care. The answer is no. How can you do this to me—to ask me to take care of your child when I am still grieving for my own? I am not made of stone. How can you put me in a position where I must turn a child from the house?' she cried with unutterable sorrow, deliberately not allowing her gaze to fall on the child in the woman's arms. 'But I must. I really cannot possibly… I cannot allow your child into my life…after what I have suffered—after what you did…'

'I am sorry.'

'You are *sorry*? Being sorry is not enough.'

His audacity took the breath from her body. She wanted to shout at him, to express all the heartbreak, pain, anger and the hatred and jealousy his alliance and marriage to Anne Lister had caused her. She prided herself on her calm dignity, her upright head and steadfast refusal to allow him to see how much he had tortured her spirit and her flesh. She would not, but she would dearly like to shout to the world of her outrage, her bitterness and revulsion at the idea and his nerve in bringing his child, Anne Lister's child, into what she now considered to be her home. The loss of her daughter was with her for ever. In her sleep she dreamed of her. She would awaken with wet eyes, her face tearstained.

'Dickon is my *son*, Arabella,' Edward said, a fierce light in his eyes. 'I have to make sure that he is safe.'

'Why? Is there to be more strife? Is that what brought you here?'

She knew this must be true since there had been a shifting of troops towards the west for some time now. Sam told of the Parliament

army moving in great swathes towards the
River Severn, with oxen and carts pulling canon
and laden with deadly loads of powder kegs. Everyone was thankful they didn't come within
distance of Bircot Hall.

'It is likely. I am to join the King's army. Malcolm Lister will not rest until he has my son in
his clutches.'

Arabella stared at him, understanding at last
why he was so desperate for her to care for his
son. 'So the two of you are still at loggerheads.'
She remembered Anne Lister's brother. She had
never liked him. There was a slipperiness about
him and he possessed a streak of ruthlessness
and an iron control that was chilling. Because
Edward was a King's man he had done his utmost to prevent him marrying his sister, but
Anne had been determined. 'I thought war
would make a good substitute for private quarrels. You are a wanted man. You have put us all
in grave danger by coming here.'

'There was nothing else I could do. I will
not surrender to them. Malcolm Lister knows
that, which is why he will use my son, knowing he is the only reason I would give myself
up to Parliament.'

'Malcolm Lister is your brother-in-law. He
would not hurt his nephew.'

'I sincerely hope not. He married in the summer before the King raised his standard at Nottingham, all of nine years ago. It appears that his wife is unable to bear him a child so he has focused on Dickon. He hates the thought of him growing up a Royalist. As siblings Malcolm and Anne were close—he adored her and, for that reason and because of my allegiance to King Charles, he never forgave me for marrying her. He harbours some burning desire for revenge. He would take Dickon from me if he could and see me hanged. Do I have to remind you that the man is a Parliamentarian?'

Without another word he turned on his heel to speak to the two men who accompanied him, his long legs eating up the ground with each stride. Arabella thought she never knew of any other man who could in so short a time fill a room with his presence and become the master of a house as if he owned every stick and stone of it.

Arabella saw he had grown more worn, his face lined—the result of the endless anxieties that pressed upon him, but it was all still there: his self-assurance, his arrogance, his strength and his overbearing will which would let none cross him. There was still the twist to his strong mouth, that powerful, passionate certainty that though Edward Grey might be against the rest of the world, the fault was theirs, not his.

Having deliberately refrained from looking at Edward's son, Arabella now looked at the woman holding the boy. She was young with dark hair and a wide mouth. While she was hardly a beauty, she had a wholesome look. She also looked weary, the child heavy in her arms. Her unease on trying to hold on to the boy was evident. His gaze was steady and grave, although his rosy mouth trembled with tears that were not far away.

Nanette's tears had ceased and Alice seemed to take hold of herself. She spoke to Margaret. 'Will you take Joan upstairs, Margaret—and see what you can find in the way of a bed and some food for her and the child? They must be tired and hungry.'

'Thank you,' Joan uttered, her voice soft and strained. 'We've been travelling all day. Something to eat and somewhere to lay the child would be welcome.'

'Sir Edward,' Alice said when he returned to them. 'I am Alice, Stephen and Arabella's elder sister. I can understand if you don't remember me—it has been a long time.'

'Of course I remember you,' he said, taking her hand and raising it to his lips. 'How could I forget? Our families were close before the war. When you visited your father in London, you were always welcoming and charming as I recall.'

'It's kind of you to say so. I bid you welcome to Bircot Hall.'

Arabella bristled at her sister's words. Edward Grey had destroyed her trust once, she was not so hasty to invoke such favour for a man whose motives she could not discern.

'I am sorry that you see my home in a state of turmoil.' Alice's eyes shone with tears, but she did not acknowledge their presence. 'Without our menfolk, as my sister explained, we have suffered greatly at the hands of the Parliamentarians. We have had several Roundhead patrols since. Mercifully they left us alone, but that does not guarantee that they will the next time. Robert, my husband, holds you in high esteem. It is indeed an honour to have you in our home.'

Edward inclined his head. 'Thank you. Your hospitality is greatly appreciated.'

Arabella almost choked on the words that rose and stuck in her throat. How could Alice betray her when he had treated her, Arabella, so badly?

As if sensing her anger, Alice gave her a look

of reproof. 'Calm yourself, Arabella. This is war and no time for private feuds.'

So chastened, though unable to conceal the resentment she continued to feel for Edward Grey—a resentment that increased when she observed the amused twitch to his lips—Arabella dutifully clamped her own together.

'We have had no news of my husband for months, Sir Edward,' Alice said. 'All I know is that he is in France.'

'I am sorry I cannot help you, Lady Stanhope, but if he is in France then he will be safe.'

'I thank God for that. It will be good to see Stephen again. If you are to stay overnight, the stables are at your disposal,' Arabella was quick to say. 'At least they are warm and dry.'

'Arabella, where are your manners?' Alice chided her once more. 'Sir Edward and those with him are our guests. The house may be in a sorry state, but it has more rooms than we know what to do with.' She smiled at Edward. 'They are at your disposal. Now please excuse me. I will arrange for them to be made ready. The hour is late and I must put the children to bed.'

Having removed his cloak, Arabella gasped when she saw a dark stain on Edward's jacket.

'You are wounded.'

'I received a sword thrust in the shoulder during a skirmish with a small band of Roundheads on the way here. They were spoiling for a fight. Fortunately we fought them off—although Stephen held back to make quite sure we weren't followed. It's a common enough wound. One of the men dressed it, but it continues to bleed.'

'Come with me and I will tend to it,' she said curtly.

Taking up a candle, she walked across the hall to the kitchens, through which the still room was located. It was where Alice liked to mix her own remedies. Arabella often helped her. It was clean and quiet and fragrant with summer smells of thyme, rosemary and lavender, berries and seeds, and herbs that were readily available in the hedgerows.

Glad of the opportunity to speak with her alone, Edward followed her. Her skirts swayed gently as she walked and the line of her back was straight and graceful. Removing his jacket, his sling and his sword, he slipped his arm out of his shirt sleeve to expose the not-so-clean bandage covering his injured shoulder. Sitting on a stool, he waited for her to proceed.

Trying to barricade herself behind a mask of composure as she held up the candle, Arabella's gaze was reluctantly drawn to his exposed flesh. Lighting two more candles better to see, carefully she cut away the blood-soaked bandage. His bare, muscled arm and shoulder gleamed in the soft light. It was excruciatingly intimate to touch his flesh. It was warm and firm. He was strong, sleek but not gaunt, all sinew and strength, his muscles solid where her fingers touched.

Forcing herself not to think about his manly physique and to focus on the raw wound, which drove such thoughts away, she inspected it carefully. It looked angry, a thin trickle of blood oozing from the lacerated flesh. Tentatively she felt the surrounding tissue with her finger. He winced. It was obviously painful to the touch.

'The wound appears to be quite deep. It has to be cleaned. You say it happened earlier today?'

'Hopefully it won't have had time to fester.' Watching her as she lit more candles, filled a bowl with water and gathered cloths with which to wash the wound, he said, 'You have changed, Arabella.'

'War does that to people,' she answered, her manner brusque as she proceeded to clean the wound, her pale hands working quickly and efficiently.

'I am sorry you've had to endure its hardships.'

She shot him a look. 'Why? You did not start the war.'

When she began to wash the wound his expression tightened and he gritted his teeth. Her heart wrenched, having no wish to cause him more pain. Yet she was quietly pleased by the sight and it gave her some satisfaction of him being less that formidable.

'How long have you been at Bircot Hall?' he asked.

'Two years now. We really are quite impoverished. We have managed to put some of the house back to some kind of order. The property will be restored later, when it can be afforded—when the war is over. We hope it will be soon—although when King Charles was executed we thought it was the end of Royalist hopes.'

'Not when the Scots proclaimed his son King of Great Britain and after Cromwell routed the Royalists at Dunbar.'

'You were there?'

Edward nodded, as memories of that bloody battle slashed like a blade through his mind's eyes. 'I was there. I was one of the lucky ones. I managed to escape over the border and back into England, where I made my way south.'

'We have heard that King Charles is heading south with a Scottish army. Is this true?'

He nodded, avoiding her gaze. 'It is. I will join him when I know Dickon is safe.'

There was a stillness in the air, a foreboding that sent a cold shiver down her spine. 'I can't bear to think there is to be more fighting.'

'We are all weary of it. There have been times when we were defeated, but we are not destroyed.'

'And new plots are being devised to continue the fight every day. If you are killed? What then?'

'If you agree to let Dickon remain here for the time being, should the Royalists be defeated, then I would ask you to take Dickon to my sister in France.'

'I see.' Pausing in her task, she cast him a wry glance. 'Your audacity knows no bounds. You ask too much of me, Edward.'

He met her gaze steadily. 'I know. I am desperate, Arabella,' he said softly. 'My property has been confiscated. My son is all I have left. I have to know that he is safe. The war will end—but not as you or I would like. The way Cromwell has trained his army is something else. Never in England, until now, has there been an army like it. For the first time soldiers are properly trained. They proved how well at Dunbar.'

Looking into his eyes, she saw there were

haunted shadows and she guessed that, like every other soldier who had survived, the ugliness of the wars had left lasting scars on his mind. 'So—what are you saying? That there is no hope?'

'Unless the King can produce a miracle, the cause is doomed.'

'I fear we are all doomed whatever the outcome.'

'You sound bitter, Arabella.'

She gave him a cold look. 'Bitter? I remember those months after Marston Moor, when everyone thought the war must end. It seemed impossible then that it would start up again. How soon they were to be proved wrong. And now look at me. My husband is dead—along with our child. My father was killed at Naseby and my brother is preparing to prolong the fight. I have no home to call my own and I have been forced to throw myself on my sister's charity, whose house has been violated by men who care nothing for the cause but only for what they can plunder from the homes of decent people without respect to their persons. Yes, Edward, I am bitter. Bitter that there are those not satisfied and continue to stir up the ugly storm of war, determined to drag it out to the bitter end.'

'No corner of England has remained untouched by the evils of war, Arabella. In every shire and every town, families have been divided and much blood spilled. With the failure to find a political solution all England is in confusion. Many remain loyal to the king.'

'As a man or as a symbol?'

'The latter, I think. When the end comes there will be no recovery.'

'King or Parliament—it's not as if war decides who is right—only who has the power to rule.'

'I fear you are right. Royalists are fleeing in their hundreds to the Continent like rats deserting the sinking ship.'

'If they loved their homes more, they would stay behind and share the burdens of defeat with their womenfolk.'

Edward was silent while she wrung a bloodied cloth out in the bowl of water, then, 'Do you bear malice toward me—for what happened between us?'

'Malice?'

Briefly Arabella closed her eyes. It was painful to recount such memories, especially when she had become so accustomed to burying them—or trying, for no matter how hard she had tried she had not succeeded. Secretly she had missed him more than she would have be-

lieved possible, for how could she ever forget
how volatile, mercurial and rakishly good looking this man was?

She recalled the pain she had felt when told
he had renounced their betrothal, the horror and
humiliation of it. She had promised herself that
never again would she allow herself to be so
treated.

Reaching deep inside herself, she pushed
thoughts of his rejection of her away. Thinking
like this served no purpose. There was nothing to be gained from these haunting thoughts.
Shaking the shroud of the past from her, she
set herself firmly to this one task of tending
his wound. Besides, she had other matters on
which she must focus now—his child and what
she was going to do about him.

'Why should I bear malice? I can understand
it must be a grim prospect indeed for a man who
is compelled to exchange marriage vows with
an unappealing woman merely to satisfy his
family. You wanted Anne Lister, I knew that.
Despite her family being for Parliament, the
moment you were introduced you were smit-
ten by her.'

He nodded gravely. 'That I cannot deny.'

'You merely married the woman of your
choice.'

'Aye. And look how that turned out,' he replied, his lips twisting bitterly, seated on the stool at the side of the table.

'I heard and I am sorry.'

'Are you, Arabella?'

'I believe she left you.'

'After eight months of marriage she went back to live with her brother—her father having been killed at the beginning of the war.'

'I—also heard that she wanted some kind of judicial separation.'

'She was carrying my child. I refused to give her one.'

Lowering her eyes, Arabella wondered how he had felt when his wife told him she wanted to leave him. Had Anne's rejection of him hurt him as much as he had hurt her, Arabella, when he shattered all her hopes and dreams?

'If she had not been with child, would you have let her go?'

He nodded. 'I would not have kept her with me against her will. She was not like you, Arabella. Commitment was not much in her thoughts when she married me.' He studied her face closely. 'I should not say this, I know, but I did miss you when we parted.'

'No, Edward, you should not. You left and for me nothing was the same any more. What we have to share is no more than a distant memory, as old and useless as the lame nag the Round-heads left behind.'

'I hurt you.'

'You made a promise you did not keep.'

'No, Arabella. My parents made a promise on my behalf. As yours did.'

'That does not alter the fact that you let me down. I got on with my life when you married Anne Lister. I believe the wedding was held in the presence of the King.'

She smiled thinly, remembering how beautiful Anne had been. The Listers had been known to Arabella's family, but because of the Listers' allegiance to Parliament they were never friends. As the only daughter of doting parents and the sister of three adoring elder brothers—two of whom had lost their lives at Naseby—Anne had been spoiled and indulged all her life. She harmed everything she touched. With a sly look and a mere inflection of her voice she could cause pain to the happiest of hearts.

Arabella had often asked herself why Anne was like she was, inflicting cruelty for its own sake, taking a sensuous delight in seeing an-other's pain. Arabella could see her now—those slanting green eyes beneath the brown hair, that hard, red-lipped mouth. It seemed incredible to

Arabella that anyone could have been deceived by her. Yet her power to charm had been overwhelming. People fell under her spell like skittles knocked over.

But Arabella had not been taken in, not for a moment. The moment they had laid eyes on each other, both of them had been aware of a mutual hostility. It hadn't mattered to her one iota that Edward was a King's man—indeed, she had preferred the rich trappings of royalty than the spartan, puritanical way of life her family tried to force on her.

But Anne would have none of it. She had been determined to have Edward and married him without her brother Malcolm's consent when he was away with his regiment. Once she had what she wanted she flaunted herself shamelessly when in the company of Edward's friends. Edward's appeal was diminished and she was entirely without mercy. Their heated quarrels were notorious and it was no secret that Anne had begun to look elsewhere for her pleasure.

'Anne had a large inheritance from her mother,' Arabella went on. 'So, yes, Edward, you married well. When you ended our engagement when the first conflict was over, like many more Royalists who had no intention of abandoning the cause, you needed funds to raise a troop of horses. You would have been a fool if you had let her slip from you and didn't seize her fortune for yourself.'

His face hardened. 'You think I am that mercenary?'

'You gave me no reason to think otherwise.'

'However you interpret it, it served my purpose. At the time the whole future of England was at stake. Desperate means called for desperate measures.'

'Are you saying you didn't love your wife?' she ventured pointedly.

'I thought I did. I was wrong and you were right. I needed money. Emotions did not count.'

'Emotions, but not honour. Your actions were not exactly subtle and did you no credit in my eyes.'

He looked at her for a long considered moment before saying, 'You are a different person, Arabella. I feel I am meeting you for the first time.'

'And do you approve?'

'I approved before—however badly I behaved towards you.'

'Then why did you leave me?' She looked at him steadily as she waited for him to answer, yet not wanting to hear it. 'Please don't tell me.

I knew Anne. She was very beautiful—and exciting. No man could resist her. You were no exception—and I was very young and inexperienced in the ways of the world.'

'But now you are a woman.'

'I had to grow up quickly when I married John.'

'Were you not happy with John Fairburn?'

'Marriage is not always what we expect.' More than that she would not say, but with her head bent over her task so he could not see her face, she thought of silent meals, of the brutality she had been forced to endure in her cold bed, of John constantly chastising her for any transgression, however small, and she said nothing.

'After John died followed so soon by our home being sacked and burned when the Roundheads came calling, with Stephen away and London being an unsafe place to be, I came to Alice.' He was watching her intently. Arabella could feel the heat of his gaze burning through the fabric of her dress. 'I shall be a while longer,' she said, struggling to sound casual and unconcerned. 'Are you comfortable?'

'Perfectly.'

She jumped at the sound of his voice so close to her ear. Her eyebrows sloped gently above her eyes and furrowed slightly as she continued to clean away the dried-on blood from around the wound. Her hair fell across her eyes in such a way as to provide a drape from his penetrating gaze that so disturbed her.

'Please put your head to one side. This is very precise work.' She was finding it difficult to concentrate with him so close, close enough for her to breathe in the smell of his skin.

'Is it in your way?'

'Yes, it is. It's blocking the light.'

He tilted his head back. 'Is this enough? Can you see now?'

'It's fine.'

The cold of the still room was welcoming, but it could not keep pace with the heat building up inside Arabella's body. She had not seen him for five years. She should be immune to him by now and it angered her to know he still had the power to stir her deepest emotions.

She remembered how, before he had ended their betrothal, he had teased her and playfully tugged her hair as though she were still a child, unaware how her blood thrummed in her veins and her heart beat quickened in her breast, as she yearned for him to look at her the way he looked at Anne Lister.

Chapter Two

Edward noticed how Arabella gnawed her bottom lip with her small white teeth as she became absorbed in her task. With her head bent he wanted to place his hand on it, to feel her warmth, to touch her skin. He wanted to ask her more about her life. He saw something different about her, something that had not been there before. It was a look that comes with maturity and suffering.

Suddenly she looked up and a pair of velvet amber eyes met his. They wrenched his heart for they were filled with sadness and soul-searching vulnerability that spoke of her loss and made him wonder just how deeply the ugliness of war had affected her. No one was immune to the loss of loved ones, but to see it on one so young affected him deeply.

Had she found happiness in her marriage?

Her brief reply to his question told him she had not. Edward had never met John Fairburn, but he had the impression from others that he was not a likable man and harsh in his treatment of others. When Arabella had spoken about the death of her daughter he had seen a look of total desolation in her eyes. It was the sort of look that could break even the hardest heart. It had taken everything in him to stop his hand reaching out to her, to tell her again how sorry he was for her loss but, all things taken into account, it was wiser to sit still while she tended his wound—and watch and listen to her breathe.

He couldn't believe how changed she was. The awkwardness had gone and even though she was as slim as a willow sapling, she was the most stunning creature he had seen in a long time. No matter how his eyes searched her face and form, he could not find that gangling girl from before they were betrothed, who had hid behind her mother's skirts and skittered shyly away when he approached.

In the past, of course he had seen her, been aware of her, had always enjoyed her company once she had lost her shyness of him, but he had never really looked at her, not properly, not deeply, as he was doing now. But he had not forgotten how bright her eyes were, how soft

and generous her mouth and the small, tantalising indentation in her round chin. Nor had
he forgotten the softness of her heart, her gen-
uine warmth, and the trust he had seen in her
eyes when she had looked at him. They were
the things he had remembered when, in his desperation to find somewhere safe for Dickon, he
had thought of Arabella. Dickon was the most
important person in his life. He would sacrifice
or endure anything for his son.

Even after everything that had happened in
the past, he knew she was the one person he
could trust with his son.

From the moment he'd recognised her in the
hall, he'd found her nearly impossible to keep
from openly staring. Her red-gold hair tumbled
freely about her shoulders, a shining, flaming
glory to the torch that was her beauty. Her amber
eyes had called to him. Her smooth, creamy
skin, glowing beneath the softness of candlelight, beckoned his fingers to touch and caress.

Edward, wallowing in his own misery over
his failed marriage to Anne, didn't know why
it should be, but when he had heard of her
marriage the thought of Arabella in the arms
of another man had made his gut twist. That
was when he felt the impact of the mistake he
had made.

At the time Anne had seduced him with her beauty and her body. She was exciting, enticing and their coming together had been as swift and as wild as a summer storm, their impulsive wedding the act of a desperate man. He had been unable to resist her. But happiness had eluded him. Just two months into their marriage their passion had burned itself out. He'd known her body, but he'd never managed to touch her soul. Nothing had prepared him for the shame or the pain at her subsequent betrayal.

Meeting Arabella after five years, who would have thought that she would have grown to such beauty? Normally self-assured, strong and powerful, Edward felt a certain unease at the way she made him feel off balance and hungry for something he couldn't put a name to. She stirred something in his soul, a sense of wonder and yearning that he'd forgotten was possible. The hunger was soul deep and it scared him.

Arabella stood back. 'There, it is done. The wound will leave a scar, but it should not trouble you much.'

'Damn the wound. What about us?' His words were impulsive, spoken in the heat of his roiling emotions and without thought.

She met his gaze levelly, cool, composed and in complete control of the emotions raging inside. 'Us, Edward? How dare you suggest such a thing? I am no longer that awkward, sensitive girl you knew. I have changed. We both have. You made your choice five years ago, and if you were any sort of a gentleman you would leave me in peace.'

'Come now, Arabella. The prospect has a certain allure, you must agree.'

'I am sure you find allure in most things, Edward—and most women.'

'You accuse me unjustly. I only ask that you do not block your heart against me.'

She stared at him across the distance that separated them, a multitude of desires hanging in the air, a multitude of doubts filling the chasm between them. How could she believe him? How could she believe anything he said? She did not trust this intimacy—it was her own response to it that she feared the most.

'My heart is my affair, Edward. But where we are concerned, I advise you to look elsewhere.'

Turning on her heel, she swept from the room.

Returning to the hall, Arabella felt her spirits lift considerably when she saw that her beloved brother Stephen had arrived. Her face broke into a wide smile as she ran into his arms and felt his close about her.

'Oh, Stephen!' she said laughingly, drawing back and looking up into his familiar face. 'I cannot tell you how delighted I am to see you again. It has been too long. Far too long.'

It was three years since last she had seen him and she observed how those years had taken their toll. Of medium height and with light brown hair that fell to his shoulders, he was leaner than she remembered, his eyes not so merry as they had once been and his face lined with worry. But with a moustache and small beard in the style of the executed King Charles, he was still a handsome man.

'It has, Arabella.' He studied her closely, his eyes tender. 'How are you?'

She smiled gently. 'Things could be better, but we get by.'

'And you have suffered much.'

'Yes, but I had Alice to help me through it and I've had much to occupy my time here. Have you seen Alice?'

'Not yet. She's settling the children. Thank God when the Bircot estate was sequestered she was allowed to continue living here and receive a percentage of the income. I gather this is the case with many of the wives of men who fought for the King and continue to support the cause.'

'That is true, but as you will recall she had to

go to London to plead for it personally before the committee concerned at the Goldsmiths' Hall. Robert may have fought on the King's side, but wherever Alice's sympathies are directed, she did not. She has done no wrong and cannot be held responsible for what he did—there can be no guilt by association.'

'We must be thankful for that.'

'There have been times when she has been quite desperate.'

'She is not alone. The taxes and fines imposed upon anyone who supported the king are extortionate. Is she able to pay them?'

'Yes. I was able to help her there. John's lawyer managed to save a small property he owned in Bath from sequestration. When I came to live with Alice and the fines on Bircot rose to such a degree that she could not pay them, I sold the house in Worcester to help.'

'That was indeed generous of you, Arabella. But when your husband's house was destroyed in Wales, why did you not go to Bath and live there?'

'I had a child to care for. Alice suggested I come to Bircot. Having no wish to live by myself, I agreed. Alice wrote, telling you that the Roundheads were encamped at Bircot and took almost everything we had. There was also an incident when Alice and the children would have been turned out and the house occupied by a Roundhead officer had smallpox not been rife in the area. One of her children was ill with a fever at the time. Mercifully it turned out not to be smallpox, but Alice did not enlighten the Roundhead intent on taking up residence at Bircot Hall and casting her out. For this reason she was allowed to remain in the house and he left with great haste.'

'Has she talked about going to join Robert in France?'

'Of course she would dearly love to join him, but it's likely they would lose the house and land were she to do that. She finds it hard. Separation from her husband adds a further distressing element to her life.'

'Poor Alice. I hope it is soon over and some form of order returns to England so those in exile can return.' He glanced around the hall. 'Where is Edward? You have spoken to him?'

Arabella's expression became cool. 'I have just been tending his wound in the still room. No doubt he will appear when he's donned his shirt.'

Stephen glanced at her sullen features. 'I am sorry, Arabella. I know what you must be thinking, but I had no choice but to bring him here. Do you still bear him ill will?'

She nodded. 'Yes, I suppose I do, but it doesn't matter any more. Too much has happened to me in the last five years to spare a thought for Edward Grey.'

Stephen studied her serious face, unconvinced by her remark. 'Marriage to John was not an easy time for you, was it, Arabella?'

'No,' she answered, seeing no reason to hide the truth from Stephen, who had known what John was like. 'But he is dead now and he can't hurt me any more.'

'I blame myself. I was the one who brought him to our home. Had I known Father would seize upon the opportunity to marry you off to him, I would not have done so.'

'You have nothing to blame yourself for, Stephen. It wasn't your fault.'

'It is generous of you to say so.'

She smiled. 'I mean it.'

'I—hope you don't mind Edward coming here, Arabella. He is worried about his son. There really is no one to care for him. It would be a great help if he could remain here for a time—with you and Alice. It will be good for Dickon to be among children.'

He turned suddenly when Alice appeared

across the hall. Striding to meet her, Arabella watched the touching and emotional scene between brother and sister as they greeted each other after so long an absence. Margaret was upstairs settling the children.

'I'm sorry to hear about the troubles you've had, Alice,' Stephen said as they approached Arabella. 'I'm proud of the way you are coping.'

Alice smiled. 'I do my best, Stephen, although I confess it isn't easy without Robert. It's a comfort and a great help having Arabella at Bircot Hall, and Margaret is a great help with the children.'

'I look forward to seeing them. They will be well grown, I imagine.'

'They are and my eldest, Charles—he is seven now—favours you in looks, Stephen.' Giving him a sidelong look, she said, 'But is it not time you had a brood of your own? You have been a bachelor too long.'

He laughed, tweaking her cheek playfully. 'When I meet a woman with your beauty and attributes, dear Alice, I shall, but until then I shall remain single and free.'

Alice sighed in mock surrender. 'What are we going to do with you? You are strong and handsome and you have many fine qualities, Stephen.'

'Thank you, Alice. But I am not handsome like Edward, I fear.'

'Are you not?' she remarked with a twinkle in her eye. 'As I recall when we were all at home, the serving maids didn't think so. Speaking of Edward, have you seen him?'

'Not yet. I will go and find him.'

'I trust you and those with you are hungry. We have limited provisions, but I will soon put something together.'

'That would be appreciated. We haven't eaten since early morning. And you and Arabella must join us. England may be a dark and dreary place under the rule of Cromwell, the luxuries and amusements we so loved in the past denied us, but we will sit and eat and be a happy family whilst we can.'

'You are not going to stay long?' Arabella asked, unable to hide her concern.

He shook his head wearily. 'We cannot. We only have a few hours here.'

She looked up at him with fear-bright eyes. 'You are going to join Charles Stuart?'

'I must, Arabella. I remain loyal to the end. It is my duty.'

Alice expelled a deep sigh as she watched their brother walk away. 'It is so good to see him again, Arabella—and to have a man in the house once more.' She searched her sister's face anxiously. 'How badly is Sir Edward hurt?'

'He shall live,' Arabella replied, sinking wearily into a chair by the hearth and resting her feet on the fender. 'The wound is clean and will soon heal.'

Alice nodded, sitting across from her. 'And you, Arabella? Seeing Edward after all this time must have come as a shock.'

'Yes. I thought I would never see him again.'

'What will you do about the child?'

'What can I do? I am left with little choice.' She looked across at her sister. 'If I refuse to look after him, you will, won't you, Alice?'

'If necessary, yes.'

'Then it seems he is here to stay for the time being.'

'The child has lost his mother. So many lives have been ruined by this war. We must do what we can to help.'

'Yes,' Arabella uttered quietly. 'I suppose you are right.'

The two sisters sat silent for a long moment, each with her own thoughts. At length Alice sighed softly and stood up.

'They'll be hungry. I asked Bertha to prepare food before I took the children to bed. I'll go and help her.'

* * *

They dined in the large dining parlour off the hall. A branch of candles stood on in the middle of the great oak table and cast a reasonable light in the high-ceilinged room.

It was a subdued meal charged with emotion. Stephen sat at the head of the table with Alice and Edward seated next to each other across from Arabella. The two gentlemen who accompanied them were introduced as Sir Charles Barlow and Laurence Morrison. Both had seen much action in the King's service. It was decided that they would sleep in the rooms above the gatehouse, where they could keep watch on the road should unwelcome guests approach the house.

Having already eaten, Arabella and Alice sat and watched the gentlemen hungrily devour the mutton stew, jugged hare and vegetables. Having refilled the drinking bowls, Arabella studied her siblings, wishing that they could be together like this for always. Margaret joined them, slipping quietly into a chair at the table, her eyes wide with awe and more than a little admiration, Arabella duly noted, as they remained fixed on Stephen throughout the meal. It was a long time since visitors had graced their table and, if the rapt expression on Margaret's face and the vivid bloom on her cheeks were to be believed, never one so handsome.

It was inevitable that with four military men about to ride off and join Charles Stuart marching south in what appeared to be a last attempt to regain his throne, the conversation turned to military matters. Edward, his dark brows drawn together in a frown, contributed little to the conversation as he stared moodily across the table at Arabella. Sitting back in his chair, he studied her with unnerving intensity, the blue of his eyes having turned indigo in the dimly lit room, heavy black locks spilling to his shoulders.

Despite her efforts Arabella felt weakness within as she gazed at that handsome face, the taut cheekbones and that full lower lip with its hard curl. Meeting his eyes, she saw something slumberous and inviting in their depths. He seemed to be reading her mind. Heat suffused her. Immediately she looked away, trying hard to ignore his brooding gaze.

Later, back in her bedchamber, Arabella eyed her bed without enthusiasm. Tired as she was, she felt no urge to sleep. Her thoughts kept straying anxiously to Edward and what it was he expected of her. Her thoughts and emotions were a jumbled mass of confusion. How dare he put her in this position! How presumptuous he'd been, to assume she would take his child as her own! And seeing him now, after all this time, only served to bring back the anger and confusion she had felt by his rejection.

His appearance had also resurrected unpleasant memories of her marriage to John. Fair haired, reasonably handsome and with pale wide-set eyes, on first sight she had been dazzled by him and hung back shyly. When her father had ushered her forward, John had laughed and said, 'Modest, I see.'

'Aye—and dutiful,' her father had replied, happy with the impending match. When Edward Grey had thrown her over he had worried that he would have trouble finding a marriage for her, so he'd been unable to believe his good fortune when Stephen had brought John Fairburn to their home and John had shown an interest in her.

Arabella remembered how she had smiled and curtsied, prepared to be ruled by her father's counsel, but when John raised her up and she felt how cold and flaccid his hand, she had shrunk back. Immediately she had misgivings about the match. John had felt her recoil and, apart from a narrowing of his eyes, he had let it pass. When she had voiced her unease to her father, he had told her John Fairburn was a good match and all would be well, but it was up to her to make sure that it was. If John Fairburn did not take her, then there was little chance of anyone else. There was no dowry. After three years of war and support of the Royalist cause, her father had nothing left.

'He is handsome enough,' he had told her, 'an only son with a fine house where you will be mistress. What more do you want?'

Deep-blue eyes, warm firm hands, deep laughter. Someone to swell her heart at the sight of him, to make her senses sing. Edward Grey, she had thought bleakly.

And so she had married John Fairburn. Every time he touched her she shrank away. He boasted of her beauty and everyone said how lucky she was, but no one knew how she suffered in the great bed she shared with her husband, how he would control her every thought.

When she found she was with child it had altered everything. A child, she thought, a child of her own she could love. Desperate for a son, John had left her alone, taking his perverted pleasures elsewhere. When Arabella had produced a daughter, uttering his disgust he left to join the Royalist army.

For the first time since her marriage Arabella

had been happy as she held her daughter in her arms and she did not shed a tear when news was brought to her of John's death. Tragically her happiness was destroyed when her daughter died shortly after she came to live at Bircot Hall.

The pain had almost ripped her in two. She had loved her daughter so much and she missed her. Her arms were empty, her life was empty. In her wretchedness she had told herself there was nothing more to live for. She had prayed that the feeling would pass, that she would learn to live and to love. But Edward's cruel betrayal, followed by the cruelties of her marriage to John and the loss of her beautiful Elizabeth had left their mark. It would be a long time, if ever, before she would allow herself to be so hurt again and to put her trust in a man enough to marry him.

Restless, her arms aching for her child, knowing there would be no sleep for her this night, she turned her back on the bed and went out. The door to the room where Margaret had put Joan and the child was ajar. Arabella paused and stared at it, her heart beating a tattoo in her chest. On hearing a faint whimpering coming from inside the room, unable to help herself she tentatively reached out and pushed the door open just enough for her to peer inside. A candle had been left burning on the dresser and a fire burned low in the grate.

Joan was fast asleep. She was breathing deeply, little snores coming from between her parted lips. The child beside her was clearly distressed. On seeing Arabella he slid off the bed, wobbling towards her and holding out his arms. Not without human feelings and unable to resist an unhappy child, she knelt and looked into his tear-soaked eyes.

There was so much emotion in that face and the sobs coming from the little mouth wrenched her heart. As if it were the most natural thing in the world to do, she picked up the weeping child and cradled him in her arms. Taking up a spare blanket and murmuring words of comfort, she wrapped it about him, the ache in her breast as acute now as when her own child had died.

Holding him close, she crossed to the fire and sat down with him in her arms.

'Shush,' she murmured, placing her lips against his curly head. 'You are safe now, so go to sleep.'

The silky head nestled of its own accord against the warm breast in a gesture so instinctively caressing that it took Arabella's breath away. The child's brooding dark-eyed gaze was working its way into her heart, and when a quiet, rare smile crept across his face it was a thing of such beauty that it wrung her heart. As though a window had been flung open, something inside her took flight and she was flooded with so much joy that it brought tears to her eyes. She remembered how it had felt to hold her own daughter so close and, remembering her loss, she experienced an emotion that was almost painful in its intensity.

Shoving his thumb in his mouth, after a short while Dickon quietened and his eyelids fluttered closed, his thick lashes making enchanting semicircles on his pink cheeks. The warmth of the fire and the security of her arms soon sent him to sleep. He was going to be handsome, she thought, just like his father. Instantly there was a resurgence in her of the magnetism that drew her whenever she saw Edward. It burned into her ruthlessly, making her heart turn over. Her eyes continued to caress the child—Edward's flesh and blood—and she acknowledge him for what he was.

Reluctant to carry him back to bed, she relaxed with him in her arms. The curtains hadn't been fully drawn and the moon shone through a break in the clouds into the room. She began to think of the strangeness of her life, of her marriage to John and how Edward Grey had come back into her life, a stranger to her in many ways. There had never been a physical closeness between them, but there had been a closeness in other ways. He had always sought her company, but because he was eight years her senior, she had sometimes felt shut out from his thoughts. Clearly she had disappointed him otherwise he would not have cast her aside for Anne Lister.

The tugging of her heart twisted into an ache that flared every time she remembered. She wanted to be more understanding about what he had done, that he had gone on to have a child while her own had died, but she couldn't no matter how hard she tried.

Suddenly an image of John came to mind and a chill slithered over her flesh. Marriage to John had not been what she had dreamed of. There was no wild searing passion, which, as young as she had been, she had known she could feel for Edward.

Arabella did not hear the loose wooden floorboard on the landing creak, so absorbed was her attention on the child.

Edward stood in the doorway, transfixed at the sight of Arabella with his son cradled in her arms. There was something so intimate, so ethereal about the scene that he found it difficult to look at the expression of wonder on Arabella's face. He hesitated a moment, watching as the flickering light from the fire shone on her hair, which hung loose and fell over her face as she bent over his son. He admired the colour and the texture. Her body had the requisite warm softness and she still had the firm-fleshed litheness of youth, the languid grace which awoke his all-too-easily-awakened carnality.

She was unaware of his presence until he walked quietly into the room and stood looking down at her. She started, clearly surprised to see him there.

'Edward!' she gasped, her eyes flitting from him to his son, hot colour springing to her cheeks, as though she had been caught out in some misdeed. 'I—I heard him crying. His nurse is asleep and I did not wish to wake her. See, he is asleep now.'

A ghost of a smile lit his face—his expression softened slightly. 'How could he not be, cradled in such soft arms? Here, let me take him.'

'Don't wake him.'

With infinite care Edward took his son from her and carried him to the bed, placing him beneath the covers. His face was creased with concentration as he performed his task. He stood looking down at him for a moment before moving back to Arabella.

'Dickon is a lovely boy,' Arabella said. 'He favours you.'

'Yes, I know. I thought I would look in on him before I go to bed. Arabella, I wish to apologise.'

Standing up, she studied him, her eyes, big and luminous in her pale face, inquisitive but cautious. Her head was raised proudly as she looked at him, keeping her hands folded tightly before her. 'Apologise? For what? That you renounced your promise to me for another woman, or that you have disturbed me here at Bircot Hall?'

'Both, I suppose,' he said, combing his hair back from his brow with his fingers. 'I wronged you, Arabella. I acknowledge it freely. I swear to you—'

'Oh, no! Do not swear! When you came here you no doubt thought I was ready to forget and forgive what you did to me. In all that has happened in the intervening years, I believe I had forgotten—but you reminded me the moment you walked in the door.' She gave him a level stare and, not knowing that her words were like knives being thrown at him, she said, 'There was a time when I trusted you. I was so young and filled with girlish fantasies that I believed we could build a happy life together—something quite wonderful. But you, ruled by an overweening arrogance and pride, betrayed me. I can only say how glad I am that you strayed before we spoke our vows. It spared me a lot of heartache. I weathered the pity of my friends and family because I had lost my intended husband. The humiliation would have been intolerable indeed had you begun an affair when I became your wife.'

Edward had paled, the flesh drawn tight over his cheekbones. Her words created an agony inside him. He wanted to comfort her, to hold her, to say her name, for the thought of her suffering made him wish he hadn't acted so foolishly over Anne and left her so brutally. 'I would not have done that.'

'How can you know how you would have behaved?' she cried, the pain in her unconcealed. 'Men make fools of themselves over beautiful women all the time. Anne Lister could not bear not being the centre of attention. Every man had to look at her. All she had to do was cast her eyes at you and you were ensnared.'

He shook his head. 'Arabella, listen to me.' Reaching out, he gripped her shoulders and stared down into her face before he went on.

'With every beat of my heart I regret what I did. I know that you've had double your share of troubles for your years. But believe me, I would never wish you harm. Sometimes I can't help wishing I could go back and do things differently—but then I wouldn't have Dickon. We cannot change the past.'

She shook his hands from her shoulders and took a step back. 'I know.'

'I hurt you. I see that.'

'I cannot pretend that I wasn't hurt. I was— very much,' she said, a sliver of remembered pain spearing her.

'When I arrived at Bircot Hall and saw you, I was taken aback by how much you have changed. I know I have changed, but I hadn't expected you to change, too.'

What he said was true. He still had the face of a man in his prime, but the careless good humour had gone from his eyes. They were wary now, with a certain hardness and seriousness in their depths. The change was brought about by all he had seen and done in the long years of war.

'But I have, in many ways,' Arabella said. 'When you left me I thought I would not recover. But I did. I was well and alive. I was determined to put it behind me—I thought of myself as a phoenix, risen from the ashes. Then I was lucky—at least, that was how I thought it was at the time. I met John and I had a child, only to lose them both.'

Tentatively Edward moved a little closer to her, but she stepped back, determined to keep her distance. He could almost feel the tension of her body. Her stillness was a positive force, like that of an animal poised for flight. One false move and he would lose her. He could read nothing on her closed face. Her chest rose and fell as she breathed, but apart from this she was watchful and utterly still.

'I realise I might have caused you trouble coming here. Believe me, I would not have done so had there been an alternative. When I heard my property was to be confiscated, concerned about my son and despite the risk of capture, I went to London. I found Dickon alone in the house with the servants.'

'You told me your estate in Oxfordshire has been confiscated.'

He nodded. 'No doubt the house in London will have been seized by now. All activists have had their estates confiscated. As you know, since Parliament came to power, all lands granted by the King to landlords are now illegal and the laws set by King William have been removed.'

'And what is to happen to the land that has been taken?'

'It will be returned to the people. That is what the Commonwealth means—a common wealth for all. Everything of value that I owned went to fund the Royalist cause. This war has made a pauper of me.'

'This war has made paupers of us all,' Arabella uttered bitterly.

'It will be returned when the King comes into his own.'

'*If* the King comes into his own. I am not optimistic about that. From what we have heard, few are prepared to join the royal standard. The King, after all, is at the head of a band of Presbyterians. If anything, the patriotic revulsion of the English against the Scots has increased.'

'You are right, Arabella. But it is a cause I will die fighting for if necessary.'

'So, with nowhere else to turn, you thought you would bring your son here.'

'Anne's brother was in London. It was only a matter of time before he came and seized the child. Before he fled London, knowing my situation, your brother suggested I bring him here, to you. I understand your reluctance to agree to look after Dickon for me, but there is nowhere else I can take him. Will you do it?' He saw the indecision on her face before she turned to gaze down into the fire.

She turned from him, but not before he had seen a flicker of pain in the depths of her lovely eyes before she looked away. 'You ask too much of me, Edward. It is too much responsibility.'

'Come, Arabella. You have just held him in your arms. How can you refuse me this?' he persisted. 'Have the courage to help me—or else you are not the woman—'

Spinning round, her face was set stubbornly, the light in her eyes fierce. 'Your meaning does not escape me. You were about to say I am not the woman you thought I was. If I refuse to do as you ask—which is a perfectly natural thing considering your betrayal—you will think ill of me.' She shrugged. 'If you do, why should I care? For too long I have known you do not see me in an attractive light.'

'That is not true. You are one of the finest people I know. You know my decision to renounce our betrothal was because of my foolish infatuation with Anne, rather than anything to do with you.' His hand came up to touch her tumbled hair, then he drew a caressing finger down her cheek. Feeling her flinch from his touch, he dropped his arm. 'I wronged you. At the time I was too stubborn to admit my error.

I am asking for your forgiveness, for I know well that you must hate me and in all fairness I cannot blame you. I blame myself—more than you or anybody else possibly could. I'll never stop blaming myself until the day I die. Which is why, perhaps, it's so important to me that you can find it in your heart to forgive me. I have grief enough, Arabella. I am saying that I hold you in the highest regard and that my feelings for you may surprise you. Laugh if you will and that will be my punishment. But it is true.'

Arabella's look was scornful. 'Please do not make any declarations of devotion that do not exist. It would be an embarrassment to us both, so pray do not continue with this jest. Considering what has gone before, I consider it to be in bad taste.'

'It is no jest. A thousand times or more I have cursed myself for a fool for ending our betrothal,' he said softly, his eyes holding hers, full of contrition. 'Don't hold it against me. I can't change what I did and, if it's any satisfaction to you, I'm paying the price for it. What I did was impetuous and cruel.'

She stared at him, her eyes telling him that she was unable to believe what he was saying. Surely she could hear the truth of his words in his voice? But he could see she refused to be moved by his words. Forgiveness did not come easily to her and in truth he could not blame her. She stepped away from him.

'Yes, it was, but I have no wish to revisit the past. Do you forget why you are here? You came here to ask me to take care of your son.'

'And what have you decided?' Edward tried to keep calm as he waited for her answer, yet the vein in his right temple beat hard against his skin. Arabella had captured his senses without even trying. His interest she had already stirred, but interest turned to intrigue with startling ease. For the first time in months—perhaps years—a feeling other than anger at the war preoccupied him. It was strong, alive and it touched him in a primeval way. He never swayed from winning his desire. Where women were concerned he was patient and the most determined. He deeply regretted the years they had been apart and felt a need to be with her.

'Very well.' She sighed, surrendering unconditionally. 'I will do it.'

Relief washed over him. 'Thank you. I cannot tell you how grateful I am—what it means to me knowing he will be safe.'

'I think I can imagine.' She looked at him, hardening herself. 'But I still don't understand why you feel you have to risk life and limb to continue fighting for a cause which by all reports is lost. Why, Edward? Is it that you enjoy the fighting so much that you leave your son with strangers instead of taking him to France to keep him safe? What if anything should happen to you? If I need to take Dickon to your sister in France, how will I know where to find her?'

Reaching inside his jacket, he produced a sealed letter and handed it to her, preferring to leave her questions unanswered. 'I have written everything down. It is my hope there will be no more fighting and I shall return, in which case I shall take him away with me.'

'And Joan? Is she to remain with him?'

'Dickon is attached to Joan, but it is only fair to tell you that she came with me unwillingly. She has family in Bath. Do not be surprised if she leaves to go to them.'

'I see. That is entirely up to her, but I hope she doesn't. I would be glad of her help.' She looked at the clock on the mantelpiece. 'The hour is late. It is after eleven. It has been a long day. I must go to bed.' She walked to the door. He followed her.

'Goodnight, Arabella. I trust you will have a restful night.'

For some reason he could not fathom, he

reached for her hand and pressed a kiss on her fingers. A subtle gasp, barely a whisper, passed her lips and he smiled into her eyes.

Arabella turned and left him then. He was watching her go, this she knew. His eyes were so very compelling that she wanted to turn and look back at him, but she forced herself to carry on walking. His fingers, firm and warm, had squeezed her hand gently, as if for comfort. Suddenly she had been intensely aware of him, his body, his warmth, the scent of him. Something had flooded through her—desire, she thought, quickening her breath, heating her blood.

A terrible, unfamiliar heaviness rested in her heart as she returned to her chamber. She undressed and climbed into bed and, because she was so weary, she managed to sleep a few hours, but, on waking, she could not stop turning over in her mind the events of the previous night and the changes Edward's arrival had brought to her life. How could she have agreed to take care of his son? But when he had asked her, when he had waited for her to answer, there had been a challenge in his voice, in his eyes as well.

Nor could she deny that the sensations that

had stirred within as he pressed his lips to her fingers had been alarming indeed. When he had entered the room and caught her holding his son, she had tried to ignore the nearness of him, the smell of him, the feelings and emotions that had been overwhelming despite all her efforts to stem them.

When she was young, she had been in awe of the man her parents had told her she would marry. She had also been almost afraid of the force and sheer power in him. Everything about him had been larger than life and she had thought marrying him would be the equivalent of riding into battle on a spirited, powerful horse.

She had been deeply hurt and humiliated when he had discarded her and made up her mind to forget him. But he was not an easy man to forget. When he had entered the house with that enormous pride, and thrust himself back into her life, she'd known that same sense of reckless excitement she'd experienced all those years ago.

By coming to Bircot Hall he had brought disruption to her life. She was resolute in her determination that not until she had been reassured of his benevolence would she grant him her friendship.

* * *

The morning was bright with sunshine, the sky a cloudless blue, the rain clouds that had been present the night before having disappeared with the dawn. The land was still wet and glistened in the bright light, and the trees were thick with dark-green leaves.

After eating a hasty breakfast and eager to be on their way, Stephen and Edward would take their leave of Alice and Arabella in the courtyard. The two gentlemen who accompanied them were already mounted, their horses restless. Edward had not yet appeared, for he was saying farewell to his son.

'God go with you,' Arabella said tenderly as she kissed her brother. 'I beg you take care.' She could not dismiss the fear in her heart, or her sense of dark foreboding that she might never see him again. 'Where exactly are you bound?'

'We have learned that the King has entered Worcester. We will join him there. It is the only Royalist stronghold left. It will be the King's last attempt to gain his throne and he needs every man he can get. It's his last hope.'

When Arabella stepped back and stood beside Margaret, who was quietly watching the scene with tears in her eyes, Alice threw her arms around her brother's neck in a final farewell. As Stephen looked over Alice's shoulder, his eyes rested on Margaret. Gently detaching himself from Alice's arms, he went to the young woman and, taking her slender hand, raised it to his lips.

Margaret's pale face flushed with pleasure at receiving attention from a man whom from short acquaintance she had come to admire intensely, a man she found appealing to her senses. Her eyes smiled her appreciation. Arabella couldn't hear what he said, but she was glad Margaret had not gone unnoticed by Stephen.

Chapter Three

When Edward came out of the house Arabella looked towards him. There was an air of melancholy about him. He scarcely seemed to notice what was going on about him as he dabbed his brow with his handkerchief and strode to his horse. Arabella wasn't so insensitive and heartless as not to realise how he must be feeling on parting from his son. She could well imagine how difficult that must have been for him. The leave-taking had clearly affected him deeply. She found she could not bear that withdrawn look on his face and went to him.

'You have said farewell to Dickon?'

He nodded, his expression grim. 'Alice's children are amusing him. He will hardly know I've gone.'

'I'm sure that is not so. He will miss you.

But…tell me, Edward—is Malcolm Lister likely to come here looking for you?'

He gave her a penetrating look. 'Why do you ask?'

'When he finds Dickon is not in London, what then? Will he not enquire as to his whereabouts?'

'The servants saw me. Malcolm will know I have taken him.'

'Which is a father's right. But you are a fugitive. As Dickon's uncle he will want to know where you have taken him. With your close relatives either dead or in France and knowing you and Stephen are close friends, will he have reason to come here? I ask because I am concerned.'

'Understandably so and I have reason to believe that Malcolm will go to any lengths to find him. It is not beyond the bounds of possibility that he will remember that you and I were once betrothed. It would not be difficult finding out that you are living with Alice and that he will come here. I advise you to be on your guard at all times—although at this present time with the Commonwealth army marching towards Worcester, I can only hope he will be occupied with military matters.'

'What I recall of Malcolm Lister is that he

is a man to watch and he has the long nose of a bloodhound. We must hope he does not come here.'

'It cannot be ruled out. Perhaps we will meet in armed combat. If not and we both survive the battle, I can guarantee he will seek me out afterwards. He wants to hurt me. He thinks he can do that by taking Dickon and seeing me hang.'

He was looking at her intently and his magnetic eyes stirred her painfully. 'I pray that does not happen.'

Edward's eyes creased with pain. 'It grieves me to have to leave my son. But I must go. I have striven for peace, but still I must fight. If there is to be another battle, then so be it. It is the price men like me have to pay to bring the King into his own. I would have contempt for myself if I did not do my duty towards my King and country.'

Her eyes suddenly moist, Arabella lowered her head, not wanting to dull the edge of his courage with her fear. 'I know and I understand your duty well. Should Malcolm Lister come here I will do my utmost to hide Dickon. That I promise you. Be assured he will be well looked after.'

His eyes flickered in appreciation and the corners of his mouth lifted in a crooked smile.

'I know you will—and he will have young children to play with. His life so far has been peopled with adults—it is not good for him. If there is to be yet another battle, which I fear there will be, in my darkest hours your kindness and loyalty to my son will comfort me.'

She met his eyes, wondering if he would return. Ever since the war began, life had been one long series of partings. Tears shone in her eyes. Why did she care so much? He might have wronged her in the past, but she could not deny the physical attraction she felt for him. And then there was his son. Already Dickon was beginning to steal his way into her heart. That poor child had been through so much already. Anne Lister might have been low down in her estimation, but she had been his mother. Having been blessed with the most wonderful mother in the world, Arabella could not begin to imagine the pain of being raised without a mother's love. *Please God, don't let him lose his father, too.* Suddenly she knew that it mattered terribly that Edward came back safe—for Dickon's sake, if not for her own.

'You will come back. Have no fear,' she said, her voice light, hiding the pain filling her mind. 'Do not concern yourself about us. I will keep Dickon safe.'

Edward glanced across at Stephen, who was mounted and ready to go. He glanced back at Arabella with his disconcertingly blue eyes. When a smile tugged at her beautiful mouth, unable to resist the temptation to taste its sweetness, he bent his head and kissed her hard and fast on the lips, a kiss of anger and need and lost possibilities, the pressure of his mouth lingering longer than was customary.

When he released her his eyes were still on her, gauging her, watching for every shade of thought and emotion in her.

'Take care, Bella,' he said, his voice husky with emotion. He touched her cheek with his finger, as if commending her visage to memory against the moment when they must part, then turning from her he walked to his horse. Taking the reins, he looked back at her. His face was drawn and bleak in the harsh sunlight. 'What you said to me last night—that I must enjoy the fighting—you are wrong. I do not enjoy what I do. An army is a harsh and brutal world to inhabit. Death is constant and soldiers carry their lives in their hands and look death in the face all the time.'

For another second they looked at each other, silent in the stillness of the morning. Arabella was overwhelmed by the urge to go to him, to reach up and touch his face. Immediately she pushed the feeling away, angry at her weakness. Then he hoisted himself into the saddle and was riding after the others through the gatehouse.

She watched him disappear from her sight, touched by an inexplicable sensation of loss. For all its intensity the kiss had been brief. The touch of his mouth on hers had sent a jolt through her system, which had for a moment left her incapable of coherent thought. She was unable to banish the memory of his mouth on hers. Her lips were warm and tingling from the farewell kiss, confirming it had actually happened, that and a heart full of unfamiliar emotions simmering inside her.

Putting her fingers to her lips, she stared after him. She had not expected him to do that. It was strange, she thought, how she could still feel it long after it had ended. At that moment it seemed to her that she had been set upon a stormy sea of emotions that had left her breathless and confused.

Clearly he had not changed. Not his reckless attitude or, to her dismay, the way he made her feel. She'd been alive to his touch, filled with a sweet longing that seemed to promise something wonderful that was just beyond reach. The way he had looked at her. The tone of his voice when he said her name. He had wanted her. The signs had all been there.

She looked down as something white fluttered at her feet. It was his handkerchief. She picked it up, holding it close to her chest, and his scent, a blend of wind and rain and leather and horses, was everywhere. She wanted to run after him and call him back and have him kiss her again with the ghosts of the past all around them. But she could not and so let the opportunity slip through her fingers. She felt empty and alone once more.

How could she have allowed such a thing to happen? With her emotions running high she had foolishly allowed herself to be borne away on a wave of passion. She despised herself for succumbing so readily to his coercive masculinity. Did he think he could go to another woman and come back and take up where he had left off?

Having witnessed the kiss, Alice came to stand beside her, her eyes fixed on the gatehouse.

'So, Arabella,' she said quietly, 'if the kiss I witnessed is an indication of future expectations, it would seem Sir Edward's intentions to court you are about to be resumed.'

Arabella was strangely reluctant to speak of

Edward, for reasons that were hardly formulated even in her own subconscious, but she could not evade Alice's questions. 'Yes, he kissed me and I let him. He—he is a soldier going to fight. He might not come back. But it meant nothing. Edward left me—rejected me for another woman. It's a long time ago, I know, but I have not forgotten—nor have I forgiven him.'

'Do you remember how angry Father was when he renounced the betrothal—and Stephen, come to that? But they seem to be staunch friends now.'

'It's the war, Alice. The conflict has thrown them together in ways we could not have imagined before that. Both our families have lost so much—loved ones and our homes.'

'Yes, we have. It will be hard for all of us when this is over. Nothing will be the same again.'

Riding with his companions towards Worcester, Edward found his thoughts wandering to Arabella. It was painful leaving Dickon behind, but he was shocked to discover how much he would miss Arabella. He had vowed that after Anne, with her treachery and deceit, his emotions would never again be engaged by a woman. But Arabella was not Anne.

He'd had to lose her to appreciate the prize he had lost.

She had been naïve, an innocent, and he had brought shame on himself for hurting her as he had. He felt a profound remorse that he had given her reason not to want him. He despised himself for the callousness with which he had broken off their engagement and he desperately wanted to make amends, to close the chasm that had opened up between them.

What Arabella had been through had toughened her. She was hard to read. He had hoped she might have put their past behind her, but they had parted bitterly all those years ago and he sensed a wariness about her now for which he could not blame her. But there was something about her, something that made him feel more alive than he had felt in a long time when he looked at her.

The kiss he had given her had been spontaneous, shocking him with its sweetness, its intensity. It had never happened to him before—at least, not since he had met and married Anne. Meeting Arabella again—all grown, a woman now—he found her intriguing and fascinating. But she was not ready to give her heart. Where he was concerned she never would be and he could not blame her for that.

* * *

In the days following Stephen and Edward's departure nothing eventful happened at Bircot Hall.

Arabella watched Dickon running around the hall with Alice's children. He was laughing and it warmed her heart to see him enjoying the game. At first he had been such a solemn child, so quiet, with a serious way of looking at her with his big blue eyes. This was exactly what he needed, other children to play with.

It was with enormous regret to Arabella that Joan had done exactly what Edward said she might do and left Bircot Hall for her home in Bath. Arabella had thought it would affect Dickon, that he would pine for her, but much to her relief he didn't seem to mind being without her. Arabella was touched that he turned to her. Dickon had worked his way secretly and profoundly into a corner of her heart. She was the one who watched over him, who washed him, fed him and put him to bed and told him the kind of stories children like to hear. She was the one he ran to when he tumbled over and she brushed away his tears.

Alice had reason to rejoice when she received a long-awaited letter from her husband Robert in France. Like many Royalists who had fled across the water, with little to do he was finding life tedious. He was considering joining the French army, as many English exiles were doing. He made brief mention of several gentlemen Alice might know who were of like mind, including one man by the name of Fairburn who had left Paris before he arrived. Robert had not met the man and knew nothing about him other than his surname and that he came from Wales and, rumour had it, bore a strong resemblance to the John Fairburn who had been killed at St Fagans—which was where Arabella's husband had met his end. He considered it a coincidence since Arabella had married a man by that name and wondered if he could be one of her husband's relations.

He asked about the children and while Alice went on reading, Arabella continued to think about the man called Fairburn Robert had referred to with a stirring of unease. Why this should be she couldn't say. After all, John was dead—he had to be dead. After all, had she not buried him? she thought with a stirring of alarm—and if the man was a relation then it didn't concern her. On that thought she put it out of her mind, but there were moments when she least expected it that it surfaced to cause her further unease.

* * *

Information began to filter through that there was fierce fighting in and around the city of Worcester. The days were spent in an agony of mounting tension for everyone at Bircot Hall. Passing travellers provided worrying news that Charles Stuart was besieged within its defensive walls by Cromwell's army. They heard that Cromwell had broken through and of vicious fighting in the streets, which ran with blood.

Arabella felt fear stab at her. Where were Stephen and Edward? She couldn't bear to think that they might be wounded or lying unattended and in pain somewhere on the streets of Worcester or on the battlefield, or even worse—killed. It was impossible to find out. There was nothing she could do, nothing any of them could do but wait as one anxious day ran into another.

It was almost dark. The children were in bed and, feeling the need for some fresh air before going to bed herself, Arabella went outside. Everything gleamed wetly after the shower of rain they'd had earlier and a breeze was tearing the clouds apart to reveal glimpses of the brightly shining stars. After strolling round the courtyard she was about to go inside the house, but on hearing the sound of horse's hooves on the stone paving, she looked towards the gatehouse though which a horse and rider emerged, leading another horse.

'Edward,' she whispered, her heart leaping with sudden joy and relief. It was three weeks since they had left—an eternity of waiting. Her eyes passed to the horse he was leading. A man was slumped over its back. Her stomach lurched and she whispered her brother's name, 'Stephen.' He appeared to be unconscious.

Lifting her skirts, she ran towards them in alarm. Bringing the horses to a halt, Edward dismounted quickly.

'Edward—oh, thank goodness you are back.' Emotions tumbled within her as, still shaken from his sudden arrival, she was so very glad to see him even though she knew his presence and that of her brother meant danger for them all. Not wanting him to read these sentiments in her eyes, she turned her attention to her brother. 'Is Stephen badly injured?'

With a week's growth of beard and his clothes stained and torn with the traumas of battle, the mud and blood having dried on them long since, Edward nodded. His face was grey and strained with exhaustion, his eyes bloodshot, bleak and darkly circled. 'He has a musket ball in his chest. He's lost a great deal of blood and needs attending to at once. We managed to escape in the aftermath of the battle. It's taken us two days to get here. Roundheads are crawling all over the place. He's been unconscious for the past five hours.'

'Sam,' Arabella called over her shoulder. 'Come and help. It's Stephen—he's wounded.'

'The horses are conspicuous,' Edward said. 'Have someone put them out of sight, as far away from the house as possible, and rub them down. If they are found, they will raise suspicion and questions will be asked. They will also be sequestered by the Parliamentary army.'

Together the two men lifted Stephen from the horse, nearly falling under the weight. Tom, Sam's young son, took the mounts' reins and led them away as Alice came running out of the house to see what all the commotion was about. On seeing her injured brother being hauled along and the large bloodstain on his buff coat, she assessed the situation immediately.

'Bring him inside. We must get him upstairs and into bed.'

Managing to get him up the stairs, Edward and Sam set their burden down in a bedchamber. While Alice went to fetch the things she would need to tend her brother's wound, with

Sam's help Edward worked frantically to remove Stephen's blood-soaked clothing.

Arabella stared anxiously at her brother. He was hardly recognisable beneath the gunpowder-streaked face and matted hair. His face was drawn and pale and his bare, powerful chest heaved painfully. His eyes kept flickering open, but the effort of doing so proved too much after so much blood loss and exhaustion, and he closed them again and drifted back into oblivion.

'I didn't want to bring him to the house,' Edward said wearily. 'I realise we put you all in danger, but he needs urgent care if he is to live. We will have to move him again, somewhere safe, but his wound must be attended to first. It won't be long before a Roundhead patrol comes to search the house. They're searching everywhere, leaving no stone unturned in their search for the King and Royalist fugitives who managed to escape Worcester.'

'The King has escaped?' Alice asked, entering the room carrying strips of linen and hot water.

'The Parliamentarians were greatly superior in numbers and firepower. Hundreds of Royalists were killed and hundreds more are being rounded up in the town. Careless of his own safety the King kept his courage to the last. He exposed himself with valour.'

'One mustn't forget that he is the grandson of Henry of Navarre,' Alice commented, rolling up her sleeves better to tend her brother. 'If he had perished, the head of the House of Stuart would pass to his brother James. I wonder what will happen should King Charles be taken? I imagine it would prove a quandary for Cromwell. Would he follow his father to the scaffold?'

'I think it will meet with strong opposition from the English people,' Edward replied, 'whomever they supported during the wars. At the end he consented to the advice of those who wanted him to withdraw. He left the town with some of his friends. The Roundheads' pursuit of the King is relentless.'

'Let us pray they don't find him and that he gets well away,' Alice murmured, looking down at her brother and touching his brow. 'He is feverish.' Staring at the ugly wound, she sighed despairingly. Soaking some of the linen in hot water, she wiped away the dried blood from his chest. 'I'm relieved the ball has penetrated the left side of his chest and is no threat to his heart, but it is still there. How I wish we could send for a physician, but I fear we cannot. It would be too risky. We must do the best we can.'

'I will attempt to remove the ball,' Edward said, shrugging out of his coat and proceeding to wash his hands.

Arabella went to him and handed him a towel. 'Are you sure you can you do it? It will be no easy task.'

He shook his head, meeting her gaze. 'I have to try.' His eyes softened as they caressed her anxious face. 'Try not to worry. This will not be the first time I have operated on a wounded soldier.'

After soaking a knife in alcohol and pouring some on to the wound, he got to work, careful not to disturb Stephen more than necessary. Stephen groaned in his unnatural sleep and his face was slick with sweat, but mercifully he didn't wake.

It didn't take Edward long to locate the offending musket ball and extract it, dropping it into a bowl. Standing back, he wiped his brow with his forearm. He was drenched in sweat. He looked exhausted and, with his hair falling forward into damp curls, he looked younger and strangely vulnerable. He looked at Arabella as she collected up bloodied cloths.

'As long as the wound is kept clean he should

recover well enough. The ball went deep, but I don't think it's done any serious damage. He has lost a lot of blood, but he is strong.'

As if in answer to his friend's remark, Stephen's eyes flickered open, although it was with great difficulty that he focused them on the anxious faces surrounding him.

'Where am I?' he mumbled, fighting with himself to keep from falling back into oblivion.

'You're at Bircot Hall, Edward,' Alice explained, taking his hand. 'Edward brought you here. You're safe for the time being. He's just removed the ball from your wound so you will be feeling sore for a while. Do you understand?'

He nodded, closing his eyes as a wave of pain swept through him. He gripped her hand hard. 'Yes—I understand—but for God's sake be careful.'

'We will move you to somewhere safe soon.' She looked at Arabella. 'I'll have Margaret make a honey poultice,' she said, smearing salve on the wound. With Arabella's help she finally wrapped strips of linen around his chest as a bandage.

'Take Sir Edward downstairs, Arabella, and get him some refreshment while I stay with Stephen.' She glanced at his blood-spattered shirt. 'And you might find him a clean shirt. Find

Margaret and ask her to come and assist me, will you?'

'What about the servants?' Edward asked, looking from one to the other. 'Can they be trusted?'

Arabella nodded. 'We have few servants left, but the ones we have are very loyal—for the King. I will speak to them.'

'It is imperative that should the Roundheads come to search the house, they find nothing.'

'Then we must find somewhere safe where you can hide. God willing Bircot Hall will be spared.'

'Unfortunately I very much doubt it.'

Unaware that Edward and Stephen had arrived, Margaret was in bed, but not asleep. When Arabella told her what had occurred, she whispered a quiet prayer and went to help Alice.

Edward was waiting in the hall for Arabella to join him. Hearing her soft footfall on the stairs, he turned his head to look at her. He watched her glide gracefully down the stairs. Something stirred in the region of his heart when he met her eyes. Her beautiful red-gold hair was drawn off her face, revealing the long, slender column of her throat. She wore a plain dark-blue dress which emphasised the slenderness of her waist. It was relieved only by a fine white linen collar. He could not deny that what he felt for her was more primitive than anything he had felt for a woman in a long time. She was looking at him, her eyes never leaving his face, and he saw the sorrow and sadness of all she had experienced in the past.

Before Edward had turned to look at her, quietly descending the stairs Arabella had taken a moment to look at him. The fire crackled in the hearth and he stood staring into the flames. His handsome face seemed carved in stone. His expression was fixed, his eyes betrayed no emotion.

'Here,' she said, handing him a brandy. 'You look as if you need it. You look tired.'

Edward looked deep into her eyes. Anxious as she was, there was something strikingly lovely and dignified about her slender form as she held out the glass.

There was a moment of silence between them as he took it and drained the contents. 'I feel positively spent. Although it's hardly surprising. I have not seen a bed since before the battle. When we escaped, with Stephen wounded and wanting to put as much distance between us and Worcester, I had to keep all my wits about me. We kept off the roads for most of the time—especially during daylight. The dark offered us some protection and I thank God we had the horses.'

'You were right to bring him here. And you, Edward? You suffer no ill effects from your own wound?'

'None. It is forgotten,' he answered briskly, and Arabella knew it would be. He was not the kind of man to dwell on weakness. 'But tell me—how is Dickon?'

'He has settled in well. He's a lovely child and loves being with Alice's children. You were right about Joan. She left to be with her family.'

He nodded. 'I thought she might. I was hoping she would stay. Where is he?'

'All the children are in bed.' She smiled. 'But I doubt you'll wake him if you would like to see him.' She moved to stand beside him, feeling the heat of the fire on her face. 'I am so grateful for what you have done for Stephen and I know I speak for Alice as well.'

'I'm beginning to envy him the attention he is receiving from his loved ones. Will I not get even a little sympathy?'

The teasing in his voice did not conceal his anxiety of the situation and to steer his mind away from her injured brother, she said, 'It must have been difficult—after all you had to endure in Worcester.'

'I have been in so many life-and-death situations with Stephen over the years that it's a miracle we've survived.'

'I think you will live for ever just to spite death.'

He flashed a smile, a dazzling heart-stopping smile. 'Perhaps I will. Who knows? But my concern now is to find somewhere we can hide until the Roundhead patrols move on. I truly regret causing you trouble. I knew that coming here was foolhardy. I have put you at grave risk.'

'Where else could you have taken Stephen if not to the home of his sister?' she asked, tucking away a wayward lock of hair burnished by the fire's glow. 'Besides, every day involves risk of some kind.' She looked at him in the firelight, unaware that her amber eyes were glowing with golden lights. The light glinted off the planes of his face and the ache in her chest that she always tried to ignore when she was with him pulled harder. She felt the urge to touch his face, to feel the heat of him, to anchor her rioting emotions in the physical reality of him. The feeling exploded inside her on a flood of heat so powerful she was almost overwhelmed by it.

Moving away from the hearth, he stopped,

his attention caught by a basket of freshly picked herbs Margaret had left on the table. He lifted a sprig of rosemary to his nose and smiled.

'Rosemary,' he murmured. 'For remembrance.'

'Yes,' Arabella said, lowering her face so he could not look into her eyes. But there was too much to remember, too much pain. Most of the herbs in the basket had wilted in the warmth of the hall, but the rosemary was still strong, its scent filling the air like a welcome guest. 'Would you like another brandy—or something else, perhaps?'

Placing the rosemary back in the basket, he looked at her and shook his head. 'Not just now, but it's a fine brandy. I'm surprised the Roundheads didn't purloin it when they came here.'

Arabella smiled. 'It was well hidden. In anticipation of what would happen if the Roundheads came, Alice had the foresight to bury it—along with other things she didn't want them to take.'

Edward laughed. 'Very wise.'

'In fact,' Arabella said, suddenly animated as a thought occurred to her, 'they were buried near the old shed which is used for storing fruit on the far side of the orchard. It would make an excellent place for you to hide.'

His eyes sharpened with interest. 'Show me.'

'Now?'

He nodded. 'We have to move Stephen quickly. The soldiers could be here at any time. If we are found, your sister could lose everything.'

They went through the huge kitchen where all around them utensils winked and glittered in the light of freshly lit candles. They passed larders and a buttery before opening a door that let them out on to a separate courtyard and stables. Carrying a candle lamp in her hand, which flickered weakly in the gentle breeze and barely held the darkness at bay, Arabella led the way to the orchards. The grass was long and difficult to walk through, the branches of the apple trees bent with the weight of fruit which they would do their best to pick when the time was right.

Her eyes darting about, she trod with care, not wishing to draw attention should someone be there. Edward followed, but she hardly knew it. He could move with the silent grace of a panther when he chose.

The orchard gave way to thick woodland of oak, beech and sweet chestnut. They made their way through the undergrowth and it was only a matter of minutes before they reached a low shed tucked away in the trees and covered with long tendrils of clinging ivy. Arabella lifted the latch on the door and pushed it open, cringing when it creaked loudly, disturbing the silence of the night. A startled fallow deer bounded off into the trees and a large bird in the undergrowth flapped its wings in annoyance and flew noisily away.

'If you think the shed is a suitable place, we will ask Sam to oil the hinges. As you see, it is quite isolated so you should be safe, although with all the to-ing and fro-ing between the shed and the house there will be a definite path worn in the grass through the orchard. I will ask Sam to cut it in the morning.'

'How many servants do you have here?'

'We just have Sam and his wife Bertha and their son, Tom. They had another son who, like my father, was killed at Naseby fighting for the King.'

Stepping inside, Arabella held the lantern high. Edward followed her, having to lower his head to get through the door. The shed wasn't roomy and cobwebs hung from the ceiling, but there was a small window and it was warm and dry. The earth floor was littered with several wooden boxes containing a few shrivelled apples and plank shelves were fastened to the walls. The air was stale and sluggish with a lingering smell of apples, but the building was sound.

'What with the war and lack of servants, the orchards have become overgrown,' Arabella said, placing the lamp on a shelf. 'The shed isn't visible from the house and unless you know it's here you would miss it completely. At this time of year the trees offer protection.' She looked at him as he took stock of his surroundings. 'Well? Will it do, do you think?'

He nodded. 'It is ideal—away from the house and well hidden.'

'We will have a couple of pallets and some bedding brought across and water for washing. There's no knowing how long you will have to be here.'

'I don't intend to stay long, Arabella.'

'Why? What will you do? Where will you go?'

'The Roundheads will look for us here. It is my intention to get to France.'

Arabella looked at him in amazement. 'But— in this present climate that is madness. The war is over, Edward, over and done with. Do not add your own death to this tragedy.'

'It is not over, Arabella. Life is not without risk. I have cheated death many times—on and off the battlefield. I do not want what I fought for to be in vain. The fight will go on. It is my hope that the King will reach France.'

'And what then—a new plan of campaign?'

'Perhaps. I cannot betray the King. I would defend him with my life.'

Weary of the incessant conflict and wondering when it would all end, Arabella shook her head. When she spoke there was no hiding the bitterness in her voice. 'Like Stephen, you will remain patriotic to the end. I hope Charles Stuart is worthy of your loyalty.'

'I ask you not to judge me too harshly, Arabella, for whatever your feelings are concerning the wars and the King you cannot deny that he has a moral duty to recover his kingdom— the one he inherited from his father. The Commonwealth has confiscated almost all Royalist lands and, unless the King regains his throne, they are gone for ever.'

'I know that and Charles Stuart has my undying loyalty, even though there are moments— when I'm feeling at my lowest—when I wonder if it is all worth it. It is sad that his loyal subjects have bankrupted themselves for a lost cause.'

'It didn't seem like that when we were fighting for it. It is unthinkable that I desert the King. He needs support now more than ever. When he comes into his own, all that has been stolen from those who remained loyal will be returned.'

'You really believe that will happen?'

'I have to. Are you not anxious about the future and what it holds?'

'I think about it all the time and what will become of us all. The world as we knew it before the wars has gone.'

'Sadly that is true. It is up to us to build a new life. There will be changes.'

'There have been changes already. Any form of entertainment is frowned upon—even Christmas cannot be celebrated. I suppose we will have to make the best of life under the Commonwealth.'

'Which I refuse to do. That is why I will go to France.'

'And Dickon? Where does he fit in to all this?'

'I shall take him with me.'

She stared at him, incredulous, unable to believe he would do something so reckless. She wanted to tell him to go, to take Dickon with him and disappear from her life, to do to him what he had done to her. But she couldn't. A feeling of impending loss stabbed like a knife at her heart. If Edward was taken before he left England, she couldn't bear to think of Dickon being alone with no one to care for him. How afraid he would be, alone, among strangers?

'Edward, I beg of your to think about this. It is safer and much more comforting to stay here than to travel to Bristol or wherever you intend trying to take ship for France.'

'My mind is made up.'

'But—but Dickon? He is so little to undertake such a perilous journey. You will find it difficult evading capture with a small child to take care of. You go if you must, but please don't take Dickon. Leave him here—with me. At least he will be safe.'

He shook his head. 'No, Arabella. I want him with me.'

'I will bring him to you when this is over.'

'You would do that?' He was clearly moved by her offer.

'Yes, I would. I will do what I think is right—and it is not right to drag a small child about the countryside crawling with hostile soldiers who would kill his father if they got their hands on him.'

'Perhaps you are right, but I have made up my mind.' He studied her with piercingly shrewd blue eyes.

'And what about Stephen? What will he do when he is recovered, do you think?'

'I am sure that when he is strong enough he will want to join me and the other Royalists who have fled to the Continent.' He looked at her with his discerning gaze. At length, he said, 'I am wondering if I can enlist your aid.'

Containing her surprise, Arabella raised an eyebrow, hoping to convey her scepticism. 'Forgive me if I seem confused. Five years ago you did not need me or my aid, yet suddenly you appear and ask me to take care of your son and now something else.'

Though his expression was strained he managed a slight smile. 'We must put the past behind us, Arabella.'

She realised he was serious about asking for her help yet again. She did not know what it could be, but she felt a strange tingling in the pit of her stomach. 'Tell me. What is it you want me to do?'

'Come with me to France. I have no right to ask this of you, I know, but you are right when you say I will be hard pressed to take care of Dickon alone and I cannot leave him behind.'

For the spell of a few heartbeats she stared at him incredulously, her eyes enormous in her pale face. She was unable to believe he wanted to take her on so perilous a journey. But he was not asking her for himself, she told herself with a stir of disappointment, but to take care if his son. There was no one else he could ask, none except her. It was she upon whom he depended, to whom he looked to take care of his son, because he assumed she would relent as she had done before. But it was a tempting prospect, especially if it meant she could spend some time with Dickon.

He was leaning against the wall, arms folded, watching her with that unnervingly level gaze as she struggled to form a reply.

'It is a fine thing you ask me to do. The threat of danger is very real.'

'For all of us. It is my intention to make for the port of Bristol—if not, then to the coast, perhaps south to Cornwall, depending on where the Parliamentarians are thin on the ground.'

Perplexed, and feeling a little defeated, she shook her head and crossed to the door. 'I don't know,' she murmured honestly. 'You take me by surprise. I cannot answer you now. In truth, I have no wish to go to France. Why should I? Everything I have is here at Bircot Hall. Besides, Alice will be against it, I know.'

'Are you not old enough and sensible enough to decide for yourself?'

'Yes, but why me? Why not someone else?'

'You know my reasons, Arabella. Yes, the

journey will be perilous, but you are the only woman I can trust to take care of my son should anything happen to me.'

'Then I beg you to leave him behind.'

'I cannot do that. He is my *son*. He is all I have left. I want him with me. Is that so unreasonable? You had a daughter. Would you not have wanted her with you?'

Arabella stared at him, wishing he had not mentioned her daughter. Turning from him, she swallowed down the hurt. 'Not if it meant putting her life in danger. Unlike you I did not have the choice.'

Edward had revived painful memories for her and he regretted his words as soon as he had said them. 'I'm sorry, Arabella. My words were badly said and not meant to hurt you. You must miss her.'

The compassion and understanding in his tone moved her. 'Every day,' she answered softly. 'Sometimes I cannot bear it.'

He came to stand behind her. The shed was small and suddenly felt unaccountably warm. She swallowed, catching her breath, her entire body filled with unwelcome yearning. She knew she should go, to tear herself away from the spell he was weaving. It was dangerous to linger, but she could not bring herself to leave.

His presence filled the shed and seemed to press against her flesh. Her hand was resting on the latch and, reaching out, he took it in his long, firm fingers, slowly turning her round to face him, his arm closing round her wrist. She swallowed, wondering if he could feel the pulse throbbing there, beating erratically beneath her skin with the steady increase of sensation, excitement and anticipation. The heat of him was tangible. Her own shadow loomed on the walls of the shed, his loomed larger.

Looking up at him, she watched the shadows play across his face in the candlelight. He impaled her with his eyes that made the colour flame in her cheeks. It stirred sensations she had felt when he had kissed her. She pulled herself up short. It was a small warning, but a warning she should take heed of. From the moment he had reappeared in her life, too often for her peace of mind Edward could get under her guard. She should learn to step back, to keep tighter rein on her attraction to him, but he was not an easy man to ignore.

'Well?' he asked softly. 'What is your answer to be?'

His voice was level, but when his eyes met Arabella's, there was a sudden, perilous silence. The intensity of his gaze was profound. His presence, his very nearness overwhelmed her. She couldn't think clearly. She told herself it was wrong, foolish to let her thoughts run away with her like this, that no good could come of it. She was not naïve of what happened between a man and a woman—no woman who had been married could be—but being in the confines of this shed unsettled her. The very quietness unsettled her. But mostly Edward Grey unsettled her.

She wanted to look away, to ignore the hunger in her loins, but she couldn't drag her eyes from his mouth, his face, and thinking about what it would be like to feel his body close to hers, to let her hands touch his flesh, to press her lips to the pulse that beat in the hollow of his throat and breathe in the scent of his skin. She was the first to look away as she considered his request, suddenly uneasy, aware that her cheeks were hot and flushed.

'I need time to think about it.'

His breath was warm on her face and sent a shiver down her spine. Releasing her wrist, he raised his hand and drew a finger gently along the line of her jaw, then down her throat. She shuddered with surprise or pleasure, she knew not which, but she did not want him to stop.

'Edward,' she whispered. Her dark lashes lowered across her eyes. She was afraid, but she did not know what it was she feared. She was suddenly so warm—it was as if she had fire in her veins.

'You are beautiful, Arabella,' he said, extending his caress to her cheek.

'No,' she murmured, shaking her head and raising her eyes to his. He was watching her, his face close to hers, as contented as an animal whose prey is neatly cornered. 'You are manipulative and demanding and only saying that to persuade me to say yes.'

'I speak the truth. You are still beautiful whether you come with me or not. You have looked after Dickon well,' he said, leaning forward and fixing that acute gaze on her face once more. 'Please, Arabella. I'm at my wits' end wondering how I'm going to get to France with him alone.'

'But wouldn't we slow you down—a woman and child?'

'Perhaps, but I am determined to take him with me.'

Arabella chewed her lip. She had agreed to care for Dickon at Bircot Hall, but she didn't want Edward thinking that he could rely on her. Yet she didn't want to let Dickon down the way Edward had let her down. But loving and caring for him had forced her to face her own limitations. She was getting too close to the child, so close that she hated to think of parting from him. But she would have to hold back, for how could she protect herself from his father?

Yet what if something should happen to Edward? What would happen to Dickon, alone and defenceless, a child at the mercy of a cruel world? Edward was standing there, watching her with quiet desperation and a need that was entirely separate from what he wanted her to do with Dickon in his eyes. At that moment he appeared darker and more dangerous and more unpredictable than she could recall.

Chapter Four

Arabella was struck by Edward's vitality and her own awareness of his masculinity. An ache awakened in her loins as his finger continued to move over her flesh, stroking her face, caressing her cheeks, her lips. She caught the scent of his flesh and lust stirred within her.

Very slowly he dropped a kiss on her forehead, a kiss as soft as the brush of a butterfly's wing, trailing his lips, so capable and so sure of their path, to her cheek as he drew her into his arms. Her breath coming quickly, she waited expectantly for his lips to touch hers. When they bypassed her mouth to her other cheek, she turned her head, capturing his lips with her own, emboldened by the intimacy of the surroundings and her own need.

She opened her mouth slightly under his, his short growth of beard brushing her flesh. She had never initiated a kiss and kissed him with a hunger she had never shared with her husband, and he responded in kind. The ardour of her response surprised him, she knew it, and she savoured the fleeting sense that she had surprised the most unpredictable man she had ever known. Answering her need, he deepened the kiss, his tongue probing and thrusting as their breaths mingled, warm and as one. He kissed her with that possessive ease that could clear a woman's mind of all thought.

When he finally released her lips she searched his face with a kind of wonder. Her lips still burned from his kiss. Recollecting herself and extremely conscious of her wanton response to his initial caress, very slowly and reluctantly she pulled herself from his arms and stood back from him, heat burning her cheeks. Despite everything he had done to her, despite her moral certainty that he should come to regret casting her off, she still longed to touch him, for him to touch her. He angered her, he infuriated her, yet never had she felt as alive as she did now and she desire him as ardently as she ever had.

'I'm sorry. I didn't mean to do that. What must you think of me?'

Their eyes met and each was aware that something had passed between them, something

so strong that it had taken them completely un-
awares. The intensity of his gaze told Arabella
that he wanted to bend his head and place his
lips on her full, soft mouth once more—and if
he was thinking that she wouldn't resist then
he was correct. He had kissed her possessively,
thoroughly, igniting a spark between them to a
smouldering fire. He looked at her knowingly,
fully aware of the hunger he had awakened
within her. He combed his fingers through his
tangled hair and she noticed how they trembled
slightly.

'It wasn't you, Arabella. I should have known
better.'

He was so intense that the air around him
seemed to tremble with it. He drew back from
her and opened the door, looking out into the
blackness that shrouded the shed. Arabella remained silent. Now that he no longer looked
at her, she gazed at the tall black figure, at the
haughty set of his shoulders, the implacability
in his stance and his averted head.

When he kissed her the way he had just done,
it was easy then to forget the resentment, the recriminations. Perhaps this was what she needed,
but when he released her, so sure of himself, her
pride came to the fore and she berated herself
for her body's betrayal. A kiss was only a mo-

ment of weakness. It did not break down the barriers of a bitter past.

At length he turned and looked at her. In the dim light his blue eyes had gone dark and hard between the narrowed lids and he spoke with chill precision. 'I have made up my mind to go. Forgive me. I should not have asked you to go with me, but I fear for Dickon if I am taken. Whatever you think of me, I did not kiss you to attempt to persuade you. That is the truth.'

A spear-thrust of pain slithered through her breast, but she spoke as steadily as he. 'Please don't go. Edward, think carefully. Cromwell will have sent soldiers in every direction to trap any Royalists who fled Worcester. What chance will you have with a small boy to care for?'

'I must.'

Arabella knew he could not be dissuaded. Embers of desire had been fanned just now, embers that had licked at her greedily and almost engulfed her. But a silent objection lingered and a small, uncomfortable voice in her head said, *What if he is simply using you?* The suggestion was unwelcome and she pushed it aside. The thought that this might be so was not to be borne. She was angry: more angry with herself for failing to learn from experience than with Edward for his persistence.

But she knew what she had to do. She would do as he asked, though she refused to examine why. All she knew was that he was offering her something infinitely special and she could not allow it to escape her. If she lost him now, she knew something inside her would wither and die. In a terrible painful moment of perception, she knew a sense of loss so strong it stole the breath from her body. She wanted to hold him back, for if he went without her she would lose him for ever.

She was shaking inside, but she lifted her chin and looked him straight in the eyes.

'Very well, Edward. I will do as you ask. I will go with you to France. But right now we have the more pressing matter of getting this shed ready for habitation. You have fought a battle and ridden far. You must be tired and hungry. We will talk about what is to be done in the morning when you are rested.' Her eyes were sombre as they lingered on his blood-stained clothes. 'We will have water brought across so that you can wash and some fresh clothes. Although it will be no simple matter bringing Stephen here.'

Everything was got ready quickly. Rushes were strewn on the floor of the shed. Sam and his son carried truckle beds and blankets. Food and water were carried across and fresh clothes that belonged to Alice's husband. By the time everything was ready Stephen was conscious and able to walk with aid.

When Arabella told Alice that she had decided to leave with Edward and Dickon, an uncomfortable silence fell.

Alice was incredulous. 'You are going with him!' she exclaimed, finding her tongue. 'Have you lost your senses, Arabella? Do you know the full import of what you are doing?' Her mouth settled into a grim line. 'Whatever possessed you to agree to such an outrageous thing?'

'I cannot let him travel with Dickon alone. Why, anything could happen to Edward—if so what would happen to his son? Before the war, for a woman to travel alone with a man who was not her husband would have given rise to condemnation, but the war has made people less concerned about morality.'

'You are of age and a widow so I can't stop you doing this foolish thing. But I beg of you to reconsider. Do not go rushing off with Edward like this. You are acting without thought of the consequences. You must stop and consider what you are doing.'

Arabella tossed back her head. 'I have decided, Alice. I accept what you say—I am of age and a widow with no child. Our parents are dead and there is no one who needs me, so I have no one to consider—except, perhaps, Dickon. Apart from his father, who may well be arrested at any time, Dickon is alone. We have that in common at least. So I have a right to choose what I do.'

'Choice you have, Arabella—you have always had it, but the choice to do the right thing. Your concern for the child is commendable and I know it is no good trying to dissuade you. I am simply afraid of what will happen to you when you reach France and there is no one to guide you. I believe what you are doing is perilous to your safety and the time you will spend with Sir Edward dangerous in other ways.'

'What are you saying?'

'Oh, Arabella, listen to me,' said Alice, reaching out and gripping her arms, looking hard into her eyes in an attempt to force some sense into her. 'Sir Edward is an attractive man. Do not let him play with your sensibilities. Physically you may not be able to resist him if you spend too long in his company. There is also the matter of the grief you still carry in your heart for Elizabeth. You cannot replace your daughter by taking Dickon to your heart. There will come

a time when you will have to let him go, you
must know that.'

Their eyes collided and Arabella looked
away, mortified that her face had reddened.
She was beginning to realise that something
beyond her control was pulling her into a web,
enmeshing her, and from which it seemed she
would never be allowed to escape.

'Yes, I do,' she said quietly, and she did, perfectly well. Alice was right, she did still mourn
Elizabeth. She had ceased to weep outwardly
and the pain and sadness had receded, but only
another child could fill the emptiness and loss
she still felt. 'But I cannot let Edward embark
on such a perilous journey alone with a child
to care for.'

Suddenly Alice's face tightened and the look
that accompanied this was needle sharp. 'Has
he persuaded you in some unscrupulous way
already? I saw him kiss you, if you recall, before he left for Worcester. He has not seduced
you, has he?'

Arabella was forced to smile. 'No, Alice,
nothing like that. My decision to go with him
was entirely my own.'

In the confusion that followed the battle at
Worcester, one thing was certain. The Royalist

cause was in ruins. The bloody defeat brought despair to all Royalists. Those who were not taken prisoner to be marched to London or transported to Barbados were fleeing for their lives. Nowhere was safe from search by Roundhead patrols. It was only a matter of time before they came to Bircot Hall.

In the meantime they had to make sure that the fugitives remained hidden. It was no easy matter keeping their presence from the children, but it was imperative they were kept ignorant in case Roundheads came to search the house and questioned them. The little ones could not have kept the secret.

Edward hated being so confined and his patience was wearing thin. His mind was active and unease prowled through him like a wild animal penned in a cage. Margaret, who was anxious, her main concern being for Stephen, fed him broth to build up his strength and Alice dressed his wound daily. It was healing well, but he remained weak. Arabella kept away from the apple store, but she did send some books for them to read and cards to help pass the time and relieve the boredom, but Edward soon tired of them.

Arabella was confused by her feelings for Edward. One half of her wanted to seek him out, to hear his voice, to see him, for him to touch her, while the other half was more cautious. She might have agreed to accompany him to France, but she was uneasy about the implications with regard to herself. Since making him comfortable in the apple store, she had kept him at arm's length—emotionally and physically.

It was a dreadful time, a time of waiting and living on a knife edge, not only for the fugitives but for the people who sheltered them. Arabella was frightened, yet she realised this kind of thing must be happening in many houses north, south, east and west of Worcester. There was courage, for if the soldiers came and found them sheltering Royalist fugitives they would all be hanged.

Events thrust themselves upon them ten days after the battle when a small detachment of Roundhead soldiers rode through the gatehouse, intruding into their home and destroying its peace. Sam had posted Tom to be a lookout for them so they were prepared and quickly warned the fugitives.

Arabella was in the hall with Alice. Margaret and Bertha were in an upstairs room with the children. The two women stood side by side, taking strength from each other, their eyes fixed on the door. The air was charged the way it was before a storm.

Alice gave Arabella's hand a comforting squeeze. 'We will need all our wits about us to play our part, Arabella. Without a male presence, it falls to us, the women, to uphold the family's honour and do our duty.'

'We can do no more,' Arabella whispered.

They listened to the jangle of harness and the sound of men dismounting, the ring of booted feet on stone as they strode to the door. They both started when it burst open and three men walked in. The man in front halted, staring at the two women.

A shiver of apprehension and fear scurried up Arabella's spine as she watched the swaggering soldier wearing the orange sash of the Parliamentary force stride towards them. His face was hard and uncompromising. She shrank back as horror streaked through her.

He studied the sisters with an intent bright gaze. His eyes were a cold calculating grey, his expression uncompromising. 'We are here to find out if you are harbouring any Royalist rebels who have fled Worcester. If you are, I demand you give them up.'

Alice lifted her chin and met his eyes steadily.

'I would like to welcome you to my *abode*, sir, but I fear I cannot.'

His eyes narrowed, assessing her, no doubt wondering if her emphasis had been deliberate. 'You have little choice in the matter.'

Fear coursed through Arabella. Did he intend to seize Bircot Hall wilfully?

'There are no fugitives in this house,' Alice told him firmly.

'I would hardly expect you to hand them over if there were,' he uttered coldly, his sweeping gaze taking note of everything in the hall. 'We will search the house ourselves in case one or two found their way inside while you were abed.'

'Do as you will, but you will find nothing. As you see,' Alice said, indicating the torn wainscoting that had once been hung with the finest tapestries, 'we have not been spared the realities of war. Your men have been here before. It is thanks to them that the house is riddled with holes from top to bottom. They left no stone unturned.'

He removed his close-fitting helmet to reveal his cropped hair. 'If there is the faintest sniff of a rebel, we will find him.'

Arabella looked at the figure in the leather jerkin, disliking his narrow, pale face, the cold eyes and the thin mouth. He looked familiar, but she could not remember where she had seen him before.

'Who are you, sir?' A faint, contemptuous smile touched his lips and she felt the malevolence in him. Her heart was hammering low against her ribs as he strode slowly towards her, his eyes never leaving her face.

'Sir Malcolm Lister, Colonel in the Commonwealth Army.'

Arabella went cold. She should have known. May God help Edward if he was found, for this man would show him no mercy.

Colonel Lister turned to his men. 'Search the house—and the stables.' His eyes slithered to the two women. 'And leave no stone unturned,' he said, quoting Alice's words. 'I am aware that this house belongs to the malignant Sir Robert Stanhope. You must be Lady Stanhope.' His insolent eyes swept Alice.

'I am indeed Lady Alice Stanhope,' Alice said coldly, meeting his eyes squarely and straightening her spine. 'We are a simple family going about our business, hoping the troubles will end so we can return to our normal lives.'

'That is what we all wish for, Lady Stanhope, as soon as we run Charles Stuart and his supporters to ground. And your husband?' His glance swept the hall, as if seeking places where the fugitives might by hidden.

'He is in France. You find nothing but a house full of women and children, Colonel, and three servants.' She gave him a thin smile. 'This is a time of hardship, Colonel Lister. We keep a minimal household here at Bircot Hall.'

'Nevertheless, I will have this house searched from top to bottom,' he said in a low, accusing tone.

'Search all you like, Colonel, but you will find nothing.'

'We shall see about that.' He nodded coldly, his eyes sliding to Arabella. 'And you. You must be Mistress Charman.'

'Lady Arabella Fairburn,' Arabella corrected him. She forced her voice to sound calm. 'I married Sir John Fairburn, who was killed at the battle of St Fagans in forty-eight.'

'I was there. The Royalist forces—made of amateurs armed with nothing but clubs and billhooks—were routed.' Colonel Lister's eyes narrowed and he eyed her strangely. 'I recall Sir John Fairburn. Dead, you say?'

'Do you have reason to doubt it, sir?'

He shrugged. 'I thought he'd fled across the water with his tail between his legs.'

A cold tremor shivered its way down Arabella's spine. 'You must be mistaken, sir. He was returned to me and I buried him.' Her mind began to work frantically. Of course John was dead. Hadn't the men who had been with him seen him fall? Hadn't she watched his coffin lowered into the ground? She hadn't seen his body, but she'd had no reason to question it.

There was no tenderness in her memories of John. She *had* to believe it. He had to be dead. If he wasn't, then she couldn't bear to think of the consequences. And yet, hadn't the letter Alice had received from her husband in Paris placed doubts in her mind that he might not be?

'Before that you were betrothed to Edward Grey, as I recall, Lady Fairburn,' Colonel Lister said.

'I was,' she answered, more than a little uneasy about his comments about John. 'As you know, he reneged on the agreement he made with my father in favour of your sister.' She saw a flash of something unpleasant in Malcolm Lister's eyes and she sensed the malice he held for Edward rippling beneath the surface.

'Much good it did her. Edward Grey fought at Worcester. It is known that he fought alongside Charles Stuart and that he escaped. Have you seen him? Has he been here?'

Arabella's lips twisted with disdain. 'Why

would he do that? He is hardly likely to come to a house where he knows he is not welcome.'

Colonel Lister smiled thinly, but there was something else there, too, something malicious and condescending. His eyes were very bright and Arabella had the uncomfortable feeling that he could see right inside her, that he knew that she was lying.

'But how would he know you were here? Your husband lived in the Vale of Glamorgan, as I recall—where his wife would be.'

'The house was burnt to ashes and two of the servants butchered before your soldiers left Wales, Colonel Lister. Their behaviour was indefensible.'

He shrugged, unmoved. 'Such acts and atrocities are not uncommon on both sides. It is war. I know Grey was in London before he went to join Charles Stuart. He spirited my nephew to God knows where.'

'Perhaps he sent him to France where he knew he would be safe,' Alice said. 'I believe he has a sister in Paris.'

'Perhaps, Lady Stanhope. Perhaps he has done just that. He escaped Worcester with your brother, Stephen Charman. It was reported that Charman was wounded during the battle and escaped with Edward Grey. Despite what was between him and your sister in the past, where would Grey take a wounded man if not to his family?'

'Stephen was wounded?' Alice gasped, feigning shock and surprise. 'I pray to God he still lives.'

'And I pray your prayers are answered, Lady Stanhope. That way we will catch two birds with one stone, for I doubt Edward Grey would abandon his friend in a ditch.' His smile held a hint of steel. 'Rest assured. If they are here, we will find them. Be so good as to have the children and your servants assemble in the hall.'

A sudden chill touched Arabella's neck. She felt it all the way down her spine. What if he should recognise Dickon? She had failed to ask Edward how well Malcolm Lister knew his young nephew.

Aware of her instinctive recoil, his eyes narrowed. 'Is there a problem?'

'No. I will go now and bring them down.'

Arabella went quickly to find Margaret, her mind working frantically. What if he wanted to question the children? They would have nothing to tell. What if he asked their names? Please God he would not ask. They had all gone to great pains so the children would not know about the two men hidden in the apple store on the other side of the orchard.

Margaret looked fearful when she entered the bedchamber. The children were gathered round her, Dickon asleep on her lap. Arabella couldn't believe her luck.

'Quickly, Margaret. You have to go down to the hall. Take the children. The soldiers are searching the house.' Taking a blanket from the bed, she wrapped it around Dickon's sleeping form and took him in her arms, almost covering his face and praying he would not wake up just yet. 'It is imperative they do not see Dickon,' she whispered so the children would not hear. 'His uncle, Malcolm Lister, is leading the search. If he should recognise his nephew, all will be lost.'

Understanding fully, Margaret ushered the children out of the bedchamber and down the stairs. 'Now you must be very quiet,' she said as she went along. 'We don't want to antagonise the men who are searching the house.'

Malcolm Lister watched the children file across the hall and stand beside Sam and Tom, who were watching the Roundheads belligerently. Arabella sat next to them, holding Dickon close.

'The children are yours, Lady Stanhope?' he asked.

'Yes—as you see the youngest is sleeping,' she said, indicating the closely wrapped bundle on Arabella's knee.

He nodded and turned away from the nervous gathering of frightened people. Crossing the hall, he mounted the stairs to join the soldiers searching the house.

As Arabella watched him go, it seemed to her that she had stopped breathing. Her stomach knotted with fear. She thought of the two men hiding across the orchard and it was as though a cold hand clutched her heart. What if they discovered them? No. She could not think of the dire consequences now.

They listened to the tramping of feet, the splintering of wood as pikes were thrust into the panelling, doors flung open and furniture being turned over. They searched from the attics to the cellars. Some of the soldiers were searching the stables and when this was done and nothing was found, they came to help the others tearing the house apart. It seemed to go on and on and no one spoke, all eyes were focused on the stairs. Thankfully Dickon slept on, oblivious to the fear and destruction going on around him.

* * *

When the search was finally over and had proved futile, Colonel Lister returned to the hall. An angry frown creased his brow. He was clearly disappointed that his arch-enemy, Edward Grey, continued to elude him.

'Well?' asked Alice. 'Have you found anything—anyone hiding?'

Arabella looked up to find him watching her with a hard, intent gaze. The sight of his sly eyes set something crawling under her skin. Averting her eyes, she tightened her arms round the child.

'No.' He paused and his audience knew he hoped to prolong their fear. 'We will take our leave of you, but I trust you will think twice before you grant succour to any rebels who might find their way to Bircot Hall. The consequences are dire to anyone found harbouring traitors.'

'Of course. Good day, Colonel Lister.'

His face darkened as his eyes passed from Alice to Arabella. 'Edward Grey will be found. I *will* find him. That I swear.'

Arabella met his gaze defiantly and did not move, did not speak, lest her fear show. She noted the sword he was fingering, almost lovingly, as if he wanted to unsheathe it to run someone through. She saw the hate he carried for Edward in his eyes. But it was gone in a flash.

Sam followed the colonel and his soldiers outside. The house was quiet once more. For a while the small group of inhabitants did not say a word, but stood in the hall and waited. Finally Sam returned.

'They've gone. They've ridden away.'

Arabella let out a huge sigh of relief. 'Thank God.'

'We dare not go to the shed just yet,' Alice said quietly. 'They may have left someone to watch the house.'

'I agree,' Arabella replied, looking down as Dickon stirred in her arms and smiled sleepily up at her before opening his mouth in a contented yawn.

'I'll go and see what damage has been done.' Alice looked at Sam. 'Come with me, Sam, and help put things to rights.'

Not until the following morning did anyone dare venture across the orchard to the shed. Sam had warned Edward and Stephen of the arrival of the Roundhead patrol and, knowing they would be at their wits' end wondering what was happening, it was Arabella who went to tell them what had transpired.

Stephen was sleeping, as he so often was. Alice said it was not a bad thing and would help with his recovery.

Edward drew Arabella outside the door so as not to disturb him.

Despite the seriousness of their predicament and the news she had brought him, when she looked at him she was conscious, as always, of an unwitting excitement. Feeling her cheeks grow hot, she bent her head, the movement sending a sliver of sunlight over her bright hair. Then, raising her head, she met his gaze, every muscle stretched against the invisible pull between them.

Taking her arm, he drew her into the shelter of the trees.

'Well, Arabella? What happened when the soldiers came? Were you harmed in any way?'

'No,' she was quick to assure him. 'The house did not fare well, they searched everywhere—and the stables.'

'Thank God they did not extend their search further afield. How many were there?'

'Half a dozen or so, but Edward, the man leading them was Malcolm Lister.'

Edward's face darkened for an instant as he strove for control. 'Dickon? Please tell me he did not see Dickon?'

'No. Your son slept on my knee throughout and did not wake until they had left. He was wrapped in a blanket so his face was not exposed. Is he well acquainted with him? Would he have recognised him?'

'Maybe not. As far as I am aware he has not seen him since he was a babe.'

Edward listened to the rest of what she had to say without speaking. It was not until she had finished that he said, 'Malcolm Lister. Knowing of my friendship with Stephen, I suspected he might come here. I fear he will come back. We cannot delay much longer. I cannot risk him finding me—and Dickon.'

'If you wait for Stephen to recover, you could go together,' Arabella suggested hopefully. 'I could come to you later with Dickon.'

He shook his head. 'Together we would be too conspicuous. No. I will keep to my original plan.'

'It is obvious Dickon is special to you. You must love him very much.'

'He is the centre of my world—an infinite concern. I never expected to feel that way about anything before he was born. I would never have credited how profoundly I could be affected by a giggle and a grin from an infant. He claimed my heart, Arabella.'

Arabella had little knowledge of his private life, of what his feelings had been for his wife—presumably he had loved her once. But because of the all-consuming love she had felt for her own child, she could understand why he was so desperate to keep his son safe.

Her lips curved in a tremulous smile. 'I know. I'm not surprised. He is adorable. And a lucky little boy to have such an affectionate father. I—envy you your son, Edward.'

Hearing the catch in her voice, he could have kicked himself for being so insensitive to her feelings. 'Good Lord! Forgive me, Arabella. I didn't think…'

'Please, it doesn't matter.' She took a step away from him, her tone becoming tight with emotion as it always did when an image of Elizabeth came to mind. 'I'd best be getting back. There are things to do if we are to leave soon.'

She turned to walk away, but he seized her elbow and pulled her to a halt. 'I'm sorry, Arabella. Look at me.' Slowly she turned back to face him. His smile was crooked and soft. 'I like you better angry than when you have a wounded look in your eyes or when you retreat into cool civility.'

He touched her cheek with his finger. It was a possessive, intimate gesture. It was suddenly as if she couldn't move. Her breath caught in her throat at his alarming proximity and her heart skipped a beat for there was no escaping that bright gaze. His finger was soft, softer than she could have believed, his touch gentle. She was tempted to close her eyes, tempted to lean into his caress, tempted to discard every warning her head was screaming at her.

Taking a deep breath, she smiled slightly and moved back. His eyes were soft and tempered her fears. 'I am fine. Truly. It is only that, sometimes, when I think of Elizabeth, it hurts so much.'

'Of course it does. I can understand that.'

She nodded. 'So, what do you want to do—about leaving?'

'We will leave in the morning—first thing.'

'What do you need?' Arabella asked, knowing it was no use arguing further about leaving Dickon behind. His mind was made up.

'A cart of some sort would be a start—and that old nag in the stable you mentioned. To use one of the horses we arrived on would draw attention to us. Horses are scarce and anyone showing too much wealth suspicious. We must appear as poor farmers travelling to Bristol to visit family. Ships go from Bristol to the Continent all the time. It will be dangerous so we'll have to be on our guard. The port will be watched. For the purpose of disguise we will pass ourselves off as man and wife and travel under false names.' He eyed her with a raised, questioningly amused brow. 'Any suggestions?'

'No—I—I haven't thought...'

'Then I will call myself Will Brody and you will be—'

'Amy,' she offered quickly. 'I'd like to keep it simple and I've always liked Amy for a name.'

'Amy it is, then. Amy Brody.'

'Right. I'll go and begin preparations.'

Preparations were made for them to leave and soon it was daylight. Edward's expression was without emotion as he reviewed his plans with Arabella. Through it all she listened, periodically running her hand over her brow as she tried to take it all in.

'One hard and fast rule. If we want to survive, we must not forget our disguise and do nothing to draw attention to us. Do not forget our assumed names for a moment. If I am taken, you may share what might be my fate.'

Arabella was touched by his concern for her survival. Or was it merely because without her, his son would be alone? 'I cannot believe I am going to France with you.'

'We will have food with us, but not too much to raise suspicion if we are searched. We will take blankets in case we have to spend nights under the stars. Fortunately it is warm enough.' When he had told her about the journey they would make he looked at her carefully. 'Do you still agree to come?'

'I cannot condone what we are going to do—something that might easily result in your capture. But I can see that it is necessary. I cannot let you do it alone.'

His eyes searched her face. 'Are you afraid of what we are about to do?'

'Not afraid. Apprehensive.'

He nodded, meeting her open, honest, intelligent eyes. 'That's to be expected.' She was gentle and compassionate, yet he believed she had the physical strength to do what had to be done, to do what he planned, and from what she had told him of her life since they had parted, she also had the mental strength.

'I want you to promise me something, Arabella. Promise me that if I am caught and you and Dickon are free you will still go to France. That you will do all in your power to reach Verity.'

As his words penetrated her mind her body became rigid. 'And leave you here? I have no illusions as to what will happen to you if you are caught. Already you are a condemned man.'

Gripping her shoulders, he looked down at her, his expression taut, his eyes fierce. 'Do you think I don't know that? I have to face facts and so must you. If I am taken, only death will prevent me from joining you in France. Promise me that you will take Dickon to my sister.'

She nodded dumbly, her throat swollen so much it hurt. 'Yes. I promise.'

Edward was almost unrecognisable. He had not shaved since before Worcester and a thick black beard covered half his face. His clothes were ill fitting and patched and a battered old slouch hat covered his dark and curling hair, which he had carelessly tied back. Arabella looked no better in her much-worn clothes and an old cloak Bertha had given her. She carried a purse holding the money they would need to see them to Bristol and their passage to France.

She looked down at her dismal attire with considerable amusement. 'We certainly look the part.'

Edward stopped what he was doing and, placing his finger beneath her chin, he tilted her face up to his.

'You may be attired in the simple clothes of

a countrywoman, Arabella, but you are more beautiful than you realise—far more so than any of the ladies who flutter about the grand halls in Paris.'

Laughing up at him, she removed his finger. 'Flatterer.'

'It's not flattery.' Edward's face was serious.

The sun softened his handsome features—yes, even with his untidy beard he was still handsome. There was an intensity in his deep-blue eyes which made her heartbeat quicken. His lips drew back into a smile, his teeth gleaming and strong between his parted lips.

'What chance has a common soldier with all the preening lords you will meet in France?'

Arabella laughed, refusing to take him seriously. 'I have no interest in preening lords. And you are not a common soldier.'

He gave her a long silent look which surprised her, for he was not usually lost for words. 'When we reach Paris and you are decked out in silk and satin, you will be like a princess.'

Coming to stand beside them, her arms filled with blankets for their journey, Alice smiled as she took in their attire. 'You certainly look like a modest couple. Anyone seeing you will be convinced you are what you pretend to be.'

The word 'couple' brought a pink flush to

Arabella's cheeks. Edward merely grinned and, taking the blankets from Alice, put them into the cart.

'Don't forget to be on your guard at all times,' Alice said, looking with concern from one to the other. 'Perhaps getting out of the country is the sensible thing to do. The sooner you reach the coast and board a ship bound for France, the better. Sam has been to the village and tells me that a proclamation has been circulated seeking the King's capture and a reward of one thousand pounds for his whereabouts. Some people would sell their soul for that much money. Anyone whose loyalties are not with the King will be on the lookout for any man resembling his description. The posters that have been put out describe a tall dark man over two yards high.' She gave Edward a pointed look. 'The description could be you, Edward. Have a care.'

At this news, all Arabella's fears came to the surface and she had an impending feeling of doom. Because of this the dangers to them were greatly increased. Edward and the King were much alike and mistakes could be made.

Alice hugged her sister warmly. 'When you reach France, write and let me know you have arrived safely. Promise me.'

'I do. I promise.'

Alice turned to Edward. 'My sister is a woman of integrity and honesty and she will endeavour to do her best for the welfare and protection of your son. She has a rare and generous soul and I love her dearly. Take care of her.'

Seeing Alice's anxiety, Edward smiled. 'Don't worry. I will do all in my power to look after her. You can depend on it. Now come, Arabella. It's time to go. We have a long way to go and can delay no longer.'

Arabella took her seat on the bench beside Edward, settling Dickon between them. He was quiet but excited to be going on a journey. Edward took the reins. The old horse that had served his time so well at Bircot Hall was between the shafts. Arabella turned to look at Alice and Margaret one last time. She had not left Bircot Hall since she had arrived after John's death three years before. Now, to be cut off from the security of her family brought a tightness around her throat and a hollowness in the pit of her stomach as they passed beneath the gatehouse and the two of them disappeared from view. She was unsure of the journey ahead of them, unsure that everything would go as planned, but it was too late to turn back now.

'I hope you know how to drive this contraption,' she said as she was almost catapulted into the air when the cart bounced over a rut, causing Dickon much hilarity.

Edward looked at her and laughed, relieved to be doing something positive at last. 'What is there to know? The horse does all the work.'

Chapter Five

It was a strange kind of existence as Edward and Arabella travelled away from Bircot Hall. Dickon was excited about going on a journey with his father and Arabella. His eyes were wide and bright as he sat between them on the wooden seat. He had no idea where they were going or why, but for now it was all one big adventure.

They travelled on quiet tracks, for not only were they more likely to run into Roundheads on main thoroughfares but they were also notorious for thieves. Arabella was relieved that Edward had a flintlock pistol in his belt. They avoided villages, only stopping in deep undergrowth to eat the food Alice had prepared.

Despite the ever-present dangers of discovery, and seeing how difficult it was for Edward to play the part of a common countryman,

Arabella loved being out in the open air and for the first time since Elizabeth had died she felt young and alive. The September weather favoured them. She loved autumn, with the smell of harvest in the air, the orchards with trees hung with soon-to-be-picked apples and pears.

When Dickon fell asleep Arabella made him comfortable in the back of the cart, tucking a blanket around him, conscious of the fact that she was arranging the coming weeks and maybe her whole life about his father. What was it about Edward Grey that had made her decide to do this reckless thing?

They'd been on the road for hours. Arabella was tired and hungry and sore from bumping up and down on the wooden seat.

'Where are we going to spend the night?'

'There's sure to be a tavern in the next village. We will stay there.'

'And if there isn't a tavern?'

He turned to look at her and a ghost of a smile lit his face. 'Does a night under the stars appeal to you?'

She laughed at his suggestion, meeting his eyes. 'If the weather is kind to us, then I will not mind. We have enough food to last us for a couple of days. It might also be better to avoid coming into contact with others unless we have to.' She turned to look at the sleeping child. 'I don't think Dickon will mind. He is treating it all as an adventure—as I did when I left Wales to come to Bircot Hall.'

'Stephen told me you went to live in South Glamorgan.'

'Yes—in my husband's house. His parents were dead and he was an only child. The house was lovely—not far from the sea.'

'Were you happy living there?'

Looking straight ahead, she spoke without much enthusiasm. 'I liked the country.'

He turned his head and looked at her, saying carefully, 'And your husband? Were you happy in your marriage, Arabella?'

She heard the concern in his voice and a pre-occupied expression drew over his face, showing that his mind was working swiftly. 'It was not what I expected,' she answered honestly, unable to tell a lie. 'John could be—difficult.' She wanted to add that her husband had been a dark, vicious man, his manner cold, but unwilling to humble or humiliate herself, instead she said, 'He did not always treat me kindly.'

'I am sorry to hear that.' The quiet sincerity with which he spoke struck a chord in Arabella. 'Did he hurt you?'

'Emotionally, yes. He was not an easy man to live with.'

Edward became quiet and the silence bit keenly into her nerves.

'I'm sorry to mention it, Arabella.' There was outrage in his tone.

'Don't be. I found a way to live with my marriage.'

'But you were not happy.'

She considered the question. 'I was safe and well fed. John wanted a son.' She remembered how disgusted he had been when he had been told he had a daughter. Her hands were trembling and she hoped he would not notice. Then her eyes found his and she spoke frankly, with much relief that someone else knew. 'After the birth of Elizabeth, with sporadic fighting breaking out, hoping to be well rewarded if Parliament were overthrown, he went to take up arms for the King.'

He looked at her, his face holding a rare look of softness. 'And he was killed at the battle that took place at St Fagans.'

'Yes.'

'Then he cannot hurt you further.'

Arabella recalled the contents of Robert's letter and later what Colonel Lister had told her about John and that he might not be dead, but she refused to believe that. He had to be dead. He must be dead. Her throat tightened and her hands clung to the seat when she thought what it would mean to her if he wasn't dead. She looked at Edward. His eyes were fixed on the road once more and he was solid, steady as a rock in the middle of a world that would spin wildly out of her control should John not be dead.

But if he wasn't dead, where was he?

As she looked at Edward, in a moment of clarity she saw him as if for the first time: the frown lines on his brow, the firm, strong angles of his face, the strength of his jaw and the firm sensual line of his mouth. She knew what that mouth felt like, how it moved over hers, and she felt the warmth that threatened to uncoil inside her. For a moment she wanted to reach out to him, to have him take her in his arms, to feel the solid security of his chest, to let herself feel safe.

She was shocked by how much she desired him. She could not deny it no matter how through sheer force of will she tried. The effort weakened her, defeating her will until she was floundering, longing for more.

Only now did she realise how familiar he had become to her. How important he was to her.

* * *

Edward had heard the sudden catch in her voice when she had been talking about her husband and it disturbed him greatly. The soul-stirring sadness and raw vulnerability had struck him as hard as a fist in the gut and he wondered just how much ugliness she had been forced to endure married to John Fairburn.

Intuitively, he had known something had not been right with her marriage. He guessed at the bullying she must have been subjected to, but he was careful to hold his opinions back. It was not his place to pry into her personal life, but he felt moved to sympathy.

The hours were long as the old horse's tireless trot ate up the miles. Dusk was fast approaching. Only the gentle undulation of the Cotswold Hills were rosy with the setting sun. The land and the hillsides were black with shadows. Every now and then they would pass travellers on the road, but as darkness closed in they saw no one.

Tired and hungry and aching from being jolted about on the wooden seat, they found a place to spend the night in a clearing sheltered by trees and away from the road. Arabella prepared their supper before washing in a nearby stream. When Dickon became fretful she made a game of sleeping outdoors, making makeshift boats out of twigs and leaves and floating them on the stream, playing peekaboo and telling him stories she remembered from her own childhood. Cradled in her arms he listened intently, but gradually his eyes fluttered closed and he slept.

Smiling down at him, his small dark head peeking out above the covering blanket, looking up she saw Edward leaning against a tree watching her with an odd expression on his face.

'He's tired,' she said softly, sitting on the grass and drawing her knees up in front of her. 'He should sleep until morning.'

'He seems to trust you.'

'I'd like to think so. Dickon is a quiet boy. I suspect there hasn't been much happiness in his young life.'

His gaze was studying her, searching her eyes, lingering on her face until her cheeks grew warm with his quiet perusal.

'You're right—and I know that's my fault. Others have been employed to look after him since he was born, but they cannot compete with a mother's lifetime care. Because of the war I've been occupied with other things and unable to spend the time with him I would have liked. I confess that it worries me. Every time one of them he's become attached to leaves it is like a lesson in heartbreak.'

'That's probably why he's such a quiet boy. But he needs other children as well as his father. I saw how happy he was with Alice's children for company.'

'His safety is my prime concern, but it will also be good for him to be with Verity. She has two children, Maria and Thomas—Thomas being just a little older than Dickon. It's time he had some stability in his life.'

'She'll be surprised when you turn up with Dickon and me. But he's still very young. Children are resilient. They adapt.'

'I hope so. I intend to be there for him in the future, to protect him. I had to act quickly to keep him from falling into Malcolm Lister's hands. He wants to make him his heir.'

'He could do that without taking him away from you.'

'No. He wants to take him and mould him into what he wants him to be—as he would his own son if he had one. I can't let that happen. No one knows how long we will have to remain in France. With my father dead and my sister in France, my estate seized by Parliament and myself declared a traitor, one thing is certain. I cannot—I will not return to England while it is ruled by Cromwell.'

'Maybe, in time, pardons may be issued to those who supported the king, if they agree to abide by the rules of the Commonwealth. Would you return if that happened?'

He shook his head. 'I cannot plan beyond the present. I—and many like me—have fought too long and too hard to do that. I am a hardened soldier, Arabella. I will not live and abide by the laws of the Commonwealth. If making my home in France is the price I have to pay, then so be it.' Shrugging himself away from the tree, he came and sat by her on the grass. 'I'm glad Dickon has found someone to look up to in you.'

The absurdity of his statement made Arabella smile. 'I've only known him a short while so I doubt he will miss me when I go back to Bircot Hall.'

'I disagree.' His eyes held hers, communicating their sincerity. 'You don't have to return to England.'

'Yes, I do. My care is only temporary. When Dickon is settled with your sister, I will come back. I remember Verity. She was several years my senior, but she was always kind and never treated me like a child.'

'Unlike me.'

Even in the dusk, she could see his eyes sparkle with mischief. 'Sometimes.' She laughed to soften her rebuke. 'Although in those days I suppose I did seem terribly young to an experienced soldier of your years.'

'There's still the difference in years as there was then.'

'But I was still very much a child in many ways, an innocent, far more naïve than I care to remember—far more than the women with whom you usually kept company.'

'You were very young, Arabella,' he said, taking her hand in his. 'I remember the day you were born. I remember my mother taking Verity and me to see you, making us pick some flowers from our garden to take to your mother.'

'My goodness! Did she really?' She laughed, finding the picture he had planted in her mind warming. 'Of course I don't remember,' she remarked, with a mischievous quirk to her brow.

He laughed. 'I would not expect you to.'

'Did you see me?'

'Of course. You were tiny, with the tiniest little fingers,' he said, raising those same fingers to his mouth and brushing them with his lips. 'You really were a pretty little thing, although you slept all the way through our visit.'

'I remember when I was a child—I couldn't have been more than five years old—and you would come to ride out with Stephen. I would cry because you wouldn't take me with you—even though my father had given me my own pony by then. I thought you were very handsome and I soon realised I wasn't the only one who thought so. All the girls I knew thought the same as me.' She laughed, unable to shake off the effects of his winning smile and the feel of his hand hold hers. 'Although I soon realised you were adept in brushing away admiring young maids placed before you by their parents hoping you would look at them and form an attachment.'

'I had eyes only for you, Bella. You were the one I became betrothed to.'

She sighed resignedly, unwilling to spoil the intimacy of the moment by raking through the unpleasantness of his later rejection of her. 'I regret it didn't last.'

'So do I,' he replied softly, staring into her translucent eyes that had ensnared his somehow. 'You no longer resemble that precocious, happy child I knew. Now you are a beautiful and fascinating young woman, a woman I respect, and that is how I will treat you. But you must forgive me if I forget myself now and then and attempt to draw you closer. I have been too long a soldier that I forget how to be a gallant.'

She had no idea how her hair hanging loose tempted his fingers. Her eyes sparkling and clear, her lips trembled in a smile. 'But you do not forget how to flatter a lady, Edward.'

'It is not flattery.' His face was serious.

A lock of his dark hair had fallen forward across his brow and the fading light softened his angular face. With the silence around them broken only by the water in the stream wending its way over its rocky bed to the River Severn, the potency of his gaze was intoxicating, sending tingling down through her body. They sat without moving, their gazes arrested, held in silent communication of attraction. Arabella's mouth became dry and her heart quickened its beat. She longed for him to kiss her as he had before and ran her tongue over her bottom lip, unaware of the sensual invitation of her action. His eyes still holding hers were dark with desire.

Suddenly a memory assailed her of the clumsy and aggressive assaults John had made on her body and her flesh went cold. A new, dark fear crept through her. Had John scarred her mentally so that she was unable to respond to another man's touch, a lover's touch? No, she thought, her mind rebelling at the thought, she would not grant him that kind of power over her. She would not allow him to triumph over her in death. And had she not responded to Edward when he had kissed her at Bircot Hall? She had certainly not been repelled by it—quite the opposite, in fact, despite his dishonourable behaviour to her in the past. She was haunted by the whispering memories of the passionate response of her body to the intimacies he had shown her. She was tormented by the rapture she had tasted in his kiss and the passion his touch had ignited.

Edward could give her pleasure and that was all she wanted—a tender, skilful lover. In fact, she would not object if he were to kiss her again. A sudden longing for him to do just that must have shown in her eyes, for he exhaled sharply.

'Arabella.'

Leaning a little towards him, she watched his eyes darken. His lashes lowered, his eyes focused on her lips. Instinctively she leaned a little further, willing him to kiss her. But he made no move. The sound of the rippling water ticked off the seconds as their gazes locked. Instead of kissing her lips, Edward raised her fingers to his mouth. A subtle gasp, barely a whisper, passed her lips, and he smiled, releasing her hand.

'I think it's time we retired. Lie down,' he said softly, breaking the silence, and Arabella imagined that there was the small hint of a plea in his voice. 'We have a long journey ahead of us tomorrow and you need to rest.'

Getting to his feet and fetching a couple of blankets from the cart, he handed one to her, spreading his own on the ground. Taking hers, she moved away from him to sleep closer to Dickon.

'You don't have to sleep so far away, Arabella. I won't bite.'

She looked at him. 'I don't expect you will.'

'Then what are you afraid of?'

She stared at him as he settled on his blanket, wrapping it around his long body.

'I am not afraid. I merely wish to sleep beside Dickon in case he wakes.'

'Goodnight, Arabella. Sleep well.'

Bravely suppressing a worrying thought at sleeping out in the open, Arabella still didn't know if she trusted Edward totally. He had asked her to travel with him to France to care for his son on the journey, but he had said nothing of his purpose for her. When she had told him she would return to Bircot Hall when Dickon was settled with his sister, he hadn't tried to persuade her to remain in Paris. What was she to do? Edward possessed a mysterious power to stir her blood. He assailed her senses whenever he was close.

Fortunately the night was warm and the grass soft and springy, providing the perfect mattress. Sitting down, she wrapped the blanket around her and lay back, watching Edward do the same. Suddenly sleepy, she yawned behind a hand and, closing her eyes, she listened to the sounds of the night, the quiet rustling of some unseen animal in the bushes, the soft wind riffling through the leaves and the gentle munching of the horse. She longed for the oblivion that would give her respite before the sun rose.

They were on the road again when the morning sky was still streaked with the lingering salmon-pink-and-gold tones of dawn. The morning air was damp and crisp and filled with the lingering smells of leaves and earth. Arabella was chillingly aware of how vulnerable they were. Edward was quiet, wary and watchful, looking out for Commonwealth soldiers. They did see the odd small troop, but no one took any notice of the bearded peasant hunched in his wagon with his wife and child beside him.

When they were just ten miles from Bristol

they spent the night in a tavern on the edge of a small hamlet with a village pond. Dickon was tired and after eating his supper he was soon asleep on the small cot in the room all three of them were to share. They had told the innkeeper they were man and wife, and to have asked for separate rooms would have raised his eyebrows and probably his suspicions that they were not what they seemed.

In the quiet of the room, both pairs of eyes were drawn to the only bed.

Arabella saw Edward's eyes brighten as if his thoughts had risen in some eager anticipation. When he looked at her, his eyes were steady and remained still. She was drawn into those eyes. She wanted him so much. She moved closer, seeking solace from the turmoil of her emotions. Edward represented safety and security.

'I think you're going to have to help me,' she whispered. 'I've never been in a bedroom before with a man who is not my husband.'

His reserve and wariness that had been present all day disappeared. His eyes held hers in one long, compelling look, holding all her frustrated desires, all the restraints she had forced on her nature for so long, everything she had been keeping to herself in the days they had been on the road.

'Arabella… Any minute now I may forget I shouldn't be here, alone with you.'

'Please don't go.'

With that unequivocal invitation, without restraint he closed the distance between them. His arms curled around her and once again she felt the immense thrill of being held against him. She was overcome by a passionate desire to surrender herself to him. As his lips touched hers, despite the roughness of his beard which brushed her face, a sharp intake of breath betrayed her longing for him. The force between them had grown powerful and impatient, and the longing could no longer be denied.

His breath was warm, his arms strong, powerful and safe. The blood pounding through her ears obliterated all will and reason and all she could feel was an immense and incredible joy. It was like a wild and beautiful madness. Running her hands over his chest, she sighed, her mouth against his lips.

'I don't know why,' she whispered, 'but despite everything that has happened between us in the past, I have wanted you to kiss me for so long. I have never felt this way before.'

With iron control, Edward raised his head and, through the heat of passion she had aroused in him, he looked down into her lovely face upturned to his. That one kiss had been too much and too little, leaving them both hungering for more.

'Stop and think what you are doing,' he urged softly. 'I have wanted to kiss you again ever since I kissed you when I was leaving for Worcester. Ever since we left Bircot Hall, there have been times when you have made it hard for me to resist you.'

'You do not have to do that any more, Edward. I want to be with you—even against my better judgement.'

He smiled, looking directly into her eyes, drawing his finger down her cheek to her nape and through her tousled hair. 'You really are the most unprincipled young woman, Arabella.'

'Widow, Edward. I am a widow, not a chaste young woman. I'm a different person to the one you knew.'

'Everyone changes.'

'Life has made me what I am. What happened between you and me five years ago doesn't matter any more. I'm not strong enough to go on hating you—if I ever did. Although I tried hard to convince myself that I did hate you for playing with my feelings, then walking away from me without a backward glance. But circumstances have changed all that.'

He was silent, a deep frown furrowed his brow and his eyes deepened as he struggled for control. 'But it does matter, Bella,' he said with unexpected gentleness. 'It matters to me and I will never forgive myself for hurting you. Of all the women I have known, not one of them possessed the heart and mind and gentleness of you. I am sorry you did not find your ideal husband in John.'

Raising her hand, she touched his face gently with her fingers. 'Please don't let us talk about him. Not tonight. Especially not tonight.'

He smiled slowly, a smile that lit his eyes, and when he spoke his voice was marked with humour. 'Would I be correct in thinking that you would have no objections if I asked to share this bed with you—that I will not be relegated to the chair?'

Arabella cast a glance at the hard-backed chair, wrinkling her nose with distaste. 'I would not be so cruel as to do that. We both need a comfortable night...' She hesitated, biting her lip nervously. He noticed and questioned it with a frown. He was waiting for her to invite him into her bed. The knowledge calmed her. To combat a fear one must meet it head on. 'Please don't avoid me, Edward. I want you to be with

me. I—I know you will think I am quite shameless, but I want you to make love to me.'

'I don't think you are shameless. What if I
said that I want to make love to you, too, Arabella? What if I said it is all I've been able to
think about since we left Bircot Hall? The attraction between us has been denied for too long.'
His voice was husky and there was such intensity in his gaze that she could not look away.
She saw something more behind that enigmatic
gaze, which quickened her pulse rate alarmingly.

'I would tell you that I have no objections to
that. I am not asking for a commitment. That
would only complicate things. I—I just want
you to make love to me, to give me that one experience I never thought I could have.'

She searched his eyes to guess his mood.
They were dark with desire and a predatory
hunger, and as she looked at him in the warm
intimacy of the room, with Dickon far away in
his own world of dreams, another side to Arabella emerged, pushing the old one away, an
Arabella without conscience, without shame.
She felt something that was completely physical, hinting at joys that could be hers. It was telling her this was a moment not to be missed—a
night for pleasure like she had never experienced before.

Gently Edward placed his hands on her upper arms, drawing her to him, lowering his head and pressing his lips close to her own. His mouth moved over hers with gentle persuasion. Her return kiss was tentative at first, as if she'd had time to reconsider what she was doing, but as his heat flowed into her, she began to relax. She felt the evidence of his desire for her pressed against her body. Her head began to spin. What was he doing to her? A situation that had once become a matter of principle had become as slippery as a freshly caught trout.

He was not forcing her as John had done and as he lengthened his kiss she felt a reckless excitement that completely banished any conscience that remained, that overcame guilt or fear that told her she should not be doing this. Her eyes closed in surrender. Her lips parted beneath his and her body became a flame with anticipation of what was to come. All the strange, intense emotions that had existed between them from that first kiss when he had been leaving for Worcester were released and she returned his kiss with a passion so powerful she was shocked by it.

After what seemed to be an eternity, he raised his head and smiled, a slow smile that heated her blood. He raised a finger to brush a lock of

hair from her face and tuck it behind her ear.
His finger slid from her ear to the curve of her
cheek that left her dizzy. Her breath caught in
her throat, so close was he, his heated gaze sim-
mered with intent. He touched the outline of her
lips before gently running his thumb languidly,
persuasively over the flesh in a way that if she
had any objections, they would vanish like the
morning mist.

Focusing her eyes on his face, she could see
the firmness of his mouth, could see the tightness of his jaw, could smell the heat of his skin
which she welcomed, though she would have
protested any such admission. She was consumed by her growing desire. She swayed a little, for she felt the heady aura of his masculinity,
his vigour. The next moment he again claimed
her lips with warm, possessive ardour. When
he at last lifted his head their gazes locked and
despite all that had transpired between them
she wanted to feel his heat within her, his body
close, his hands upon her flesh.

She knew it was wrong, that she shouldn't be
doing this, but his lips felt *right*, his arms felt
right—everything about him felt *right*. She was
starved of love, her body was starved of love.
What did it matter what had gone before when
his mouth and his hands, his body, could give

her so much pleasure? She told herself that it
didn't matter if he didn't love her, that there
could be no lasting future for them. Had she not
decided on a life without convention, to make
her own choices?

He held her close so that she could feel the
beating of his heart and she knew he was fighting against the need to possess her completely
before they were both ready. She reminded herself of her husband's rough handling of her and
it was not hard to remember how she'd had to
force herself to submit to him. But at that moment she could think of nothing but the fire this
man could awaken with his touch.

Taking his mouth from hers, he lifted her up
and carried her to the bed, placing her on the
covers. He undressed her slowly, his eyes caressing every inch of her body. She might not be
a virgin, but she blushed as he removed every
article of clothing and tried to hide her breasts
with her hands. He laughed softly and removed
her hands and kissed the lovely soft mounds of
flesh, and then she relaxed.

When she was naked and exposed and the
light bathed her in a soft golden glow, his gaze
swept over her, taking in every inch of her,
every detail of her slender body, her small pert
rose-tipped breasts and slender waist and long,

lithe legs, and the smile that curved his lips was one of admiration.

'You're beautiful, Arabella.'

She trembled at his tone. 'Flatterer.'

'I told you once before. I have no need to flatter you.'

Laughing lightly, she reached out and pulled him down on top of her. They kissed and clung to one another, then she suddenly pushed him away.

'Take off your clothes, Edward, and please do it quietly,' she whispered, looking concernedly at Dickon, who had turned over in his sleep. 'We don't want to wake your son.' Her breath came quickly, her skin was flushed.

'Have patience,' he murmured, standing up to remove his clothing.

When he had at last shrugged out of his clothes, she gazed at him in awe, earthy and vital and strong, all rippling muscles and sinews, and she wanted him. She held out her arms. She wanted the firm feel of his body against her bare flesh that was glowing and pulsating with life.

Stretching out his body beside hers and wanting to savour every exotic moment, he was in no rush to possess her. His experienced fingers were incredibly sensual. They stroked and teased, caressing her breasts, her flat stomach, her thighs. The quick rise and fall of her breasts, her shallow breathing, the fast beat of her heart, all told him how much she wanted him.

When his mouth moved to circle her breasts, kissing each one in turn until they hardened, the rosy nipple standing firm and proud, Arabella moaned in pleasure. Considering she was no chaste virgin, she still possessed a trembling innocence which he found incredibly erotic. He longed to bring her to ecstasy, to let her experience the pleasure that had clearly been absent from her marriage.

To his delight her legs opened at a slight pressure of his hand and she half-sighed, half-moaned beneath him as she felt the moisture from her loins as his rigid manhood pressed against her flesh. He kissed her long and deep as her fingers trailed a line up his spine, then her hands relaxed and, gaining confidence, began stroking his back, his buttocks, his sides.

The heat within Edward swelled until he was on fire. The very essence of life, the body his own had so fiercely desired, lay beneath him. Taking control, he settled his muscular thighs between her own and found her waiting for him. Raising her hips to accommodate him, effortlessly he slid inside her moist warmth.

Arabella could resist no longer. Her legs rose and clasped around his waist and she moved as he moved, moaning and sighing as he drove himself into her with masterly precision. Everything was forgotten in the feverish crescendo of desire, in the heat of motion and each pleasurable sensation, thrusting, touching all of her with a driving, primitive rhythm until the final moment of release. Deep inside, the hard contractions started and built, surging through her, burning and filling her to the very centre of her being, until the flame subsided and her body relaxed.

Her breathing irregular, her heart beating faster than normal, Edward's manhood still swollen and held in the warmth of her, still moving gently and tenderly—she knew then what it was to be a woman and felt a rare peace. Never had she experienced anything like it.

Opening her eyes, she stared up at him. Tears of gratitude and fulfilment welled in her eyes, one single tear forming on her lashes.

Staring down into her eyes, he kissed it away, stroking the hair that curled around her bare shoulder. 'Tears?' He smiled a gentle smile. 'Was it as bad as that?'

For a long moment she did not answer, but he saw the long column of her throat tighten as she swallowed with some difficulty. 'Oh, no,' she whispered, when she was able to speak. 'Quite the opposite. I thank you, Edward—with all my heart.'

'Don't thank me,' he murmured, kissing her shoulder. 'The night isn't over yet.'

'I don't want it to end. You will never know what you have done for me.'

'I think I do. You told me there was no joy in your marriage.'

'No. Making love with John, who was never tender, was never a pleasurable experience. In fact, it was quite the opposite. It was totally without passion, without consideration.' And afterwards, she remembered as the memories came flooding back, there had been pain and misery and the dark and unmistakable bruises all over—a legacy of his violence. No, what John had done was so ugly set against what she had just shared with Edward. 'I—I found the act painful and often undignified, leaving me unsatisfied and unfulfilled. I told myself that there had to be more to it than that.'

'And now you know there is.'

'Yes,' she whispered, unable to believe she had confessed the ugly cycle of brutality and submission John had put her through. 'I've never told anyone what John did to me. I couldn't. I was too ashamed. But what we have done was wonderful and I will treasure the memory always.'

'Memory?' he murmured, planting light kisses on her cheek, her lips. 'What is this nonsense? You speak as if this is the last time we will make love, Bella. I told you, the night is not over.'

'There is still a little time left for loving, I know. But our journey together may well be over,' she murmured, her body contradicting what she said when it began to respond to his closeness once more. 'We neither of us know what the future holds.' She sighed, her eyes, sultry and warm, holding his. 'It would be so very easy to fall in love with you, Edward. But considering the dangers of the situation we find ourselves in, that would be foolish. Don't you agree?'

He eased away from her to lie on his side, gathering her into the circle of his arms. Both trembled and the only sound in the room was Dickon's gentle shuffling in his cot and their prolonged rapid breathing. They lay without speaking. There was so much he wanted to say to her.

At length he said, 'I shouldn't have ended our betrothal, Arabella. Now I have found you again—after making love to you—I have reason to regret my actions more than ever. I can't tell you why I did.'

Turning her head, she looked at his handsome face set in sombre lines. 'It's quite simple really, Edward. You loved Anne Lister.'

His eyes filled with pain and suffering. 'I didn't love her,' he said with bitter clarity. 'I don't think I ever did. It was impossible to love her in the sense that you mean. What I felt for her was dark and primitive—something ugly.'

Arabella fixed him with a level gaze. 'And how do you feel now? Are you free of what it was that bound you to her?'

He nodded, kissing the top of her head. 'She has been dead over two years. If it were not for Dickon, I would not give her another thought. My concern now is to keep you safe, and Dickon, to reach Bristol and secure a vessel to take us to France.'

He wanted to reassure her, to tell her that everything would be all right, but he couldn't find the right words. There was a hollow sensation in the pit of his stomach. How could he tell her that all would be well, when he didn't know himself?

However, the night was not yet over and there was still pleasure to be had. Arabella was close and all feminine warmth, soft skin and tumbled hair. He held her in his arms, turning her to face him.

Arabella saw desire once more in his dark-blue gaze, and something more. What she saw was so profound that she was mesmerised. Her throat was tight from an aching need and she willingly gave in to the silent demand she saw in his eyes.

They made love again, more than once, and each time was sweeter, more intense than the one before. Arabella was startled by the pleasure unfolding, the fierce, probing hunger as she began to find herself. And afterwards she lay back on the pillows and slept.

It was mid-afternoon when they reached the outskirts of Bristol, where they had to sell the horse and cart at a livery stable. Arabella was sorry to part with the old horse. It had served the Stanhope family well over the years, but they had no choice. In any case they could not take the cart into the town. Edward explained to her that no wheeled traffic was allowed in the town for fear of weakening the structures of the honeycomb of wealthy merchants' cellars beneath the streets, which were used as warehouses for their goods.

Carrying only what they would need for the crossing to France, Dickon holding Arabella's hand, they made their way along the often steep, narrow streets teeming with people. Arabella looked about her with interest, at the high timber-framed houses, their upper storeys jutting out so much that they almost blocked out the light. Horse-drawn sledges were everywhere, some piled high with merchandise from the ships in the harbour.

'We'll find somewhere to stay,' Edward said, shouldering the canvas bag he carried and lifting a tired Dickon into his arms. 'We need a good hot meal and a comfortable bed.'

At the mention of bed, Arabella recalled the previous night, although it had not been far from her thoughts all day—how could it be after what they had done? Remembering the way he had looked at her, intimately and tenderly tucking her hair behind her ear, smiling suddenly, almost in surprise, as if he had found something precious, a lovely, precious treasure. Heat rose in her face and her heart raced in her chest. When she turned her eyes to his and caught his gaze, he smiled a knowing smile.

'Of course, if you prefer I can request two rooms.'

'No,' she replied, smiling softly, already anticipating the pleasure that would be theirs in the night to come. 'One will do perfectly.'

Perfectly attuned to one another, they were impatient to be together, their mouths joined in a sublime kiss, their flesh pressed together, touching each other, discovering each other, growing familiar, tender, exciting each other, that was in itself exquisite while knowing there was much more to learn, much more to come and that it would be as good, if not better, than what had gone before.

'That's settled them. I'll lose no time in making enquiries about vessels leaving for France. Hopefully it will be soon, but in the meantime we must try not to draw attention to ourselves.'

As they reached the port the scene was quite extraordinary, unlike anything she had ever seen. The quay, piled high with casks filled with rum and drums of tobacco and other merchandise, was busy, a wide expanse of ships and shrouds and skeletal rigging all a-tangle on the river. The tide was beginning to swell the Rivers Avon and Frome, quickly covering the fetid mud, gradually setting to right the vessels that had been lying at a slant, waiting for the incoming tide to right them once more. Arabella drew the hood of her cloak over her hair, drawing it across her nose and mouth to lessen the awful stench of rotting fish, the filth of humanity and the reek of hot pitch.

Seeing Parliamentary soldiers on the streets, she was relieved when they eventually secured a room in a tavern set away from the harbour and down an alley shared by a complex of tenements. The tavern was clean, its walls whitewashed. Oil lamps were fixed to its walls and the beams crossing the ceiling. Its clientele was made up of mostly seamen off the ships in the port and its food, as they would discover, was palatable.

Giving the landlord their false names and paying in advance, to the strains of a jolly tune a sailor was singing, they were shown to a room under the eaves overlooking the narrow street. A casement window hung perilously far over the street below. It was not a large room, but there was a chest, a cupboard, a mirror on the wall above the washstand and a double bed made up with clean bedding. A truckle slotted underneath would be suitable for Dickon.

After they had eaten Edward left the tavern to go to the port to see about obtaining a passage to France. He knew Commonwealth soldiers would be watching the port for fleeing Royalists, but it was a risk he had to take. He was fortunate. A small vessel, the *Albion*, was

to leave some time during the next two days for
Le Havre. The captain was ashore, but his first
mate saw no reason why he couldn't book passage for himself, his wife and child. Leaving
payment for the passage and intending to call
back later to speak to the captain, he returned
to the tavern to give Arabella the news.

Later in the day when he was returning to the
inn after making final preparations for their departure with the captain of the *Albion*, without
thinking he straightened the stooped form he
had adopted and stood tall. Removing his hat
to scratch his head, he drew the attention of a
young soldier, who had been watching him for
some time as he walked along the quay.

The soldier continued to watch him, thinking he was uncommonly tall, his hair long and
black and a black beard covering the lower half
of his face. With the whole of the West Country and beyond looking for the son of the late
King Charles, who had been proclaimed King
in Scotland before coming south with an army
of Scots, seeking glory and reward, the ambitious soldier soon convinced himself that here
was the fugitive, Charles Stuart.

Wasting no more time, he stepped in front of
him. 'Might I have a word, sir?'

With alarm running down his spine, Edward lowered his head and tried to push past his assailant. 'You're mistaken,' he mumbled. Taking stock of the situation immediately and realising that to try to run would only draw further attention to himself, he took a step to walk away calmly.

'Do not run if you value your life.'

Chapter Six

The scene through the mullioned windows downstairs in the tavern where Arabella was waiting for Edward was distorted, but it appeared some kind of disturbance was taking place. Feeling a sense that something was amiss, then hoisting Dickon up into her arms, she left the tavern.

A small crowd had gathered in the street. As she pushed her way through, it immediately became obvious that what she had feared from the outset was about to unfold before her eyes. Suddenly weakened, she had to fight to keep her knees from buckling beneath her. Her heart was seized by sudden terror. Heedless of the danger to herself she was about to dash to Edward, but some instinct made her stop herself.

'Name. What's your name?' The soldier stood his ground, his voice ringing out sharply as he beckoned to his fellow roundheads.

'Brody. Will Brody.'

Arabella cringed inwardly. When Edward said his name why, oh, why did he have to say it with the simple pride of a man of the nobility?

The soldier scowled at him, unconvinced. 'From where, Will Brody? Where are you from?'

'Gloucester.'

The soldier was distracted when an authoritative-looking man astride a large grey stallion rode into the crowd. Such was this man's aura of importance that it parted like the Red Sea to let him through. The closer he came, his features grew more recognisable. Arabella's heart almost ceased to beat.

It was Malcolm Lister.

She stared in disbelief and was tempted to rub her eyes as if that would prove this was just a terrible dream. Despair filled her as she realised Edward had not eluded him after all. Looking at Edward, who was watching him closely, she knew he had recognised him. She could only guess at the intensity of his feelings from the way he bunched and unbunched his fists at his sides.

'Who have we got here?' Colonel Lister asked the soldier coldly.

'Says his name's Brody. He looks more like Charles Stuart to me.'

Coming to a halt, Colonel Lister looked down at the prisoner. His eyes glittered in triumph when he met those of the man who was no longer cowed. He laughed then, a thin, discordant sound.

'Well, well. Who would have thought it? Charles Stuart it is not, but this man is still a prize worth having. Edward Grey.' The name rolled off his tongue with a cat-like purr. 'At last I have you. Caught like a rat in a trap. Restrain this man, lest he try to escape.'

Two men sprang forward. A rope was produced and Edward's hands tied in front of him.

Colonel Lister looked down at his enemy, his smile turned into a sneer. 'You will not escape me, Edward Grey. I have looked for you long and hard. Now I have you I know how to deal with you. As a traitor you will be taken to London to stand trial. It will be done lawfully, but do not think for one minute you will escape with your life.'

'I am no traitor, Lister. I did my duty as I conceived it had to be done. King Charles called me to his side. I did but answer that call—as many loyal Englishmen did.'

'Aye, and died for him—as he did on the scaffold. Under Cromwell the Commonwealth stands for fairness and equality among men—

men who were willing to oppose the King and have nothing to do with his plans. England will be a finer country without him and his son, who they say has been crowned King north of the border.'

'He is the lawful King of England. Others may wish to ignore the fact, but I cannot. I cannot rejoice in an England without a king. I would sooner die than live under those conditions.'

Colonel Lister's lip curled. 'We will see how we can accommodate you. Cromwell is a man of great power, a leader, who played no small part in bringing about the downfall of the King. He is to be congratulated.'

Edward answered in a cool, even voice, 'Cromwell is a brilliant soldier—a genius, in fact, but he is not a man of honour. If he were, he would not have executed the King. And you were ever of one mind with Cromwell, were you not, Lister.'

'No man makes up my mind for me.'

Edward looked up at his brother-in-law with open contempt. 'As I discovered to my regret when I wed your sister.'

'Much good it did her,' Colonel Lister ground out angrily.

'I agree. The only good thing to come out of

that was Dickon. Your hounding of me has nothing to do with Cromwell or the war. Admit it.
Because I took the King's side you were against
our union. Anne was ambitious. Her heart was
set on a life at court. Since her death your ambition to seize my son and insinuate him into
your household seems to have become an obsession. Lock me away in the Tower if you must,
but if you think you can seize my son you will
not succeed. You are insane if you think that,
insane if you believe I will hand him over to
you and your barren wife.'

Under Edward's contemptuous expression
Colonel Lister glared angrily at him, beginning
to lose his precarious hold on his temper. 'Nay,
Edward Grey, that I am not. It is not for you to
insult me—or my wife. If you look for insan-
ity, look to your dead King. It was he, with his
extravagance, his callous disregard of our laws,
and his smug assumption for the divine right of
kings, who led your fellow Royalists to war and
ultimately to disaster and cost him his crown.
He overrode Parliament and put himself above
the law of the land. Like him you are no longer
of any account. You are nothing.'

Edward smiled. 'You are wrong. I know who
I am, and on what account I hold myself—as
does the King's son—Charles Stuart. God will-

ing he will return to England and soon be sitting in his rightful place at Whitehall. He has been proclaimed King of England and Scotland. That he will be until the day he dies.'

Colonel Lister's lips tightened with derision. 'Which may not be long in coming. He will be run to earth before he takes ship for France. You can guarantee it.' Pulling his horse back, he looked at the man holding Edward Grey. 'See that he is mounted and we will be on our way. He might not be alone. He fled Worcester with a malignant by the name of Stephen Charman. Keep looking.'

As much as Arabella wished to be strong, her body trembled and she gripped Dickon to her, pulling her shawl across her face and shielding Dickon with her hand should Colonel Lister look her way and recognise her. More people had gathered round to see what was happening and for a moment a pin might have been heard to drop. But then some began to jeer at the prisoner who was now surrounded by Commonwealth soldiers, bristling with arms. Others who remained sympathetic to the King's cause stood mute, their faces blank.

Out of the corner of his eye Edward must have seen her for she saw his shoulders stiffen. Briefly he glanced her way, the look he gave

her reminding her of the promise she had made
to him, of what she must do if he was captured
and she remained free. He didn't acknowledge
her presence again. She didn't move for several heartbeats and then her insides began to
lose their tension. She did not know how long
she stood there as part of the crowd, her heart
in her mouth. It was as if she had been turned
to stone.

With her eyes blinded by tears she watched as
Edward was hauled atop a horse and led away.
Soldiers surrounded him, one of them leading
his horse by the rein, making it impossible for
him to escape. She clung to Dickon who, aware
of the tension in Arabella and sensing all was
not well, had begun to cry. All her strength was
concentrated in her arms as her eyes clung to
the receding group of soldiers surrounding the
proud figure of Edward Grey, until she could
see them no more.

The crowd slowly began to disperse. With
some effort, putting Dickon down and wiping
his tears away, holding his hand tight, she forced
her way back through the crowd, trying hard not
to think what they would do to Edward.

He was Sir Edward Grey, a close friend and
confidant of Charles Stuart, wanted for his trai-
torous activities during the Civil War.

He would be taken to London and executed. She would never see him again.

Her fear for Edward was great, but there was nothing she could do for him without jeopardising her chances of getting Dickon to France. Like a sleepwalker and filled with grief and despair, she returned to the tavern. Suddenly she found herself thrust into another world fraught with nightmares. Even as she feared for Edward's fate her mind was working. What best to do? She would not allow herself to fall to pieces. What she had to do must be done in a calm and rational way.

Nightmares pursued Arabella all the way to France as she suddenly found herself cast into the mercy of events. A woman alone with a child and all the threats that posed made her anxious. Edward was for ever on her mind, his ordeal adding to her distress, and the knowledge that when her task was over and Dickon safe with Edward's sister Verity, her link to Edward would be severed.

The sky was a collage of soft pastel colours as the *Albion* sailed into the open sea. A gentle breeze filled the sails and wood beams creaked and groaned as it rode the water. Standing on the deck, holding Dickon in her arms, Arabella inhaled a scent of brine. She looked to the horizon upon which the coast of France would soon appear, trying to ignore the misery of her situation, but it was nigh impossible. Suddenly her life had become complicated and dangerous, and nothing would ever be the same again.

The journey from Le Havre to Paris had been a long and arduous one for Arabella. It was difficult keeping Dickon entertained in the close confines of a coach crammed with other passengers and she was exceedingly glad to reach Paris. Dickon missed his father and could not understand why he had left them. With her heart heavy with sorrow and missing Edward more than she could ever have imagined, she was unable to explain to the child why he was not with them.

Stepping down from the coach, holding Dickon's hand tight with one hand and clutching her travelling bag with the other, she looked about her. Paris was all so bewildering to her. It was a busy, bustling place and she was overwhelmed by the press of people.

Like every other city on earth it was dirty, smelly and noisy and had its share of beggars, cripples and ragged waifs. Carriers, carters, merchants and vendors were all talking and shouting together, bargaining and cursing in French and a babble of different languages. She stepped quickly back, pressing herself against a wall as a servant cleared a passage for his noble master on horseback. The rotting debris in the gutters mingled with the aromatic smell of baked pies and cakes in the shops that lined the street.

Her French was reasonable so, combined with the directions Edward had given her and making a few enquiries along the way, she had no difficulty finding her way to the small two-storeyed, half-timbered, gabled house in a modest neighbourhood in a quiet quarter of the city where Verity lived with her husband and two children. There was a small enclosed garden at the back, which was ideal for the children to play in.

In a dress of grey silk, its folds catching the light, and with her deep-blue eyes and dark hair drawn back from her face with a few curls stressing the line of her neck, Verity bore such a startling resemblance to her brother that it brought a lump to Arabella's throat. Her efficiency and the way she took control of everything the moment Arabella arrived on her doorstep with Verity's nephew reminded her of Alice. She felt her spirits rise at the warmth of her welcome. Verity remembered her with fondness.

Dickon was handed over to Pauline, a young and extremely efficient female servant, her curly hair covered by a white cap. She had accompanied the family from England—the only servant the family could afford since money was scarce.

Arabella smiled a little nervously on finding herself alone with Verity following the turmoil of their arrival. 'I apologise for my appearance. It's been a long journey to get here.'

'We'll soon have you cleaned up and some food inside you,' Verity said, taking Arabella into a drawing room and indicating that she be seated.

Arabella perched on the edge of a chair in the charming room, painted and wallpapered in various pastel tones of green and gold. Next to her chair was a branch of tall candles and a piece of tapestry Verity was working on.

'Arabella,' Verity went on, clearly puzzled by Arabella's surprise arrival with her nephew and deeply anxious about her brother, 'please tell me about Edward. I worry about him constantly and am impatient to learn what has befallen him.'

Arabella bowed her head, swallowing down

a lump that had risen in her throat. 'The news I bring is so bad that I scarcely know where to begin.'

Verity seated herself across from her, clasping her hands to keep them from trembling in her lap. She was tense, expecting to hear the worst about her brother. 'Tell me. I have felt so cut off from everything since we came to France that I have no idea what is happening in England. I'm afraid the news is always gloomy. We heard there was a battle—at Worcester, I believe. It is said to be the final battle of the war and that the young King Charles is a fugitive.'

Arabella sighed wearily, relieved now that her journey was over. The discomforts she had encountered, combined with her own utter powerlessness to aid Edward, had done nothing to improve her spirits. She had not slept since leaving Bristol and had eaten only little, such was her state of depression.

'Tell me, Arabella,' Verity prompted gently, her eyes tormented with worry. 'Do not spare me. He is my only sibling and I love him dearly. You must tell me everything.'

Arabella raised her head and gazed into her eyes with such an expression of compassion that she saw Verity tremble slightly. 'He was arrested at Bristol before we had time to board the vessel for France. I think they will have taken him to London. I—I fear for his life.'

Verity stared at her, then, uttering a small cry, she got quickly to her feet, her hands going to her face. She paced the room before coming to a halt in front of Arabella. 'What can we do? Can anything be done to save him?'

Arabella shook her head. 'I don't see what can be done. You see, the man who arrested him was Colonel Lister. Malcolm Lister. I—I believe there is bad blood between them.'

Verity paled visibly, sinking back into the chair she had just vacated. 'Malcolm Lister? But he hates my brother. Ever since he married Anne… He never forgave her for marrying a Royalist.'

'Yes. Edward told me. He also told me that Malcolm Lister's wife is unable to bear a child and that he wants to make Dickon his heir.' She went on to tell Verity of the circumstances that had brought Edward to Bircot Hall, his flight from Worcester and his decision to try to reach France with Dickon. 'Fearing he would be arrested, Edward asked me to help him. He told me where I could find you should he be taken.'

Verity listened to her every word. When she fell silent, at length she said, 'You have been courageous in bringing Dickon to Paris, Arabella. As his aunt I shall be eternally grateful to you. He will be safe here with us. The journey must have been arduous for you.'

'I did not expect it to be easy. There were privations, but we survived them.'

'When I remember how badly my brother treated you in the past, I am surprised you were willing to help him.'

'I was glad to. After Worcester everything had become quite desperate. Dickon's welfare had become of great concern.'

'He seems to be very attached to you, Arabella. Poor motherless little mite. I haven't seen him since he was a babe. How I wish I had brought him with us to France, but everything happened so quickly when my husband decided to leave England. How is he really?'

'He's a quiet, serious little boy. It will be good for him to be here with you—and I am sure your children will help bring him out of himself. He is not yet three and there has been so much tragedy in his young life.'

'You are right. To be with other children will be good for him. You must meet our two later. But what of you, Arabella? I heard you had married.'

'Yes,' she replied quietly, reluctant to speak of John. She had been so preoccupied with everything that happened after Edward had been arrested that she had given no thought to John. But remembering Robert's letter and Malcolm Lister's disclosure, she wondered if she would learn more now she had arrived in Paris. Could there be some truth in it? Until she knew more she would keep her fears to herself. 'When my husband was killed in battle I went to Bircot Hall to live with Alice.'

'I am sorry to hear that.' Verity sighed. 'The war has made many widows. I feel that I must tell you that life is difficult for exiles in Paris. We do not have all our servants here and we occupy this small house whilst we remain unsettled. In the beginning we were optimistic, believing we were doing the right thing to leave England. Already the optimism is beginning to wane. Money remains the key to absolutely everything and the courtiers have an obsessional interest in their own poverty. We are all penniless and forced to live on the charity of the French and relatives in England who can afford to send money. But enough of that. Tell me how you came to meet Edward again—and I would like to hear about Alice.'

When Arabella had finished giving Verity an account of everything that had transpired, bravely hiding her fears and anxiety she felt for Edward, Verity set about making Arabella and Dickon comfortable. Her husband, Sir Gregory Rainsford, who had been visiting fellow exiles, arrived home. Of medium height with brown hair threaded with grey and soft brown eyes, his welcome was as warm and welcoming as Verity's had been.

Idealistic and filled with hope, he had fought bravely for the King when the war began. He had soon come to realise that war was no glorious adventure and his idealism had not lasted after the King's execution. Unable to live under Commonwealth rule and hoping for better times, as many other Royalists had done, he had brought his young family to France with the hope that they would be safe from the tyranny of Oliver Cromwell.

Gregory was deeply distressed to learn that Edward had been taken prisoner.

'What can be done to help him?' Verity asked, looking to her husband for the answer. 'I cannot bear to think of him at the mercy of Malcolm Lister. We cannot abandon him.' Her lips trembled and tears filled her eyes. 'For all we know he might already have been executed.' She swallowed down a hard lump that had risen in her throat. 'I pray that is not so.'

'Take heart, my dear,' her husband said, putting a comforting arm around her shoulders. 'I will do what I can to find out what has become of him. There are agents who come and go across the Channel all the time. After Worcester, London's prisons are overflowing. It will be no easy matter finding him, but I will do my utmost.' He turned to look at Arabella. 'In the meantime, Arabella, you are welcome to stay with us for as long as you wish.'

Their kindness brought tears of gratitude to her eyes. 'Thank you, you are very kind, but I will not add to your burden. Now Dickon is safe I intend to go back to England as soon as it can be arranged. I cannot stay here, safe in Paris, while—while…' She faltered, biting her lips, afraid she was about to disclose too much about the way she felt for Edward. But she need not have worried. Verity smiled her understanding, having already made up her mind about that.

'While Edward is in dreadful danger.'

Arabella nodded. 'Yes. I—I think I should go mad not knowing,' she uttered quietly, her words an admission of what was in her heart.

Verity cocked her head to one side, considering her thoughtfully. 'I think you have feelings for my brother, Arabella.'

She flushed and lowered her eyes. She would

have liked to dispel Verity's speculation that she had an interest in Edward—or that he had any in her—but she could not hide her true feelings from Verity's sharp eyes. 'I—I feel that if I can be close to him, I shall find some way to help him.'

'He is a lucky man—although hardly deserving of so much consideration when he has treated you so badly in the past,' Verity said with a faint, rather wistful smile.

'I have put all that behind me. I understand why he did what he did—I have not forgiven him fully, but with his life in the balance this is not the time for petty recriminations.'

'I understand your haste to return to England,' Gregory said, 'but my advice to you is to wait until I have information regarding his whereabouts.'

'But is it not difficult to come and go, considering the tensions in England just now?' Arabella asked.

'The people I have in mind do not let obstacles get in their way. You cannot go wandering about London asking questions. A woman alone would be prey to all manner of dangers. When we know more, an opportunity may arise to help him, and if it should, we will take advantage of it. I will then arrange for you to travel with someone I deem trustworthy who will see you to London.'

Arabella was overwhelmed with gratitude at a degree of assistance she had scarcely dared to hope for. If she were to be honest with herself, she had been dreading returning to Bircot Hall and trying to live her life as if Edward had never existed. 'I am indeed grateful, sir. I am only sorry to impose upon you in this way.'

'Nonsense,' Verity said, taking her hand and raising her up from the chair. 'I shall enjoy your stay. You have no idea how I crave to talk to someone about home. Now let us go and see what Dickon is up to—and we must see to finding you something suitable to wear. I would also like you to tell me more about how you and Edward met again. While you are in Paris we will introduce you to other exiles—one in particular. Robert Stanhope, Alice's husband, is at St Germain. He frets daily about his wife and children.'

Arabella felt her spirits lift. It would be good to meet with Robert and allay any fears he might have about Alice and their children—although if it were discovered that Alice was harbouring a fugitive she might not fare so well. She prayed Stephen was recovering well and that he could soon find his own way to Paris.

That night as she slept in a bed she had not seen the like of since leaving Bircot Hall, lulled into sleep by its softness, she dreamed that she was in London and that she was going to fling open the barred gates to Edward's prison and set him free.

The hour was two hours before midnight. There was a half-moon in the sky, frequently obscured by long ragged clouds. A light breeze stirred the tall grass that fringed the narrow stream running beside the place where the soldiers had made their second night camp. They were on the edge of a village, a busy hostelry just yards away. Edward's wrists were rubbed raw by the rope which so cruelly bound him. His captors gave him no respite and Malcolm Lister took sadistic delight in his discomfort.

Edward was unable to stop thinking about Arabella and that most exquisite, beautiful night they had spent together. Their coming together had been no ordinary experience. It had not been merely a joining of their bodies, it had been more than that. Much more. It had been a searching and finding, a mounting pleasure, a removal from reality, and then there had not been the intense explosion of release, but a pure joy, perfect and peaceful, he had never known with any other woman.

What he saw in his mind's eye was the wrenching look on her lovely face when he had been arrested. The memory of that haunted him. It tortured him, along with other worries about her. He did not know whether she had managed to board the ship to take her and Dickon across the Channel.

Most of his escort had gone to slake the dust from their throats after the long ride. One of them returned with some food for the prisoner and the three soldiers guarding him.

Weary and eager to partake of what food the inn had to offer, Colonel Lister nodded towards the guards. 'Untie his hands and let him eat.'

'But, sir,' one of the soldier said in alarm, 'he might try to escape.'

The colonel handed him a pistol. 'He will not escape. If he tries, shoot him,' he said, throwing Edward a cold look. 'Put the rope back on when he's eaten.'

He went to join the soldiers at the inn, where some kind of disagreement had broken out among a group of locals full of ale in the street outside. Fists were raised, curses yelled and a brawl ensued. The soldiers who had paused to watch shouted encouragement.

Temporarily released from his bonds, his body aching from the long ride, Edward flexed his cramped muscles, forcing blood to flow into them to strengthen them for his impending escape. With the soldiers momentarily distracted, now was the perfect opportunity, perhaps the only one he would have. He couldn't believe his luck when two of the soldiers guarding him, hearing the yells and guffaws coming from the brawl, covered half the distance to see what it was all about.

When the remaining soldier, who was little more than a youth, was handing out the food, Edward seized the moment, grasping it and throwing it in the soldier's face. In the blink of an eye he caught the soldier's arm and twisted it up his back. The youth tried to get his finger on the pistol to fire an alarm, but Edward was already raising his powerful fist. He caught the youth hard on the jaw. His head snapped back and the gun flew from his grasp as he collapsed on the ground unconscious.

His fist throbbing wildly, Edward scooped up the pistol and headed for the horses, taking the grey belonging to Malcolm Lister, the only one that remained saddled. Leading it into the trees, he went unnoticed, keeping to the shadows, away from the boisterous activity around the tavern as his captors were otherwise distracted.

Coming out of the trees, beginning to breathe more easily, he mounted the horse and rode away, heading south, hoping to negotiate for a boat somewhere along the coast to take him across the Channel.

When Malcolm Lister discovered his prisoner had escaped, a white hot rage erupted inside him. Ordering his men to begin a search, he immediately set off after him. Two days into the search and no sign of the fugitive, his exhausted horse threw him. Unfortunately the ground was hard. Malcolm Lister hit his head and was rendered unconscious.

Verity was always busy and interested in most things going on around her. In Paris she made sure that Arabella met many Royalist exiles who spent time about the court. The conversation was always very much about their return to England and continuing the fight to restore the King to his throne. It would seem they could talk of nothing else, but they did find time for pleasure.

France was in the throes of a civil war of her own, which had broken out in September. As a result the French royal family was in a state of alarm and tension, which spread to all its dependents, including the English exiles and Queen Henrietta Maria, a princess of the French royal blood and the widow of Charles I of England. Many exiles applied for active posts in the French army.

Leaving the children to be cared for by Pauline, Gregory took Verity and Arabella on a visit to St Germain, several miles to the west of Paris, which housed a great many English Royalists. This was where he had arranged for Arabella to meet Robert Stanhope. As they sauntered through the trees in the park that surrounded the beautiful palace, Arabella recognised Robert among a party of riders just returning from hawking.

When he saw her he left the group and walked his horse slowly towards her. Dismounting, he swept his plumed hat from his fair head and, smiling broadly, he greeted her warmly, genuinely pleased to see her. A tall man with long fair hair and clear grey eyes, Arabella had forgot how she always felt dwarfed when she stood beside him.

'I confess that I am surprised to see you here in France, Arabella. You are well, I hope.'

'Quite well, thank you, Robert.'

'And you are staying with Gregory and Verity, I understand.'

'For the time being.'

'Come,' he said, taking her arm. 'Let us walk and you can tell me everything I wish to know.'

Respecting their need for privacy, Verity and Gregory strolled arm in arm some distance behind them.

'And Alice and the children?' Robert asked, eager to know all about how his wife was faring and news of Bircot Hall. 'We do write, but the post is unreliable. I have had no letters for weeks. When I do, I feel that she doesn't tell me everything for fear of upsetting me.'

'Alice is well—as are the children—although she misses you dreadfully. Thankfully she has managed to stave off sequestration and pays the fines imposed on her, but not without hardship.'

'I have every confidence in Alice's ability to run and defend Bircot Hall efficiently, but I feel so wretched being so far away—leaving her to cope with everything while I stand idle in Paris. It has been a comfort knowing you were there to help—a Godsend, she told me—although I was indeed sorry to learn John was killed at St Fagans, followed so soon by your daughter.' When he looked at her his expression was grave. 'You've had a terrible time, Arabella.'

'It has been hard, but Alice helped me come to terms with what happened—and Margaret, of course.' They walked on in silence for a while, then, unable to contain the curiosity implanted in her mind by his letter to Alice, she said, 'About your letter to Alice, Robert. You—mentioned someone called Fairburn who is a soldier in the French army.'

'Yes, I did. I considered it a coincidence and merely wondered if he was related to your husband.'

'Have you learned anything else about him?'

He shook his head. 'No—although I must be honest with you, Arabella, it hasn't crossed my mind. If I do, I promise I will let you know.'

'Thank you, Robert. I would appreciate that.'

'Gregory has told me what brought you to France and that Edward Grey was arrested.'

'Yes. He has been taken to London. Gregory is going to try to find out what has become of him.'

'You were betrothed to him once, Arabella,' he said, giving her a quizzical look. 'I find it strange that the two of you were together at all.'

Arabella gave him a brief account of the events that had brought Edward to Bircot Hall and their journey to Bristol. He listened carefully, concerned.

'You say your brother was still under Alice's care when you left Bircot Hall?'

'Yes. Stephen was badly wounded at Worcester.'

'Let us hope he isn't discovered. It would not go well for Alice or Margaret to be found harbouring a fugitive.'

'They know that, but Stephen is our brother and Alice will do what she can to keep him safe.' Suddenly she smiled. 'Although I think Margaret will see he comes to no harm. She tends him night and day.'

Robert's expression brightened to hear this. 'Margaret? My little sister?'

Arabella laughed. 'Not so little now, Robert. I have to say her face lights up every time Stephen's name is mentioned.'

'Then I hope Stephen remains under her tender care for them both to realise they cannot live without each other. Margaret is not cut out for a life of piety.'

'I agree. Stephen has certainly proved to be a distraction. What are your plans now the fighting is over, Robert? Will you stay in France?'

'I have no choice for the present. If I return to England, I will be arrested.'

'Is it not possible that Parliament will grant

a pardon to the exiles and they can return to England?'

'We shall have to wait and see.'

'What would you do? Would you go back?'

He nodded. 'Yes—yes, I would. I'm done with war. I cannot bear being apart from Alice. If she came to me and Bircot Hall was left empty, it would be subject to sequestration. The estate has been in my family for five generations. It would break my heart to lose it. I would have to return and make the best of life under the Commonwealth.'

Arabella would welcome that. She, too, was tired of the strife that had existed in England for too long and all because of the old King's implacable belief in the divine right of kings.

Gregory and Verity were popular figures among the exiles. Happy to see a new and pretty face arrive among them, their friends claimed Arabella's time in Paris and she soon became sought after at any event. They were frequently invited to one salon or another where she was introduced to many handsome gentlemen and beautiful women, who, since there was little else for them to do, passed their time in idle entertainment.

The days turned into weeks and passed in a

blur. Still nothing was heard of Edward. But it was encouraging that that there was nothing to suggest he had been executed.

'Have faith, Arabella. My brother is strong. He will not give in to his captivity without a fight,' Verity said with a slight smile. Whether it was meant to reassure Arabella she did not know, but it did nothing to lessen her anxiety.

She immersed herself in social events with Verity, spent long hours playing with the children and did anything to distract her mind from thinking of Edward. But at night, in the quiet of her room, she would lie awake, staring at the ceiling, remembering every moment they had spent together, that wonderful night and the tender sound of his whispered endearments when he made love to her.

In the middle of October, King Charles, who had eluded capture, joined his mother, Queen Henrietta Maria, in exile. He received a rapturous welcome, but he was described as a sad and sombre figure.

What had happened to him since Worcester? everyone asked. Where had he been? It had taken him six weeks to reach France. There was much speculation among the English courtiers about the truth of his escape, but he did not speak the names of the courageous and daring men who had assisted him for fear of endangering them.

With no means of sustaining himself, he was reliant upon a pension granted by the government of France.

The Royalist exiles might not have won the war, but they had something to celebrate at last—King Charles was safe and lived to fight another day. And for now these poverty-stricken exiles would not allow their lack of money to interfere with their pleasure. Everyone was caught up in the dazzling spectacle of celebratory balls, of feasting and masquerading.

Four weeks after Edward had been arrested, Arabella began to suspect she might be with child. It was the only explanation she could think of for missing her flux. She did not want anyone to know and blamed her nausea on something she ate. But she began to dream about the baby and the man who was its father, but not her husband, and she thought about the passion and the gentle loving that had brought about this child. Because nothing had been heard of Edward's execution she had every reason to believe that he was still alive. When she thought of this her heart was surprisingly light.

How would he react, she wondered, when she told him? Would he be happy? Excited?

Would he make her his wife?

The more time Arabella spent with Verity, the more impressed she was by her. Verity had lived in Paris for so long that she was wonderfully au fait with everything that went on. When she told Arabella about the ball to be held at the Royal Palace, which was the residence of Queen Henrietta Maria, Arabella would have preferred not to attend.

She had no interest whatsoever in the shallow amusements of the exiles or in being admired by any of them. How could she eat and make polite conversation and dance as if everything in the world was well, when she didn't know what had happened to Edward? However, Verity, swept along on a wave of activity and eager to appear at an event which would be attended by French royalty, would not hear of her staying behind and in the end Arabella was persuaded.

'But—what am I to wear?' she asked. 'I have nothing suitable.'

Verity thought for a moment, her face undergoing various transformations. Then, clapping her hands, she suddenly said, 'Leave it to me. I have several gowns that will suit you perfectly.

I am not as slender as you, but I am sure one of them could be altered to fit you. They may not be as grand as some of the other ladies' gowns, but it is the lady inside who will make it shine.'

With the danger of discovery ever present, Edward had travelled mostly under cover of darkness, resting during the day in barns and thick woodland and any other suitable hiding place—often for days at a time since the presence of Commonwealth soldiers was everywhere. Fortunately he was not without money, so he was able to buy food.

It had taken him almost four weeks to reach Bridport, a small fishing village on the Dorset coast, where he had finally arranged for the master of a coasting vessel to convey him to France for twenty pounds.

Leaving the vessel at Cherbourg, he had managed to purchase a horse and headed for Paris. Passing through St Germain, he encountered Robert Stanhope, who told him that Arabella was still in Paris, staying with Verity and Gregory. After taking a much-needed bath and acquiring a change of clothes from Robert, he considered what to do next.

Arabella would be shocked to see him. He did think of sending word to the house first, rather than arrive without warning, but such was his impatience to see his son and Arabella, to pull Arabella and Verity into his arms and soothe away their concern and the tears they would shed when they realised he was.still alive, that he went directly.

His disappointment was acute when Pauline informed him Sir Gregory and his wife and Lady Fairburn were attending a ball at the Royal Palace. Impatient to see Dickon and told he was abed, after gazing down at his son's sleeping form he went directly to the Palace.

The Royal Palace was like a rabbit warren of Cavaliers. Not only did this gracious building house Queen Henrietta Maria's own attendants, it was beset by an array of Englishmen and their families, all exiled to France because of their adherence to the Royalist cause and all consequently feeling they were owed support.

The hallways were crowded, the room where the dancing was held filled to capacity. Standing in the doorway, he took a moment to survey the colourful and dazzling scene of lords and ladies displaying their finery. Perfume and wig powder permeated the air. In adjacent rooms could be heard the clinking of glasses, the shuffling of cards and the rolling of dice as these exiled Englishmen tried to enliven their dull and idle lives.

Dozens of couples were on the floor, stepping with as much grace and dignity to the strains of the music as was possible. Not one for large gatherings, he found the heat and sweat of so many bodies packed together mingled with perfume and wine nauseating. Many of the ladies were shameless in their low-cut gowns and flaunting manner as they laughed and teased and flirted with husbands and lovers.

His eyes swept the room, his lips curling with disdain as he decided the battles he'd fought were less intimidating than a ball at the Royal Palace. Many of those present recognised him. Having heard the rumours about his capture and not having expected to see him in Paris—if at all, for many had expected him to be sentenced to death—overcoming their surprise they gave him a hearty, heart-warming welcome.

Moving further into the room, he could feel every eye settle on him, the ladies as predatory as the males. They smiled at him as he pushed his way through and one lady dressed in a revealing coral-pink gown had the audacity to accost him.

'Why, Sir Edward Grey,' she purred, flutter-

ing her eyelashes in accompaniment to her fan.
'You are fresh in Paris?'

When he did not reply, not to be deterred, she
continued, 'You must be, otherwise we would
have heard. How nice it is to see you. I do hope
you are to be a permanent fixture in Paris.'

Having no idea of the identity of the woman,
when he replied his tone was agreeable, but his
eyes had hardened. 'I sincerely hope not. Excuse
me.' On that note he sidestepped and went on
his way, secure in the knowledge that despite
the ravages of war and the hardship he had endured since his escape, he still held some allure.
Please God let Arabella find him so.

He saw Verity first and his heart warmed on
seeing his only sibling looking so well. He let
his gaze dwell on her for a long moment before
shifting them to the woman standing serenely
by her side. She commanded all his attention,
for what he saw stole his breath away. That was
the moment when he realised just how important she was to him and the thought of her van-
ishing from his life once more was not to be
borne.

Arabella was attired in an alluring, off-the-
shoulder gown of shimmering sapphire-blue
satin, the bodice tight with full sleeves and
skirt. The swell of her breasts above the bod-

ice was distracting, and if there was a man who didn't see how well that gown fit her figure, he was either blind or dead. Her glorious wealth of hair—just begging for him to run his fingers through—was dressed in a mass of tight curls. They framed her enchanting face, resting gracefully on one shoulder.

But it was her face that caught Edward's breath in his throat. Starved of feminine beauty for so long, she was the loveliest, most alluring creature his eyes had ever beheld. Delicate pearl-drop earrings brushed her cheeks and drew the eye to her lovely face, and never had Edward envied a piece of jewellery so much until now.

Beneath her thick fringe of dark eyelashes, eyes the colour of amber that could enchant and weaken a man gazed candidly about the room, completely unaware of their mesmerising effect. Her softly pink, generous mouth was slightly parted, as if waiting to be kissed, yet at the same time warning the gathering of admiring males, drawn to her like iron filings to a magnet surrounding her, not to get too close.

How was it, he wondered, that she managed to look seductive and provocative, yet untouchable? It was that contrast and her clear unawareness that added to her allure.

He waited for the moment when she would turn her head and look at him. Suddenly, as if she sensed his eyes on her, her head slowly turned and she met his gaze. She seemed to freeze and some of the colour drained from her face, and she watched as he slowly made his way towards her, his eyes not relinquishing their hold on hers.

Chapter Seven

Rendered speechless by amazement, Arabella stood there, while her mind struggled to take in what was happening. She was afraid to move lest this man, who had haunted her dreams and tormented her days, disappeared as she gazed at that well-remembered, brooding face. Every night her sleep had been troubled because him, her dreams filled with such longings as she had never thought to experience.

His dark hair curling to his shoulders and attired in a black-velvet suit with a broad white linen collar marked him as a handsome, dangerously desirable man than any she had met before. There was a roaring in her ears and she swayed.

Taut with excitement and happiness, she watched him approach, her eyes huge, round and sparkling. Her entire being began to glow, such was her joy on seeing him again. For the first time in years she felt as though she was completely alive. Remembering her reluctance to attend the ball, she was suddenly appreciative of the care Verity had taken with her appearance, how she had painstakingly arranged her hair into elaborate curls with the heated curling tongs and the alterations she had made to make the gown fit.

Mentally she wanted to cross the distance between them, to reach out and touch his beloved face, to make sure he was real, but such was her recent alternations of fear, grief, shock and hope that all her resistance was worn out.

Her eyes registered the changes wrought by the time they had been apart. Clean-shaven, he was thinner due to his ordeal. Lines circled his eyes as if he had slept little in weeks. There was a weather-beaten look about him, but he was just as tall, just as handsome, as every woman in the room seemed to have noticed as their eyes settled on him. There was a whispered stir, a rustling among those present. When he walked across the floor he sparked a wave of interest among the ladies as they leaned forward and devoured his every move, commenting to each other behind a vigorous fluttering of fans.

Beside Arabella, Verity, having recognised

him also, was immobilised, staring at him, her hand pressed to her throat. He reached them, a smile softening his grim features. Taking his sister's hand, he raised it to his lips before folding her in his embrace. Neither of them spoke until he released her.

'Thank God,' Verity whispered, touching his cheek with affection, tears of relief and happiness swimming in her eyes. 'But where have you been? We have been so worried—you were captured—we thought…'

'The worst, I expect. I managed to escape my captors—although I had the devil of a time reaching the south coast and finding a boat to take me across the Channel. It's taken me the best part of six weeks to reach Paris, but as you see I am alive and well.'

'I thank God for it. You have been to the house?'

He nodded. 'Your servant told me you were attending a ball at the Palace.'

'Did you see Dickon?'

'I did, but he was asleep.'

'As all little boys should be at this hour. Now, say hello to Arabella. She has been quite beside herself with worry about you. It was a brave thing that she did, bringing Dickon to Paris by herself.'

Verity smiled when she turned to Arabella, who was unable to conceal the heady surge of pleasure and relief she was experiencing on seeing Edward again. It was painted like a confession on her lovely face. Neither of them spoke. The moment stretched between them, each savouring the moment and enjoying the sexual pull that drew them together.

'Thank you for keeping him safe, Arabella, and for bringing him to Paris. I am in your debt—more than you will ever know.' His voice was rich and hypnotically deep. He extended a hand towards her, impatient to be alone with her. 'Come. Walk with me. If we are fortunate, we may find a quiet place. Excuse us,' he said to those gathered round.

Finding refuge in the shadows of an adjoining room, they were relieved to find it was less crowded. They stood by the window, gazing at each other. Edward touched her cheek lightly with the backs of his fingers, his gaze holding hers.

'You are surprised to see me, Arabella?'

'Of course I am. I cannot believe you are safe—that you are here. When I saw Colonel Lister arrest you, I did not hold out much hope. I worried about you so much,' she whispered, loving him with every fibre of her being.

A smile curved his lips, the light streaming from a nearby candelabra illuminating his smile and his eyes that settled unswervingly upon her face. 'You need worry no more, Bella. As you see, I have returned to you unharmed.'

'How did you manage to escape?'

'They were taking me to London. It was the second night of my captivity, the guard was slack and I managed to get away.' He smiled into her eyes. 'I can't tell you how concerned I was about you and Dickon. You boarded the *Albion* with no trouble?'

'Yes, and we had no trouble getting to Le Havre—and then on to Paris. Dickon missed you—it was difficult explaining to him why you were suddenly not there any more. When he was settled I intended returning to England—I was desperate to know what had happened to you,' she confessed quietly. 'Verity and Gregory persuaded me to remain in Paris until we had news of your welfare.'

'I thank God they did. It was knowing you were here in Paris with Dickon that kept me going. I admire your courage, Arabella.'

'Courage?'

'You executed the task of bringing Dickon to Paris with the bravery of a soldier. But your courage isn't the only thing I admire about you, and if we were alone I would show you.' He cursed softly when another couple walked boisterously by. 'How I detest events such as this,' he growled, his eyes following the offending couple as if he could do murder.

Arabella laughed. 'They do no harm. They are simply enjoying themselves.' She gazed at his face, unable to believe he was really here. His eyes seemed to be as blue as the cornflower one minute and the next as purple as the darkest pansy, and then a combination of the two. The impact of his gaze was a potent thing. 'When they took you away I thought—I feared...'

Taking her hand, he raised it to his lips. Had they been in an empty room he would have taken her in his arms. 'Why, Arabella, what an imagination you have. I'm not killed as easy as that.' He smiled at her in an attempt to reassure her, realising then just how much he wanted her. 'Ever since I was arrested I've been unable to think of anyone but you. You haunt my dreams and I wake wanting you beside me. When I arrived and saw you surrounded by admirers— which is hardly surprising—for the first time in my life I experienced a jealousy that cut through me like a knife. You are beautiful, Arabella. You outshine every other lady present. You deserve to be gowned in silks and satins, with jewels as bright as your eyes at your throat.'

His compliment worked its way into Arabella. She flushed prettily. His words wrapped themselves around her like a warm blanket. 'To be perfectly honest, I had no wish to attend the ball. Verity persuaded me to come. I find the attention of those admirers you speak of tiresome. If only they knew that their attentions are unwanted.'

'Does that go for mine, too?'

'No, of course not. I believe you know that. You are different and when you arrived your mere presence saw off those persistent gentlemen.'

'So you see me as your knight protector. Is that it?' he teased softly.

Arabella smiled winsomely. 'I suppose you are—in a way. I've never had a knight protector before.'

'I'm flattered.'

She smiled up at him. 'I hardly recognised you when I saw you just now. You are much thinner and when we parted you had a beard.'

He grinned. 'And do you prefer me with or without a beard?'

Tilting her head to one side, she considered him, a puckish smile tugging the corners of her lips. 'I think I like you better without it. Without all that fuzz you cannot hide what you are thinking so easily and become less a man of mystery.'

He laughed. 'In which case I shall cease shaving if you can read me so well. I rather like the idea of being a man of mystery. Now come and dance with me.'

He held her eyes with his own. For a moment she stared at him. His animal-like masculinity was an assault on her senses and she was unable to resist him. In that instant, right there in a room where people strolled in and out, they acknowledged they had reignited that which had been lit between them in England and exchanged a carnal promise as obligatory as any spoken vow.

'You do dance?' he enquired quietly.

Arabella gave him an aggrieved stare. 'Of course I dance. My education covered all the finer points of a lady's upbringing. Although I was given neither the time nor the opportunity to put them into practice in my marriage to John.'

'Then we can only hope that now you are in Paris you can make up for lost time.'

Without uttering another word, with trembling fingers Arabella placed her slender hand in his. As the music started for a pavane he led her on to the floor. The floor was crowded with slow-moving figures, pacing to the rhythmic cadence of the instruments. She was relieved it was a moderate tempo and not the previous spirited dance.

When she had arrived in the company of Verity and Gregory and cast a glance over the scene, she had been unprepared for the colour and sparkle that greeted her. The English exiles gathered together might be impoverished, but they were still a sight to behold, and she thought how dull and how much poorer England would be without these aristocrats.

Unfamiliar with such occasions, she had felt as if hundreds of eyes were turned to her, but she knew that was likely only her nerves. She had fixed a smile on her face and endured a series of introductions and partnered several of the gentlemen in a dance. Before she had been led on to the floor by her first partner, a sense of panic had welled up in her stomach. She was not used to this kind of event and fervently hoped she would not make a fool of herself on the dance floor by forgetting the steps she had learned as a girl. But she need not have worried. She did not discredit herself, and now, dancing with Edward with her gown flowing in shimmering waves about her long legs, her feet flew over the floor as if they had wings. She was mesmerised by him, the deep-blue eyes almost consuming her, and each time he touched her hand a strange kind of energy seemed to flow into her.

At once her body began to react, to throb and burn as evocative memories of their loving came flooding back and a heat surged through her veins. Her composure was shaken by the various sensations that swept over her and the yearnings gnawing at her heart were nothing less than cravings that he had elicited when he had made love to her.

The dance ended and, keeping hold of her hand, he took her back to Verity. Gregory had joined her and they decided to retire to an adjoining room for refreshment.

As they left the dancing behind, experiencing a peculiar sensation of being watched and seeing a movement out of the corner of her eye, Arabella turned her head quickly, in time to see a figure disappear into the midst of people on the fringe of the dance floor.

It was nothing, she told herself, but a cold shiver passed down her spine.

With drinks in their hands, the four of them retired to a quiet table where they could talk undisturbed. Gregory held out his glass. 'To your freedom, Edward. It's good to have you back with us.'

He nodded, holding up his own. 'And to health and good fortune. Let it not be long before England realises her mistake in supporting Cromwell and the King comes to his own.'

Arabella noted the hard gleam in his eyes and her heart plummeted. 'Edward, do not tell me you are to continue the fight.'

His eyes met hers and he shook his head. 'No, Arabella. Rest assured the war is over. The Royalists are impoverished, their estates sequestered. There is no money to resume the fight and France is occupied fighting its own war. Besides, like every other European country she is eager to do business with the new order in England. We can only hope it does not last. With the austerity and dark piety imposed on the English people by Parliament, it will not be long before they begin to long for the return of the monarchy and the old way of life.'

'Have you given any thought to where you will live, Edward?' Verity asked, eager to turn the conversation away from the political situation. 'Of course I would like you to stay with us—I know Dickon would love to have you with him, but the house is small—scarcely large enough for us all as it is.'

He shrugged. 'Do not worry about it, Verity. I shall find somewhere. Exiles appear to have taken over the Royal Palace. I have friends whose situation is no different from mine. I'm sure one of them will take pity on me and offer me lodging. If not, there is always Robert at St Germain. It will not be as close to you as I would like to be, but beggars can't be choosers, can they?'

'You have seen Robert?' Arabella asked.

He nodded. 'I stopped there before coming on to Paris. He is worried about Alice and the children.'

'I know how desperate he is to see them again. He will return to England if Cromwell offers a pardon. Will you return, Edward?'

A faraway look entered his eyes as his mind travelled on the scheming and planning of which she had no part.

'Never. To do so would be to concede defeat. I will not do that while ever there is a prince left alive to sit on the throne. There is nothing for me in England at this present time. Everything I have is in Paris. Fortunately I am not entirely destitute.'

'But what you have will not last for ever,' Verity said quietly. 'What will you do? Would you consider offering your sword to the French King?'

He nodded, his face sombre. 'If I have to, yes, I will.'

They were leaving. Despite the revelries Arabella felt a certain unease. Turning her head, she looked towards a curtained alcove, seeing the heavy fabric fall back into place as if someone had just passed through. Telling herself not to be silly, that she was imagining things, she turned away. But she could not put off the feeling that she was being watched. She frowned. Something wasn't quite right. There was something strange going on and she trusted her intuition. Something simple, perhaps, but it could be significant.

The following morning when Edward came to the house, having found lodgings in the city with Lord Pettigrew, a close friend he had fought with in many a battle, Dickon was so excited to see his father again there was no pacifying him until Edward walked through the door. Dickon squealed with delight and threw himself at him. Edward laughed and swung him up into his arms.

Arabella looked on fondly, wondering how

he would react when she told him of the child—their child—she was carrying. But she would keep it to herself a while longer until things had settled down and she knew what he intended to do.

Edward had no hold over her. She was not his mistress. No promises had been made and there had certainly been no talk of marriage. She had not asked him for anything. But what if she did ask him for more? No, she could not do that. She would not want him to marry her out of obligation.

That evening they had been invited to dine with friends. In the early days of her pregnancy, Arabella was feeling slightly under the weather and would have preferred to have remained at home, but when Verity promised they would not be late leaving the party, she was persuaded. She might have been more enthusiastic had Edward been able to accompany them, but he was otherwise engaged at St Germain.

It was a large gathering, mostly exiles with several French noblemen and their wives. At the conclusion of the meal, the atmosphere became relaxed as more liquor was imbibed, the conversation louder and more animated, the favourite topic among the exiles about battles fought, won and lost.

Arabella was about to find a seat when her attention was drawn to a florid-faced gentleman in a long curling black wig, describing his escape from Worcester and before that Dunbar and St Fagans. Gregory told her that the gentleman's name was Captain George Fanshaw and he had indeed fought at all three battles. Unable to conceal her curiosity, Arabella approached him.

'Captain Fanshaw,' she said, standing directly in front of him. 'My name is Lady Arabella Fairburn. Pardon me for interrupting, but you were there—at St Fagans?'

A jovial sort with lively dark eyes, he looked down at her. 'I was indeed. Is the battle of interest to you, Lady Fairburn?'

'Yes, it is.'

'Was there a particular aspect that you are interested in?'

'My husband was killed during the battle.'

'I see. I am sorry. His name? Perhaps he was familiar to me.'

'Sir John Fairburn of South Glamorgan.'

The gentleman frowned. 'A Welshman?'

'Yes. Did—you know him?'

Thinking hard, he nodded. 'I knew of him

and I believe we did meet on occasion. If my memory serves me correctly, I seem to think the John Fairburn I know is well and truly alive. In fact, I think he came to France.'

Arabella stared at him with something akin to horror in her eyes. 'You—you must be mistaken. My husband is dead…'

'Not unless there are two men with the same name. The John Fairburn I know was wounded—that I do remember. Quite badly as it happens. He came to France to enrol in the French war, but he did not recover well and still suffers from the wounds inflicted on him at St Fagans. I have neither seen nor had reason to think of him since. If he had returned to Paris, I am sure I would have encountered him—but I seem to think he is somewhere in the south of the country.' He smiled. 'He probably prefers the warmer climes of the Mediterranean.' He looked at her with his deep-set eyes, noting her sudden pallor. 'I see I shock you.'

She nodded. 'Since he was reported killed and his body returned to his family home, then, yes. I have believed him dead these three years. Now you tell me he is alive.'

'You—saw the body?'

'No—no. I was told he was so badly wounded as to be unrecognisable.'

'Then unless I am mistaken and there are two men with the same name, you will be happy that I can confirm that your husband is alive—although who the man was that you buried is a mystery.'

'Thank you.' Arabella turned away, unable to believe what she had been told. This frightful thing could not be happening to her. She wanted to scream, to try to overcome the horror which was taking possession of her. She felt as though she were in a nightmare and that she would never wake up.

John was dead—he *had* to be dead. She couldn't bear it if he wasn't. And until he showed himself then that was how he would remain.

She frowned, thinking hard. But why would he have feigned his death? Why had he not come home? And why come to France and fight for the French king? Had he wanted her to think he was dead? It just didn't make sense.

And what did it mean for her?

She had been unfaithful. She was carrying another man's child.

There would be no forgiveness in him.

As the days passed Arabella became more and more certain that someone was watching her. Something didn't seem right. It was nothing she could put her finger on, just something she couldn't ignore. When she attended events with Verity she sensed invisible eyes watching her, and on turning she would see a figure disappearing into a crowd, a door closing or a curtain move. Common sense told her these events were not necessarily related, but her instinct was telling her to ignore common sense.

Anxious and increasingly restless since she had spoken to Captain Fanshaw, she made excuses not to go out, but after a while she could feel the walls of the house closing in. She felt like a caged bird struggling to be free, to stretch its wings. When Edward came to the house their eyes would seek each other out. The signals flashed, one to the other, and the silent, invisible cord stretched between them, and as the days passed the tighter it became.

When Edward was leaving the house after spending an afternoon with Dickon, he asked Arabella to accompany him to the door.

With the sound of children's laughter ringing in their ears, they stood and gazed at each other, both of them aware that their reunion was not to their satisfaction.

Edward's longing to take Arabella in his arms was so great that he knew he would have to devise something. She was like a diamond shining on the perimeter of his sight and he was aware of her flitting in and out of his mind. Whenever they were together they were never alone. Always Verity was present and the children. At these times there had been a need to keep their expressions closed, neutral.

Keeping his voice low, he said, 'I cannot stand this a moment longer. I seem to recall you were fond of riding as a girl.'

'Yes, but I haven't been on the back of a horse for longer than I can remember. The horses at Bircot Hall were taken by the soldiers.'

'Then tomorrow I will hire horses and we will ride out of the city. Does that appeal to you?'

Before Arabella could reply, Verity appeared, having overheard Edward's suggestion.

'Arabella has been looking a little pale of late, Edward. Perhaps some fresh air would be good for her. It is time she saw something of Paris,' she said, smiling her approval.

Immediately Edward's eyes were drawn to Arabella. Verity had voiced his own thoughts. Arabella had not seemed herself of late, and, intuitively, he knew that something was troubling her, which made him all the more determined to get her alone.

'But—would it not be best to hire a carriage?' Verity suggested. 'What I mean is—perhaps you should take Pauline with you.'

Arabella laughed at Verity's concern for her reputation. 'Pauline? Oh, Verity, that is exactly what Alice would have said. I hardly think a chaperon is necessary. I am almost twenty-three years old and a widow. As such, my status is rather different to that of an unmarried young woman. Besides, I love to ride and the activity and fresh air will do me the world of good.' What she said was true. The exercise would draw her out of the mire of uncertainty and vague disquiet in which she had wallowed since her brief conversation with Captain Fanshaw.

Verity looked from one to the other, then, with a knowing smile and a slight shrug of her shoulders, she turned away. 'Oh, well, I am sure you know best.'

Pulling on his gloves, Edward chuckled softly. 'As much as I adore my sister, Arabella, it is you I want to spend some time with. Alone. There is so much I want to say to you.' He frowned, suddenly concerned. 'Verity is right. You do look pale. Are you suffering some ailment?'

Arabella laughed. 'I am perfectly all right, Edward—and, as Verity said, it is nothing that fresh air won't cure.'

'If you're sure.'

Raising her hand, he pressed the backs of her fingers to his mouth and, parting his lips, touched them with the tip of his tongue, his eyes holding hers. Arabella felt that familiar, melting sensation spread throughout her body and she shivered.

He smiled as he lowered her hand, knowing exactly the effect he was having on her. 'Until tomorrow.'

True to his word, Edward arrived the following morning. It was a cool, overcast day, but neither of them would allow it to detract from their pleasure. It took no time at all for Arabella, gracefully perched side-saddle, to get used to being on horseback again and begin to enjoy the freedom it brought and to being away from the house. They rode through the outer environs of the city into the open countryside.

'We will stop for refreshment shortly,' Edward told Arabella as they rode towards a village in the distance, his face relaxed beneath his wide-brimmed plumed hat.

'I would like that,' she replied.

They had been riding for some time and already her stomach was beginning to rumble with hunger. Glancing across at Edward, she noted the jewelled buttons on his crimson tunic flash in the sun as he rode. She could not believe she was alone with him at last. Her heartbeat quickened when her gaze settled on his darkly handsome features and she fervently hoped he was in no hurry to return to Paris.

After partaking of a light meal at a small wayside inn, they rode on.

Edward turned and smiled at his companion, and she returned his smile. He liked it when she smiled. It transformed her face. Her large amber eyes sparkled and her mouth softened, smoothing away the frown that creased her brow all too frequently of late, the cause of which puzzled and worried him.

After a while, longing to stretch their legs, they strolled through a wooded area, climbing a slight rise, from which they had a splendid view of the city in the distance, beneath a pale blanket of cloud. But neither of them were interested in the view as they stood and looked at each other.

Reaching out Edward slowly removed the hood of Arabella's cloak from her head and he watched, fascinated as her heavy curls spread about her shoulders, the burnished tresses gleaming beneath a shaft of sunlight slanting through the trees.

'That's better. I like to see your hair.'

She laughed lightly. 'If you do not think I resemble a gypsy with my hair down, then I'm sure I don't care.'

'In my opinion it is better to look like a gypsy wench than one of those long-faced puritan women who inhabit Cromwell's world.'

'I have no puritan leanings, Edward.' Her mouth was slightly parted and she nipped the flesh of her bottom lip with her small perfect teeth in an innocently sensual gesture.

Edward felt the heat flame in his belly. Removing his gloves, he flung them to the ground and, taking her hand, drew her closer. Slowly he untied the cord at the neck of her cloak and let it fall in a pool at her feet, his eyes holding hers all the while. She did not move or speak, but her eyes darkened with desire.

Edward took her into his arms. He placed his lips on hers, kissing her with deepening hunger, and Arabella was happy to find there was no lessening of the passion he had felt when he had made love to her the night before he was captured. The sweet scent of her hair and skin and the touch of her body as he kissed her ignited his desire.

Leaving the tethered horses to munch grass to their hearts' content, they went a little deeper into the wood where they were hidden from the world.

'I think we have much catching up to do,' Edward murmured, removing his jacket. His strong hands drew her close to a hard, warm chest.

'I agree. We have been too long apart from one another.' She looked at him askance, mock-serious. 'But that does not mean I can be won over so easily, my lord.'

He laughed lightly, his arms tightening about her. 'We shall see about that.'

At once his lips were on her eyes, her cheeks, seeking her mouth. Finding what he sought, he kissed her hastily, breaking down her defences within a breath. As impatient as he was to renew their ardour, Arabella reached for him and kissed him back as if her life depended on it. The kiss was hot and bittersweet, with all the passion and tenderness of something long awaited.

'I cannot understand what it is you do to me,' she whispered, her mouth against his, her arms uplifted, her fingers threaded through his thick hair. 'I seem to become a different person when I am alone with you.'

Edward's gaze caressed her upturned face, watching her eyes darken, and her breathing quicken. 'I've missed you, my darling. You are so lovely, Arabella—so lovely that I ache when I look at you.' He was almost demented with desire for her.

They lay down on the grass. He stroked her face, caressing her and placing light kisses upon her closed eyelids, kisses so soft they were like the brush of a butterfly's wing. Unfastening the tiny buttons on her bodice, his fingers, so capable and sure of themselves, trailed a path to her neck, stroking the hollow of her throat, then moved down to cup her breasts. She murmured her pleasure as he began to knead them, his fingers passing slowly across the tautness of her rosy nipples. As his hands continued to stroke and tease, she felt her blood answering in eager response, until she was consumed with a desire, a need so strong that it matched his own. With her body awakened, she opened her eyes and looked up at his face hovering above hers.

'You are cruel, keeping me in suspense like this,' she accused softly.

He smiled. Kneeling alongside of her and leaning over, with his mouth against hers, he said, 'What would you have me do, my love? I am yours to command. I am more than willing to oblige my lady.'

The kiss he gave her brought the level of her

pleasure to such an intensity that she didn't think she would be able to tolerate it for much longer. Reaching up, she pulled his head down to hers. Twisting her hands in his hair, she savoured the taste of him, the heat growing inside her. His hands pulled up her skirts and maddeningly slow his fingers caressed her legs, her thighs.

'Please,' she whispered when he buried his face against her breasts and waves of passion assailed her. 'I don't think I can take much more.'

He sighed and his hold on her tightened. His kisses deepened and were no longer gentle. His hands, so capable, so strong yet gentle and loving, left no part of her untouched, opening her to pleasure. Her hands snaked their way beneath his shirt and they burned with the heat of him. Her body opened up to him, welcoming him, and she arched to meet him as he entered her.

In the cool November light, they became lovers once more. Locked in an embrace, when he touched her he turned her skin to fire, when he kissed her she went spiralling off into some mindless oblivion. It was as if neither of them could quench their burning thirst for each other as they moved together, twisting and rolling on the soft woodland grass, as if they were trying to force into this brief moment of happiness their stake of paradise on earth.

Afterwards they stretched out side by side, gazing up through the tops of the trees, some resilient leaves clinging to the boughs. As the passion ebbed from Arabella's body, she felt as if she were floating, the sound of her own heart beat slowly returning to normal, her breathing slowing. The languor following their lovemaking was still present and remembering his caresses and murmured endearments added to her contentment.

They said nothing for a long time as their bodies returned to normal and the world around them intruded into their solitude. They were aware of the trees swaying and rustling in the breeze, of the flapping of birds' wings. Finally Arabella stirred and, turning her head, looked at Edward lying by her side, his body touching hers. His black hair was spread out on the thick golden carpet of leaves. His eyes were closed and his handsome, swarthy face no longer showed the signs of strain which had been present since his arrival in Paris. The feelings she carried deep in her heart for him overwhelmed her. What she had experienced with him was different from anything she had known before—a blend of relief from anxiety and the restoration of her self-esteem and her physical relief in her response to him.

Sensing her gaze, he opened his eyes and turned his head to look at her. There was such tenderness in their dark depths that her heart felt it would burst with what was inside her.

He smiled. 'What is it?'

'I think we should be getting back. Verity will start to worry.'

'My sister worries over the slightest thing. She'll know you're safe with me. I want to make the most of having you to myself, without children climbing all over me and Verity's fussing. This time belongs to us. Surely we can forget the real world for a few moments more.' Propping himself up on his elbow, he smiled and bent to kiss her swollen lips. 'When I asked you to ride with me, I didn't intend for this to happen,' he said softly, his breath warm on her face.

A blush heated her cheeks. 'Yes, you did,' she contradicted with a smile. 'You knew I couldn't resist you—and I wanted you to make love to me,' she whispered, looking up at him, and, as she met his eyes, she realised how much she had come to love him, how much she had missed him, how much she wanted him, how he had brought her to the fullness of passion in a way she could not have imagined. 'No matter what happens, I will never forget it.'

'I'm glad. Are you happy, Arabella?'

'Yes. At this moment I am so happy it terrifies me. I've been alone for so long. When I'm with you my heart sings. I'm so glad you suggested we ride out together. I appreciate it so much.'

Reaching out his hand, he gently cupped her face, his dark-blue eyes glowing beneath his long black lashes and his face sculpted by the deepening shadows beneath the trees. 'I am at your service, Arabella. The pleasure was mine. Now,' he said, his voice low and lulling, 'when are you going to tell me what is wrong? You are not yourself. Is something troubling you? Verity is right. You have become pale of late and when you think no one is watching you, you have a worried look and there is such sorrow in your eyes. I feel as though there is something bothering you. Won't you tell me—confide in me?'

Her heart wrenched. She couldn't possibly tell him the whole of it. Yet she did not want to have to lie to him, nor yet to involve herself in explanations about the child. Because of the mystery surrounding John and not knowing if he was alive or dead, something held her back from telling Edward and she decided to keep the knowledge to herself a while longer.

'Is there something you don't want me to know?' he persisted, releasing her chin when she sat up, wrapping her arms around her up-raised knees.

'No,' she whispered.

'Good. I don't like secrets. Whatever it is I am on your side and ready to listen.'

He sat beside her in stoic silence, waiting to hear what she had to say and watching the complex play of emotions that played across her lovely face.

'There is something—but you will probably say it is all in my imagination,' she said, deciding there was no harm in telling him about the other thing that was tormenting her.

'You won't know that if you don't tell me.'

'I—I know it may seem absurd, but I think I'm being followed—that—I am being watched.'

He cocked an eyebrow. 'I won't ask if you are sure of that.'

She appreciated his belief in her judgement.

'An admirer, do you think?'

'No, I don't think so.'

'Has anyone approached you—spoken to you?'

'No. It's—it's just a feeling I have. I am unable to repress the feeling of unease I have when I attend any kind of gathering with Verity. It— it's as if I'm being stalked. When it is dark I think something or someone is going to jump out at me from the shadows.'

'I see.'

Edward was looking at her anxiously, his expression so troubled that Arabella tried to laugh away her alarms.

'I expect you think I am being foolish and I have to say you are probably right and that my fears are all in my over-active imagination, that I have a morbid love of mystery and a wish to be eccentric which makes me believe these things.'

'I would say nothing of the kind. If you are right and someone is watching you, do you have any idea who it might be?'

She shook her head. 'No. I mean, who would want to and for what reason?' Not for the first time she asked herself if what she had seen had been a delusion. She sighed. She didn't know what was real any more and was honestly tired of trying to figure it out. 'I shall try and put it out of my head, and so must you. Try to forget what I have said.'

As she spoke these words she began to put her clothes into some semblance of order, but a sudden thought entered her mind and settled

there. Was it possible that it could have something to do with John? It was a possibility that
had been prodding at her mind ever since she
had been given reason to believe he might not
be dead, that he had escaped the battle at St Fagans and made his way to France.

She had not let herself believe it—not then,
not now. And if he had escaped the battle, why
would he not approach her openly, instead of
indulging in this kind of cloak-and-dagger charade?

Edward was watching her, noting how her
hands trembled as she attempted to comb out
the tangle of her hair with her fingers, how she
was avoiding looking at him. 'Arabella?' The
expression on her face had altered slightly and
her eyes looked uneasy as she glanced at him
and then away, as if afraid to meet his eyes. He
became thoughtful. Instinct told him she was
hiding something. 'What is it? I feel there is
something you are not telling me.'

Her amber eyes were soft and stricken when
she said, 'Why, Edward, I cannot think what
you mean. What is wrong?'

'You tell me. You are holding something
back.'

Arabella glanced at him nervously, then
looked quickly away, fear escalating to panic.

In contrast to the deadly quiet of his voice, his expression was taut and harsh. Her mouth went dry. 'Very well. You are right. There is something wrong. You see—I—I can't say for certain, but there is a possibility that John may not be dead.'

He stared at her in disbelief. He had not expected that. When she was about to speak again, he held up his hand, silencing her. 'Wait a minute. What is all this?'

Arabella stiffened and the colour rushed into her face. 'I am sorry. I do not seem to be saying it very well.'

'How long have you known?'

'Colonel Lister seemed to think he did not die at St Fagans—and that after the battle he made his way to France.'

Edward said nothing, but his raised eyebrows and his silence seemed to question her. Briefly, like an obnoxious burden she wished to shake off, she told him about the unease she had felt since speaking to Colonel Lister and how what he had told her had been verified by Captain Fanshaw.

'And knowing this,' Edward said when she fell silent, 'you let me into your bed. Do you realise what you have done?'

She met his gaze, which had turned hard and

cold with anger, tears pricking her eyes. 'I didn't want to believe either of them. After all, I saw John's coffin lowered into the ground.'

'But you didn't actually see him?'

She shook her head dejectedly. 'No.'

Edward sprang to his feet, turning his back on her and combing his fingers through his hair. Naked pain sliced through his heart.

Desperate to explain, Arabella scrambled up and went to him, her eyes wide and fixed and unbelieving. 'Please don't be like this, Edward. Truly I thought John was dead. I could not bear to let myself believe he would be alive.'

Edward turned and looked at her, his eyes as hard as flint. 'Then you should have. Lister clearly had good reason to believe your husband survived the battle. If that is true, then God knows why he did not return home to you, why he chose to go to France instead. The fact remains that, knowing there is a chance that he is alive, you committed adultery—not once, but twice. I hoped…' He cursed beneath his breath, taking several impatient strides away from her before looking at her again. 'Like a fool I allowed myself to believe we might have a future together. You should have told me this before we left Bircot Hall. Why in God's name did you not tell me of this?'

She didn't answer him, but moved her head in a slight, helpless gesture.

Something in that movement and the bleak look in her eyes hurt Edward with a savage pain, but he would not allow himself to be moved by it. 'You should have told me—' He stopped abruptly. Questions were futile. It was too late now. If John Fairburn was alive, then as his wife she must go back to him if he presented himself. Why he had disappeared from Arabella's life, wanting her to believe he was dead, was not for him to question. He, Edward, was the one who had made love to the man's wife.

Arabella wanted to go to him, to reach out and have him take her in his arms, but his expression forbade any further intimacy between them. 'I am so sorry, Edward. But—truly—I had not imagined I would ever see him again.'

'What are you going to do?'

'What can I do other than wait for him to show himself?'

'And what then? Your marriage cannot be dissolved. That is irrevocable. The fact remains that your husband has the law on his side.'

Going to him, she stretched out a groping hand and placed her fingers on his arm in a gesture that begged for reassurance. 'Edward—'

He wrenched his arm away and said suddenly, fiercely, 'For God's sake, Arabella, don't look at me like that.' He saw her flinch as though he had struck her and he said, with cold impatience, 'We must be getting back.'

Arabella did not move immediately, nor did she answer him. The moment seemed to stretch out interminably. A pigeon flapped in the trees, keeping to the shadows, undisturbed by the two motionless people who stood looking at each other. Suddenly Edward turned on his heel and walked away from her.

It was with a heavy heart that Arabella followed him back to the horses. They rode back to Paris in silence.

On reaching the house she slipped down from her horse and looked at him. He took the reins.

'Are you coming inside?' she asked.

'Will you make my excuses to Verity? It has been a somewhat trying day and I am sure my sister will forgive me if I don't.'

'Yes—yes, of course—but where are you living, Edward—should we need to reach you?'

'I am staying with friends at the Hotel de Joubert—close to the Royal Palace. Gregory knows its situation.'

'I see.' She stared at him, bewildered by his behaviour. Her courage seemed to have temporarily deserted her. Their affair—or what she had thought of as a lovely romance—had turned into a grotesque farce. It was no use arguing because, looking at it from Edward's point of view, he had every right to be angry. As John had deceived her by faking his death, so she had knowingly deceived Edward, no matter how innocent her deception had been.

He was about to ride away when she had a sudden surge of pride.

'Wait, Edward.'

He turned and looked down at her, waiting for her to speak. Her elegant head was proudly raised and the hood of her cloak had fallen back and her magnificent mane of hair formed a halo around her lovely face. Her eyes were wide and bright with a hint of scorn in their amber depths.

'I did not tell you about John because I did not want to believe it, but I will say this. Even though your ears may be closed to anything I might say, nothing anyone can say will persuade me to go back to John. Where I am concerned I am no longer his wife. I had no life married to him—at least not one worth living. Our marriage ended when he sent an unknown man's body back to me. He wanted me to believe he was dead, so that is how he is to me. How he will remain. I may be his lawful property, but I will never belong to him. I will not go back to him. I would kill myself first.'

Edward met her eyes without blinking. Although the white-hot anger he had experienced when she had told him about John Fairburn had begun to fade, he kept his voice hard and unforgiving. 'Then let us hope it does not come to that. What happened to your common sense, Arabella?'

'The heart is a curious thing, Edward. It does not always listen to common sense.'

Arabella waited until he was lost to her sight before she went into the house. She could not have stopped him if she had tried. But how she wanted to run after him and beg him to help her, for there was no one else she could appeal to. She had not expected him to react so angrily. Not only had he been unsympathetic, he had been scandalised that she had been so lacking in restraint and lost to all sense of responsibility towards her husband.

Chapter Eight

Edward did not come to the house the next day or the one after and Arabella could only be thankful that she was spared the humiliation of facing him.

Verity became increasingly worried about Arabella. The drawn pallor of her face became more noticeable and there were dark shadows beneath her eyes that made them look too large for her face. When Verity commented on this, Arabella assured her that there was nothing wrong with her health, which led Verity to wonder if Edward and Arabella had had some kind of disagreement on their ride.

'Have you and my brother argued?' she enquired.

Arabella stopped what she was doing and looked at her. 'What makes you ask that?'

'We've seen nothing of him for a couple of days now. Are you avoiding each other?'

Arabella made a pretence of carefully folding the children's clothes that had been freshly laundered. What Verity said was true—and as much as she would dearly like to confide in Verity, she held back. Although being several weeks into her pregnancy, evidence of her condition would soon be evident and she would not be able to hide it. 'No,' she said. 'He is probably busy. He did say something about going to join Robert at St Germain for some hunting.'

Verity gave her a sideways thoughtful look. 'I am glad. The two of you seem to be getting on so well. I hoped…'

She never did get to say what it was she hoped for because at that moment there was a cry from one of the children playing upstairs in the nursery and she scuttled out.

Sighing deeply, Arabella watched her go. She knew Edward would prefer not to see her and that he was probably arranging to go and fight for the French like so many exiles were doing in order to relieve the boredom of Paris.

After an absence of several days he did come to the house to see Dickon. Pleading a headache, Arabella remained in her room, but the fact that he was in the house, even if she did not speak to him or see him was comforting—the one ray of light in her dark and dismal life.

Two weeks after the day she had last seen Edward, Arabella was looking beautiful in a gown of green-and-cream satin with a tight, pointed bodice with dropped shoulders and slashed sleeves—another of Verity's gowns that had been altered to fit—and she was relieved her condition was not yet noticeable. She was accompanying Verity and Gregory to a banquet to celebrate the marriage of two of England's noble exiles. The King was expected to be present to wish the couple well so invitations were much sought after.

But the possibility of seeing the King in the flesh for the first time was not the reason why Arabella had decided to attend. Gregory told her that Edward would be accompanying the King. After giving the matter of the child considerable thought, she had decided to do the right thing and tell him. She could not begin to guess how he would react—no doubt he would accuse her of further duplicity—but at least he would know.

No longer suffering from the discomforts of early pregnancy, which was not yet evident except for a slight thickening around her waist, in her finery she was the epitome of youthful beauty and grace. Her pallor had been replaced by a glowing radiance and her eyes shone beneath their long silken lashes, so bright they dimmed the pearls at her ears and throat which Verity had kindly loaned to her.

The wedding was being celebrated in a large house in a wealthy quarter of the city. The banqueting hall was brilliantly illuminated and the wedding feast was happy and lively. A good number of the guests were already inebriated. Footmen poured the sparkling wine and served the food scullions brought from the kitchens below. The meal seemed interminable to Arabella. The reception afterwards was attended by a large press of royalist exiles and French nobles from the ducal provinces all packed tight together.

'See,' Verity whispered, fluttering her fan and raising an eyebrow as she glanced across the room. 'There is King Charles. He is certainly worthy of our attention, don't you agree, Arabella?'

Arabella followed her gaze. It wasn't difficult to identify the King. At twenty-one years of age King Charles was tall and slender, his features dark and brooding. Arabella's heart went out to this young man who was unable to return to England to claim his throne. Perhaps one day in the future, when the people of England became tired of the austerity imposed on them by Parliament, he would be recalled to his own. Until then he would have to endure exile with other Royalists.

King Charles moved further into the room, submerged in a sea of silks and satins and a wave of perfume as ladies vied with each other for his attention. The voices in the room seemed to grow louder, but Arabella was conscious of none but Edward. King Charles smiled now and then as people accosted him, nodding genially from time to time to other guests, all the while followed by those who accompanied him, seeming reluctant to leave his side.

Verity was talking to her, but Arabella was not listening. Her attention was suddenly caught by a man who was part of the King's entourage. Her heart leapt when she recognised Edward. She was beginning to think he had decided not to come. Seeing him now reminded her of all that had passed between them. Engaged in conversation with a gentleman in the King's party, he seemed unaffected.

At last he looked her way. A world of feelings flashed across his face, then he was shoving his way in their direction.

Edward had done his utmost to avoid Arabella, but seeing her now, so close, a physical pain betrayed his feelings for her. When she had told him that her husband might not be dead after all, and knowing himself to be unwilling to conduct an adulterous affair, he had convinced himself that an estrangement from her was for the best. But seeing the unguarded longing on her face twisted his heart. For all his firm resolve not to see her, nothing could change the way he felt for her.

As he pushed his way through the throng, he took a deep breath. He had no idea how he had got through the days since their acrimonious parting when his mind and body was absorbed with thoughts of her. The ache inside him refused to subside. Why couldn't he find another woman and slake his lust?

The truth was that he didn't want any other woman. He wanted Arabella. Why should she be any different to any other woman? He only knew that she was different. Having taken a moment to observe her from across the room, seeing her laugh and wrinkle her nose at something amusing Gregory whispered in her ear, he found himself remembering how it felt to hold her pliant young body in his arms, the taste of her mouth, the sweet scent of her hair, her body, and her unashamed impatience for him to make love to her and her unforgettable response.

A part of his anatomy responded to that memory, making him realise that he didn't want to let her go—husband or no husband—if and when the man condescended to show himself. She had told him she would rather die than go back to John Fairburn, and if what she said was true, then perhaps, some time in the future, they might have a chance of happiness together.

There was so much masculinity in the way Edward moved that Arabella's heartbeat quickened in her breast as he came towards her. His broad shoulders and clear-cut profile were etched against a sea of colourful and glittering people all milling together. She held her breath, overwhelmed by a wondrous feeling of anticipation.

When he reached her he took her hand and drew her aside. 'Arabella, how lovely you look. You outshine every woman here tonight.'

His compliment brought a sudden rush of colour to Arabella's cheeks. Gazing wonderingly into his eyes, she searched for confirmation that she was forgiven. 'Even the bride?' she ventured to ask.

'Even the bride,' he confirmed. 'I wish to apologise for my boorish behaviour. Since I left you I've been living in fear that you will not forgive me and my harsh words. You must have been suffering all the torments of damnation not knowing if your husband is alive or dead. I should have been more understanding, but I could think of nothing but how his return would affect me. You have no idea what I have been through these past days. For God's sake, tell me I am forgiven?'

After days of numb despair and physical suffering, a rush of warmth and well-being pervaded Arabella's whole being. She drew in her breath quickly. Something was happening which made the whole world seem golden, glorious and wonderful. She could understand why he had reacted so furiously and uttered such harsh words. Now, seeing him beside her once more, with that drawn look on his face and the anxiety in the depths of his deep-blue eyes, betrayed how deeply he felt. She felt a sudden longing for him and an even keener awareness of her love for him. She was feeling so intense that she wanted to confess it and to tell him how the suffering she had experienced when he had walked away from her had made her want to die.

'What we have, Edward, means there should be no need to ask for forgiveness.'

For a long moment his gaze held hers with penetrating intensity. 'Has your husband shown himself?'

'No. In truth, Edward, I don't know what to do. I do not want him back in my life.'

'So you will not return to him?'

'No.'

Edward's teeth gleamed from between his lips and his eyes held a devilish light. 'Perhaps I need to be reassured.'

Arabella gave an answering laugh. 'I regret that I cannot give you the kind of reassurance you ask for with all these people looking on. I fear they would be scandalised,' she murmured as he raised her hand and pressed his warm lips to her fingers, each thinking of the time very soon when they could again find fulfilment and forgetfulness in each other's arms.

'Come,' he said suddenly, without relinquishing her hand. 'I will introduce you to King Charles. Would that please you?'

'Yes—I would like that,' she said glowingly, her heart beginning to beat a wild tattoo at the very thought. How Alice, who had always had a soft spot for the young Prince Charles before he had become King, would envy her.

Still holding her hand, Edward escorted her to Charles Stuart. In the surrounding haze she saw no one else. Had she wanted to look away she could not have done so. She was not even conscious that people had paused in their conversations to watch her approach. Even the King paused in talking to one of his entourage to look at her.

Proudly, Edward drew her forward. 'Sire, may I present to you Lady Fairburn.'

Arabella sank into a curtsy of stately reverence. 'It is indeed an honour to meet you, Sire.'

'The pleasure is all mine, Mistress Fairburn,' the King said suavely. Very courteously, he took her hand and raised her up, pressing her fingers to his lips before releasing them, keeping his eyes firmly fixed on hers. He was easily moved by the beauty of women and he was completely charmed by Mistress Fairburn. 'I am delighted to make your acquaintance. Edward tells me it is you he has to thank for bringing his son safely to Paris. I am surprised I have not yet had the pleasure of meeting you—had I done so I would have remembered, for I never forget a face, especially when a face is as lovely as yours.'

'You are too kind, Sire,' Arabella murmured, with an air of pretty confusion, her eyes irresistibly drawn to the King's face.

His gaze beneath his heavy-lidded eyes was appreciative, his interest unconcealed. She was transfixed by him for there was something so sensual in his dark eyes that she found herself flushing hotly. He was a fascinating man, and powerfully aware of his charm. He emanated a great physical power and the muscles of his hard shoulders rippled beneath his clothes. His movements for one so tall were graceful, in a lazy kind of way, and there was an air of mystique about him. He was younger than she was, for all that he appeared to have all the troubles of the world upon his broad shoulders.

The King turned to Edward. 'Come, Edward. There are others I wish to be introduced to.'

Edward moved to follow His Majesty.

'Edward.'

He paused and faced her.

'I have to talk to you. I have something I wish to say—but not here.'

'I will come to the house tomorrow.'

'Yes.' As she watched him go, a movement caught her attention. A man had just entered the room and she turned her head and looked at him. He had his back to her and she was about turn away when something about him drew her eyes and rendered her motionless.

Cold fear and an unpleasant feeling akin to revulsion slithered through her, creeping up her spine and into her heart when he turned and his face was revealed to her. The shock of it was like a punch in the chest.

For a moment she thought her eyes must be deceiving her, but she soon realised this was no evil dream. She felt she would suffocate. Sweat stood out on her brow and her heart seemed to roll over and cease to be her own. With difficulty she struggled to control her emotions. The ground seemed to move alarmingly beneath her feet.

There could be no mistake. The man was her husband, John Fairburn, and no figment of her fevered imagination. The distinguished features which had once given his face distinction were pinched and shrunken, his flesh waxen and gaunt. His light-brown hair was sparse and grey in places, curling almost to his shoulders. His clothes were fashionable, the subdued colours relieved by a broad white-lace collar.

Noting her stillness, Verity excused herself to Gregory and came to stand beside her.

'That man, Arabella? Is he known to you?'

She nodded. 'Yes,' she managed to utter. 'He is John Fairburn. My husband.'

Verity stared at Arabella as though she had taken leave of her senses. 'Your husband? But—I thought he was…'

'Dead. So did I.' Considering the turmoil inside her, her voice was surprisingly calm. 'It appears I was mistaken.'

Across the distance that separated them, Arabella met John's cold grey eyes without flinching. In some strange way she was relieved he had finally shown himself, for though she could not see him he seemed to hang in her presence for ever, to lurk in her mind. The terrors that had haunted her ever since Colonel Lister had led her to believe he was alive had vanished, but she could not overcome the repugnance she felt at seeing him again. She was going to need all her self-control to prevent her anger and hatred of him bursting out.

With a mockery of a smile, he made her a flourish of a bow and, excusing himself to his companions, who were looking at her with a salacious interest she found nauseating, he slowly made his way towards her.

'He is coming this way,' Verity whispered. 'Would you like me to stay?'

'No, thank you, Verity. I would rather be on my own.'

As Verity returned to her husband, Arabella moved to a quiet corner of the room, knowing John would follow. She watched him approach, noting his confidence and swagger were undiminished. John Fairburn was an arrogant, selfish man, incapable of feeling any emotion that did not gratify his love of himself.

When he finally stood before her his thin face was so expressionless that it might have been carved from stone. He stared at her without greeting. He was breathing hard as if he'd been running and beads of perspiration shone on his brow.

Then, suddenly, a faint smile lightened his sombre countenance, a smile that hid his teeth and made her tremble inwardly. With a great effort of will she controlled herself and faced him—a slender, deciding confidence was the best approach in confronting her errant husband.

'John! So you are alive,' she exclaimed coldly, struggling to conceal the panic that gripped her, her expression a mixture of fear and revulsion.

'As you see, my dear wife.' He glanced around, clearly irritated by the proximity of other guests. 'I would like to speak to you in private, if you please. We cannot converse in a crowd.'

'I do not please. You may say what you have to say to me here.'

His pale eyes impaled her. 'Why, Arabella, don't you trust me?' His voice was cold and disdainful.

'I have every reason not to. I believe you were already in Paris when I arrived—which is strange since no one appears to have seen you, otherwise I am sure they would have informed me. I know you have been watching me. Why did you not make your presence known to me instead of hiding in crowds and behind curtains?'

He shrugged nonchalantly. 'Why would I do that? I enjoy watching you. I always did, you know that.' He glanced around the room at the colourful and elegantly dressed gathering, his gaze resting briefly on the King. 'I like to keep myself to myself—although you and I did arrive in Paris at the same time. I did not expect to see you here in France.'

'I can understand why,' she retorted with more than a hint of sarcasm.

'I keep to my rooms mostly. I do not normally associate with such illustrious company as this, but I thought it was time you and I met. You appear to be enjoying yourself, Arabella.

You are hardly the grieving widow,' he accused smoothly.

'But I am not a widow, John, though for some perverse reason of your own you wanted me to think so.'

'I know where you live, Arabella. I also know who you associate with.' When she raised a questioning brow, he laughed harshly. 'You have become a popular figure. Your movements are commented on. You have also become re-acquainted with Sir Edward Grey, I see. How fortunate for you that his wife is dead and you believed you were free to resume the relationship that was cut short prior to our marriage—when he threw you over for another woman. How disappointed you must be to find I was not slaughtered in glorious combat.'

His mocking tone reawakened all her anger against him. He was still the same. Nothing could shake him. He still had that sarcasm and exasperating air of superiority even in the most trying circumstances. Determined not to let his jibe upset her, she tossed her head defiantly. 'Is that why you have suddenly decided to show yourself? I certainly do not for one moment imagine you have sought me out to make amends for lying to me over your death in battle.'

His smile didn't waver, but the skin around his eyes tightened. She saw his gaze hover over her breasts and she knew that, for all his airs, he was no different to what he had always been—a cruel bully. The calm, almost carefree, detachment of his astounded her. Since his supposed death she had tried not to think how intolerable he had been as a husband. Now she was reminded with a force that was very hard to bear.

Calmly, and unemotionally, he moved a step closer to her. 'You are still my wife. I could not allow your affair to continue, which is why I could not conceal myself any longer. Come now, is this not a poignant moment—a man and wife together again after so long an absence, especially after a parting you believed would be for ever?'

'I am not going back to you, John,' she told him, her voice low and hoarse with indignation. 'I would rather die first.'

'Oh, but you will, Arabella. In the end.'

His tone was subtle and sneering with contempt. It was the way he had habitually addressed her since the day of their marriage. 'I was told you were dead. That was what you intended me to believe when you sent me the coffin containing another man's body. As far as I am concerned I buried you that day. After the battle when Parliamentary soldiers came and burned the house down and took the land, my ties with you were severed.'

As cold as a block of ice, John looked at his wife completely unmoved. 'I still have the house in Bath.'

'Not any longer. I needed money, so I sold it.'

This he had not known. His eyes narrowed and glittered with anger and a nervous tic twitched at the corner of his mouth. 'You did what? Damn you! It was not yours to sell.'

She met his eyes with a defiance she would never have dared show in the past. 'Whose was it? You were dead.' She looked at him curiously. 'If you wanted me to believe you had been killed at St Fagans, why have you decided to show yourself now?'

'Because I changed my mind and decided not to hide myself away any longer.'

'You are a well-known figure. Did you really think you could remain hidden for ever? Was that what you wanted?'

'At the time. You suspected I was alive. Who told you?'

'Malcolm Lister—after Worcester when he arrived at Bircot Hall looking for fugitives. What were you hiding from—or perhaps I should say whom? Me?'

He nodded. 'Partly—mostly from myself—and what war has done to me.'

Captain Fanshaw had told her John had been badly wounded in battle. She had noted a stiffness in his walk when he had approached her. 'I heard you offered your sword to France.'

'I did. Unfortunately the wounds I received at St Fagans have left their effects so I returned to Paris. However, I have not been idle. I have made a point of finding out what you have been up to. I know you became reacquainted with Edward Grey and he sought your help to bring his son to Paris—away from his brother-in-law, Colonel Lister, who he feared would take his son as his heir.'

His calm, aloof tone annoyed Arabella. 'You are right. You have been busy, John. May I ask how you came by this information?'

'I made a point of finding out all I could.'

'I had no idea that the people in Paris were so interested in me.'

John pretended not to have noticed the force with which Arabella uttered those words. He brushed at a minute piece of lint on his sleeve and without looking at his wife he said smoothly, 'Edward Grey is your lover. I am right, am I not, Arabella? I do know so you might as well admit it.'

Arabella dug her nails into the palms of her hands to keep herself calm. The heat of anger that shot through her was acute. 'Then why do you ask?'

'I will not be made a fool of and nor will you cover me with shame by continuing your sordid affair. I will leave you now to consider what my return into your life will mean for your future. Tomorrow I will call on you and I will tell you what I intend to do. Make sure you are at home for I will not take kindly to your absence.'

John moved to stand in front of her, putting his arms out and drawing her slim, unyielding body close.

'Don't,' she objected, putting up her hands to fend him off. For a moment it appeared as though she were returning his embrace. Suddenly someone sauntered past and, turning her head, she found herself looking into Edward's cold expression.

With the green-eyed demon of jealousy clawing at his heart, Edward looked away and headed for a group of gentlemen engaged in conversation at the other side of the room. When Verity had approached him to inform him of John Fairburn's unexpected arrival, believing Arabella would be unduly upset he had hur-

ried to her side to offer his support. He needn't
have bothered. He was more furious than he
had ever been in his life. It was an entirely il-
logical fury, for surely he should be happy that
Arabella hadn't been as unhappy in her marriage as she would have him believe.

Too much had happened to Arabella that
night for her to sleep. She lay turning the problem over and over in her overstimulated brain,
looking at it from every angle without reaching any satisfactory conclusion. One thing she
did know: the man she loathed above all others with an obsession would destroy her if she
went back to him.

When it began to get light, seated in a chair
by the window she still had not found an answer to her dilemma. With her head aching she
dragged herself out of her chair and began to
prepare for the day ahead.

When John came she admitted him into the
house herself, relieved that he had come early
and hoping he would be gone before Edward
arrived. She took him directly into the drawing room as Verity had directed she must do to
speak to him in private. Closing the door, she
stood and faced him, trying to keep her knees
from trembling.

'Please say what you have to say and then go. I have no wish to prolong this meeting.'

'This meeting will take as long as I want it to—until you have packed your bags and come to live with me.'

'Live with you? Where?'

'Don't worry, Arabella, you will be well kept. Since I have been back in Paris, I spend my time frequenting an establishment where the play is high—I have to say the company is anything but exclusive—but where fortune smiles on me and has enabled me to rent suitable rooms close to the Louvre Palace. You will recall that I always did have a flair for the dice and the turn of a card.'

Arabella remembered well. John had the compulsion of the dedicated gambler. Whenever possible he would whittle away at the fortune his father had left in his care, casually gambling away enormous sums of money as if it would never end. Sometimes he won, which only encouraged him to continue.

'I remember all too well,' she replied. 'I also remember how you almost gambled your inheritance away.'

'Not any more. You might say my luck has changed. You will be comfortable, I promise you.'

'Promise me all you like, John. I will not live with you.'

'Yes, you will—in the end.'

'No—and do not threaten me. I am not afraid of you.'

'Threat? It is not a threat. It is an order. I will not have another man do to my wife what I can no longer do myself.'

'What do you mean by that?' she asked, bewildered by his remark and curious as to what could be behind it. 'Is it that you no longer want to—or because you can't?'

John said nothing, but his eyes, as he studied her, grew clouded and their expression was transformed slowly and strangely to one of vulnerability.

'Yes,' he said at last, reluctantly. 'That is the reason. You already know I was wounded at St Fagans. I took the full blast from a fusillade of muskets. When I was pulled from the fray I was alive, but only just. I won't go into detail, but the damage done to me has rendered me impotent. In other words, my dear wife, I am no longer capable of begetting a child.'

Arabella stared at him, silent and wide-eyed, as if seeing him for the first time. He could not conceal the fact that he was suddenly agitated. Curiously she observed the distress into which this normally self-assured, manipulative man had sunk. He turned from her as he fought for restraint, but when he turned back to her all trace of his distress had vanished. Briefly, an immense sadness replaced Arabella's anger. She was unable to imagine his suffering. He was watching her closely and saw the changes in her expression.

'Pity me—gloat, even, if you must, for who would have guessed that John Fairburn would be brought so low that he can no long have carnal knowledge of his wife? I have no doubt that you will say I got the punishment I deserve.'

The calculated, cold disdain with which he uttered these words acted like a bucket of cold water on the softening of her feelings.

'No,' she said in a low voice. 'I do pity you, but I will not gloat over your torment. You caused me a great deal of pain in our marriage and I hate you for it—which is understandable. But I would never wish what has happened to you on any human being. What was done to you... Was that the reason you wanted me to believe you were dead, because you couldn't...?'

A faint smile appeared at the corner of his mouth which twisted his thin face, making him look as cruel as his heart. 'As you know I have

always prided myself on my virility. I didn't
want to return to you half a man, to have to
suffer the infernal torture which you would be
for me if I could not share your bed, to remain
bound by my own impotence, eaten by desire,
interminably, knowing there would be no respite until death.'

'So you sent me another man's body in a coffin,' she said, trying to understand. Despite his
suffering, she could do nothing for him, nothing
at all. But it did not alter the way she felt about
him or remove the bitterness from her heart.

'That is what I did,' he replied, with a bitter
smile. 'I expected to die anyway, but it seems
my time has not yet come. No one knows my
secret except the man who tended me—and
now you.'

'What I find rather odd is that if you wanted
to feign your death, then why not change your
name also? You are well known—a man of considerable importance. Surely you must have realised that someone would recognise you and
your name.'

He shrugged. 'I told you. At the time I cared
little. I thought my time had come. When I realised I was not going to die from my wounds
and that I would have to go on living, I decided
to return to the world—and you.'

His gaze travelled over her. 'You know, you look different. There is something about you that…something in your eyes that…' His words trailed away and he looked at her hard, appearing to consider a thought, then he frowned suddenly. 'Are you breeding, Arabella?' Arabella's heart missed a beat and she started. Her quick intake of breath and sudden pallor answered his question. He smiled, a thin knowing smile. 'Ah—so my suspicion is true. It is Grey's, I take it? Does he know?' She shook her head. His eyes narrowed as he contemplated her stricken face in thoughtful, calculating silence, then he seemed to reach a decision. A hardness entered his eyes and his expression became animated, as if a spark had been lit. 'You will not tell him. I forbid it.'

'But—what are you saying? Of course I will tell him,' she retorted, staring at him in disbelief. 'How can I not? The child is his.'

'It does not have to be. It would appear I may have something to gain out of all this.'

'Gain? What do you mean?'

'I have always wanted a son.'

He smiled slowly, a malicious, cruel smile. Arabella looked at him aghast. The result of what had happened to him at St Fagans had given him a vulnerability and to some extent weakened him, but the cruel streak still ran through his veins like his life's blood. She remembered how it had been to live with him—ugly, violent. She hated him.

'I hope I am mistaken and that you are not saying what I think you are. You can't do that. It is up to Edward to provide for the future of his child.'

'I can do what I choose and I will. I will do anything I please.'

Arabella stood as one turned to stone, unable to think or act as she stared at her husband in horror, watching as her world began to crumble around her. Fear and panic were setting in. She struggled to conceal what she felt. With this man, her husband, whose terrifying history she knew more than anyone else, it was imperative that she remained calm and did not show her fear. She looked away, closing her eyes. She couldn't believe this was happening. She told herself that it was some kind of bad dream that would go away when she opened her eyes.

But when she did, John was still there, watching her like a cat watches a mouse it has selected for its dinner. She glared at him, her hands clenched into fists in the folds of her skirt.

'The injuries you suffered not only rendered you impotent, they warped your mind.'

'Perhaps. I have always wanted children.'

'We had a child, John—Elizabeth—or have you forgotten?'

'I remember her—a sickly girl. I know she died, but I shed no tears over her loss.'

Arabella was appalled by his callous disregard for their daughter, but she chose not to comment. To become immersed in an argument about the one good thing that had come out of their marriage would only bring her more sorrow and heartache.

'What I want is a son to carry on after me,' John went on. 'A son who will one day take over the estate.'

'But the house is gone.'

'The house was nothing but a pile of stones. It can be rebuilt. The estate is still mine.'

'Along with all Royalist properties it has been sequestered.'

'If that is so, then I will find a way of getting it back. When the King comes into his own he has promised he will return everything that has been taken by Parliament to those who remained loyal to him and his father before him. The child you are carrying is my only chance. If it is a boy he will be my heir.'

'You are willing to raise another man's child

as your own?' He nodded. 'You are quite mad—insane.'

'No, Arabella. Edward Grey has another child—a child that Parliamentarian Colonel Malcolm Lister would go to any lengths to get his hands on—to make his heir.'

Arabella stared at him, a coldness and deep fear beginning to creep into her heart.

'You intend to use it against him.'

'Exactly. I can make it possible for Lister to achieve his aims. If you do not obey me in this, it is not you who will suffer.'

'No, John. I will not satisfy your wicked schemes.'

'No? Perhaps you should look at it another way. I will not divorce you, so you will not be free to marry Edward Grey. Do you know how society treats a known adulteress? Does the prospect attract you?'

'Ever since I realised I was with child, I have been prepared to fight for—'

'For what?' he snapped. 'For a man who jilted you to marry another? What happened to your pride, Arabella? I did not take you for a fool.'

Arabella knew that what he said was true, yet she was loath to agree to the horrifying prospect he put before her. 'You cannot expect me to agree to something so serious. Do you really expect me to turn my back on Edward, to keep the fact that I am to bear his child to myself merely to appease your greed for an heir?'

'Then consider the alternative,' he said, his tone menacing. 'I shall have Edward Grey's son—Dickon, I believe his name is, the boy you have become so fond of—spirited back to England.'

There was a long silence, a silence heavy with the threat of a powerful man who would have his way whatever the consequences. His eyes had changed suddenly, becoming sharp and brilliant. She knew that change and it frightened her. It was a moment before she could bring herself to speak. John was determined, that was obvious. It was enough to see his eyes, intense and cold, the eyes of a man ready to commit any crime to slake his overwhelming ambition—and no doubt he had accomplices to assist him in his crime.

'Not even you could be so cruel. You would not take a son from his father.'

At the sight of her stricken face he laughed. 'Believe me, Arabella, I will take him to hell if I have to. Do I really seem like a person who would let the disappearance of a child trouble my sleep?'

The words dripped from his mouth, each one penetrating her heart like the sharpest blade. She stared at him as she realised the full impact of what, to her, amounted to a death sentence. For a moment she struggled inwardly to come to terms with the awful choice she knew she would have to make—and there was no choice, not really. That was the moment her anger evaporated in the face of grim reality.

Hearing him speak with such cynical detachment of removing a child from his father made her doubt his sanity. Her husband was a man from whom all human feeling had gone. She was starting to tremble, but she did not dare show it. Ever since her discovery that she carried Edward's child, she had been carried along on a wave of exultation. But now she knew that nothing was that certain.

'Let me think about it. Because of your—impairment, I realise that our marriage from now on will be a marriage in name only. That being the case, if I do agree to your terms, I ask you to respect my privacy.'

John reached out and clasped her chin, twisting her face to look at him. His breath was sour on her face. Her flesh prickled with disgust and her gorge rose.

'You have nothing to think about,' he told

her coldly. 'It's quite simple. If you want the child—Dickon—to remain with his father, you will keep silent about the one you are carrying and come with me—as my *wife*. Our marriage will be a marriage in name only. But for all intents and purposes, the child is mine.'

Arabella twisted against his hand. 'You're hurting me,' she gasped, struggling to free herself, but he was panting, his eyes fevered with excitement.

'You deserve to be hurt.' His grip tightened, twisting her flesh. 'You will not see Edward Grey again. I will not sit by while another man performs on my wife that which should be done by me. The humiliation is *mine*, Arabella. Mine. You care for him?'

Arabella nodded, suddenly tearful, realising at last the full depth of her feelings for Edward. 'I love him. I love him with all my heart.'

His look was scathing. 'Then that is your misfortune.'

'He will not take my leaving lightly.'

'I am not a man to be trifled with and I don't give a damn how much trouble he causes, he'll not get you back—or the child. You have changed. You have become too bold for your own good. A little humility would not go amiss.' His eyes narrowed. 'I see I shall have to teach you. As for your privacy—you will have as much privacy as I see fit. When the child is born I might be generous enough to share you with some of my friends—who commented profusely on your beauty when they saw you last night.'

A wave of nausea swamped Arabella. There was no worse thing a man could inflict on a woman than rape. Although she hoped that even John would not stoop so low, she would not put it past him. John was powerful, controlling and manipulative, and because there had been no way out she had accepted it, and now, with a cruel twist of fate, she was as much in his power as she had been before. How could she fight him?

Relinquishing his grip on her chin, he smiled. Arabella watched him and her eyes gleamed with such contempt, such hatred, that another man might have turned his head away in shame. But not John Fairburn. He was different to any other man she had known. He was cruel and vindictive, as his behaviour to her in the past had shown.

He turned from her and strode to the door. 'You have until tomorrow.'

Panic rose once more in Arabella. 'Tomorrow?'

'That's what I said. The sooner you are settled into my lodgings, the better.'

* * *

John was feeling satisfied as he left the house. What a pity he couldn't resume marital relations with Arabella—his grotesque impairment made it impossible, which grieved him unmercifully. He remembered how it had been when he had been wounded, lying in his own filth, seeing, knowing what had been done to him, which was why, having no wish to return to his home incomplete, he had sent the body of a man so badly wounded as to be unrecognisable back to Arabella.

But he didn't die.

He had known when Arabella arrived in Paris. It hadn't taken long for him to find out why—and that Edward Grey was her lover. Eaten up with jealousy and rage and unable to fight in France's civil war because of the damage done to him, he had decided it was time to show his wife he was very much alive. She was more beautiful than he remembered. Marrying her and possessing her had been an improvement on the jaded strumpets who had occupied his bed, too eager to perform for a coin or two and leaving him writhing with frustration.

Arabella had kindled that part of him where all the whores with their experience had failed.

* * *

When John had left Arabella stood staring at the closed door for a long time, thinking about him and what he would have her do. Something inside her turned to ice. She had lost everything she had ever wanted. Defeated, she bowed her head. A lump had lodged in her throat. She could hardly swallow past it. What of Edward? Everything in her cried out to him. She had been a fool to dream they could ever be together, she knew that now. She could not be with him. To protect Dickon she would have to stay with John.

The horror of it was almost too much and she stifled a sob with the back of her hand. She had to put her personal feelings to one side. The thought of deceiving Edward and keeping her pregnancy from him was anathema to her, but the thought of Dickon being kidnapped and taken to England to Malcolm Lister was unthinkable. She would have to obey John and go wherever he would have her go, just when she longed to remain in Paris, as near as possible to Edward. Her heart sank at the futility of it all. That she would never be a real wife to John was the only thing she could cling on to.

She had to find a way of making this right.

'What are you doing in here, Arabella?'

At the sound of Verity's voice she turned from the window. 'Just thinking.'

One look at Arabella's pale features made her concerned. 'Oh, my dear! You are so pale. What has happened? Are you unwell?'

With an effort, Arabella straightened and took a steady breath. 'No, I am quite well, Verity.'

'I saw John Fairburn leave. Is—is everything all right?'

'I cannot pretend that it is.' Taking a deep breath, she faced the woman who had made her so welcome in her home. 'John is my husband. My place is with him.'

Verity stared at her. 'But—this is so unexpected, Arabella. Is it what you want?'

She shook her head. *No*, she thought. Going back to John was not what she wanted. She wanted Edward, but if she couldn't have him, then there wasn't anything else she wanted. 'No,' she said with sudden gravity. 'But he leaves me with no choice.'

'Can he compel you to go back to him?'

'Yes, Verity, I'm afraid he can.'

'And—Edward? What will you tell him?'

'What can I say except the truth?'

'But—I think you are in love with Edward.'

Arabella's expression was one of torment. 'Verity, please don't. I—I cannot bear to think of Edward—not now.' How could she tell this caring, gentle woman that her heart was breaking? It would only upset her. She must do what she must to endure. 'I am not free. Edward must understand that a woman's place is with her husband.'

'But you do not love John.'

Arabella gave a little, weary shake of her head. 'No. I have never loved him.'

'Then I feel so sorry for you,' Verity said in a sympathetic tone. 'I did hope that you and Edward might have found happiness together.'

'It is not possible, Verity.'

'I cannot believe this is happening. Are you afraid of your husband, Arabella?'

'Yes,' she confessed, 'and the rights he has over me.'

'But—Dickon. He will miss you.'

'Dickon has his father and you and your children now. He will not notice my absence.'

'He will notice more than you seem to think,' Verity disagreed.

'It is kind of you to say.'

'Kindness has nothing to do with it. He has become very attached to you.'

Arabella felt a rush of emotions wash over

her. Verity's sincere words stabbed at her heart. 'But I must go. The longer I leave it, the harder it will be. But believe me, leaving Dickon gives me no joy.'

Chapter Nine

Helpless and defeated, with her mind in a strange, feverish state and her heart heavy with foreboding, Arabella waited for Edward to come, as she knew he would. Verity had told her he knew John had come back into her life, that he had seen them together at the wedding feast and that he had left.

When Edward arrived early in the afternoon, hearing his brisk step on the tiled floor of the hall outside, she waited until Verity showed him into the drawing room. A great weight had gathered in her chest that was almost too heavy to bear. Desperately she sought to cling to some sort of help for her plight, but she could not.

He regarded her coolly, like a stranger, distant and completely different from the man who had made love to her with such intimate tenderness. Fear stirred inside her, fear and consternation at the gulf that had opened between them. He stood looking at her across the space that divided them, and there was a sudden quickening in the depths of his eyes when they rested on her face, but there was no welcoming smile to soften his stern and masterful features. It was he, however, who broke the silence.

'Is it true? Are you to go back to him?'

'Verity has told you?'

'I want to hear it from you.'

With an agonising pain stabbing through her heart, Arabella nodded. She had never felt him so remote from her. 'Yes, Edward. It is true.'

He stared at her incredulously, as though she had suddenly changed into a different creature before his eyes. The hard planes of his face grew rigid and his blue eyes seemed to darken beneath the black brows. Her heart was wrung as she read the vast disappointment in them. There was a thin white line about his mouth.

'You said you wouldn't. Are you telling me that you love him after all?'

She stared at him, appalled that he should have asked that question. 'Love him? No—no, I do not.'

'Then what has happened to change your mind?' he asked, moving further into the room, but not far, just close enough to look at her, near enough to smell the delicate perfume of her skin. 'What has he said? Has he threatened you? Does he force you? And do not tell me you owe him your loyalty, because that I cannot believe. You led a miserable life as his wife. John Fairburn doesn't know the meaning of the word honour. The man is a ruthlessly controlling, conniving, unscrupulous bastard.'

He was sternly formal, seeming awesome and remote. Unable to meet his eyes, Arabella shook her head. Every word he said was true and she could offer no defence. She felt his sharp eyes watching her and she had to struggle to hide her distress and keep back the tears which threatened to betray her. She longed to explain that it was all a dreadful pretence, that she was still his and only his. But she must not let her tears flow as they threatened to do.

'He may be all those things, but I must go back to him—he is still my husband,' she said quietly. 'I bear his name. I cannot be with you, Edward. There is no future for us—only the past.'

'He didn't treat you well before. What makes you think it will be any different now?'

'I don't.'

'Why did he stage his death and then suddenly decide to reappear?' he demanded sharply. 'Why did he deceive you?'

Arabella lowered her eyes. As John had deceived her, so she was knowingly deceiving Edward by not telling him about his child she was carrying, and she hated herself for doing it. 'He—he has explained it to me— It is complicated.'

'Complicated? Arabella, he sent another man's body home to his wife, making you believe he had been killed in battle. What kind of man would do that?'

Arabella gave a little hopeless sigh and her amber eyes dimmed with tears. 'I know what you must think—'

'No, you don't,' he said, his voice low and fierce. 'I fear for you, Arabella, which is why I have made enquiries among those exiles who know John Fairburn. What I've learned gives me cause for grave concern for your safety. You do not have to go back to him. You have good reason not to. No one would blame you.'

She stared into the unfathomable depths in his eyes, his face set in hard and bitter lines. 'I have a duty…'

'Duty be damned! You owe him nothing. Does he know about me?'

'Yes.'

'And?'

'He—he is prepared to overlook it.'

'How magnanimous of him,' he uttered drily. 'Arabella, I am asking you to come with me.'

Her head snapped up and she stared at him in open-mouthed astonishment. 'And what can you offer me, Edward? Tell me that. Certainly nothing that can be called decent.'

'Perhaps not. At this present time all I can offer you is a fairly humble existence, and not very respectable at that, so long as you are not free of your matrimonial ties. Ever since I found you again I've thought of you as my soulmate— my other half—even though you are not my wife, which I had planned to ask you to be, for in all truth I thought you were a widow.'

Arabella regarded him sadly. 'I am sorry to disappoint you, Edward, but I have a husband and I am duty bound to go to him.'

Edward stepped back, his eyes a gleaming brilliance of hot blue. 'And you put duty before your happiness?'

'I have no choice.'

'You're right. While ever you remain John Fairburn's wife there is nothing I can do. But you know how I feel. I want to see that you come to no harm—if you will let me.'

'No, Edward,' she said firmly, raising her

head and straightening her spine in a determined effort to let him know her decision to return to John was no longer open to discussion. 'Please let it be. I beg of you. My mind is made up. I have made my decision. There is nothing I can do.'

Edward appeared to be frozen. Standing there with his hands behind his back, his feet apart, he was so tall and strong, but nothing could protect his heart from the pain. The colour had drained from his face and Arabella realised the enormity of the blow she had dealt him.

'Beg? Since when did you have to beg anything of me? I will not fight you, Arabella, but I cannot accept with good grace what you are about to do.'

He spoke quietly, fiercely, holding her with his gaze. She looked back at him, pale and trembling. 'I am sorry, Edward—I wish I could explain—'

'I'd rather you didn't,' he said, noting how the firelight from the leaping coals shone on her bright hair, streaking the copper with gold. How could he let a woman affect him as this one did? 'You must forgive me for thinking we were as one. Have you any idea how tormented I shall be seeing you living with a man no one I know can bring themselves to speak well of— not even your own brother?'

She met his angry stare and suddenly her heart lifted and a rush of colour stained her cheeks. 'Stephen? You have seen Stephen? He is here—in Paris?'

He nodded. 'He arrived yesterday. On recovering from his wound he managed to make it to the south coast and take ship for France.'

'But—that is good news. Oh—I would like to see him.'

'You will. He's at St Germain at present and is to ride with others to offer his sword in France's war. He doesn't intend being away from Paris very long at this present time and I have no doubt he will call on you when you take up residence in your husband's quarters.'

To hear the words *your husband* on Edward's lips wrenched Arabella's heart. 'Edward…' she began, stretching her hand out in a gesture of mute appeal, then letting it fall to her side when her gesture brought nothing from him but a cold glare. 'I realise that I have hurt you and that you must despise me for what I've done.'

'I could never despise you, Arabella—for God's sake, I love you,' he said, with so much passion that it wrenched her heart to hear it. 'But you have made your choice. I can do nothing but wish you well.'

His face was so closed that it made her think

of a solid, impenetrable wall. He was so encased in his anger and resentment that without another word he turned on his heel and went out.

The closing of the door was like a death knell to Arabella's already breaking heart. Only when she was sure he had left the house did she find the strength to make her way to her room, with the sound of children's voices raised in laughter and their pet dog barking, to begin preparations to leave. She was close to tears of absolute despair—about herself, about Edward, and about Dickon—that she should have come to this.

Unable to find the heart for it, she sat on the edge of the bed, staring listlessly at the walls, wondering how she was ever going to survive without Edward. Whatever he had felt for her— whether it be love or something akin to that emotion—must have turned to hatred by now. She did not expect him to forgive her.

On leaving the house Edward didn't return to his lodgings. Wanting to be alone, he directed his horse outside the city, finding something distracting about galloping across the countryside hell for leather. For those moments of complete freedom his mind was clear of all thought.

It was not until he rode past the woods where

he had made love to Arabella that he slowed the horse down and allowed his memories of that blissful day of stolen pleasure to enter his mind. A yearning so great washed over him. For what, he couldn't determine. Perhaps it was to recapture the happiness he had found with her before she had told him that John Fairburn had returned from the dead.

Ever since Edward had seen her with her husband at the wedding feast his world had begun to fragment. He could not bear to consider the possibility that she might go back to him. He wouldn't let himself believe it until she had told him with her own lips. As the hours of the night had slipped by into day, so rooted in his mind was the possibility that it became harder to banish the ugly, tormenting terror inside him.

Every time he thought of her in bed with John Fairburn, the bile rose in his throat. His nights were haunted by the image of her lovely slender body, and—and Fairburn's—moving together, as one, crying out, as she did with him, at the end.

After two weeks and nothing was heard of her, he made up his mind not to think of her. When Verity asked with concern if he had seen her he told her no and he did not expect to.

'But she must have an explanation for going back to her husband,' she said loyally.

'What sort of explanation could she possibly have?' Gregory said, unable to share his wife's concern. 'The man is her husband. As his wife she is duty bound to return to him.'

'It doesn't matter,' Edward said in harsh tones. 'Unless her husband dragged her back kicking and screaming, she is no concern of mine.'

He had left them then, his eyes showing neither interest nor concern. He reminded his sister that she had gone of his own volition and he gave the impression that he was past the point of caring. But he did care. Very much. He loved Arabella so much it hurt, and considering the treatment she had received at John Fairburn's hands in the past, how could she expect it to be any different now?

Arabella was trapped as surely as she had been trapped that day she had married John Fairburn. The following day she waited for him to come for her, hoping for a reprieve, but he was impatient and came early.

She settled as best she could into the rooms John rented. At least they were spacious and comfortable and well furnished. As the days passed a listlessness settled over her. Confined to the rooms most days, time seemed to stand still, each day seeming longer than the one before. Already she was feeling very lonely and she missed Dickon dreadfully. She was confused by all that had happened and the changes that had suddenly turned her life upside down. In a moment of confusion and despair she had committed herself to this course.

John was immensely smug with the developments. He left her alone for most of the time and he had no objections to her visiting some of the other ladies who had come to Paris to be with their husbands and to visiting the shops to purchase clothes, but he would not allow her to visit Verity.

Often when she returned home it was to discover John absent. Mostly she dined alone and retired early. He didn't return until the early hours, drunk and mercifully impatient for his own bed. He suffered immense pain from his injuries and it made him irritable and bad tempered. He bought remedies to ease it from a woman who lived by the river, but nothing took the pain away as well as drink.

On occasion he would insist she accompany him to a supper or to some other event held at one or another of his friends' places of residence—he liked to parade her among his friends. The people she met at these events were so very different from the kind of exiles she had become acquainted with on her arrival in Paris. John's associates, she observed derisively, existed in a world of languid self-indulgence and careless gaiety deserving of contempt.

John had always been a gambler, believing gambling to be an effortless way of making money. He also drank heavily as the nights he gambled wore on, the liquor increasing his readiness to take risks, but he was lucky and the money steadily piled up in front of him, allowing them luxuries other exiles could ill afford.

She heard nothing of Edward and the longer she went without word, the more her heart ached for him. Thankfully John was not at home when Stephen called on her. She was so overwhelmed to see her brother's familiar, beloved face at last that she cried tears of absolute joy and relief at having someone to talk to after the excruciating days of living with John.

'Oh, Stephen!' Vulnerable and aching to be close to him, she moved into his outstretched arms and placed her cheek against his chest, his hard, strong, reliable chest, while his arms enfolded her. 'I can't tell you how happy I am to see you. Are you fully recovered? When I left Bircot Hall you were very ill.'

'As you see, Arabella, I am quite well.' He grinned. 'I had an excellent nurse.'

She laughed lightly, which was something she had not done in a long time. 'I think you mean Margaret. I know how close the two of you became. I imagine she is missing you dreadfully.'

'As I am missing her,' he replied softly. 'I have promised to write to her when I am settled, and who knows...'

'Who indeed,' Arabella murmured, happy for her brother. She was extremely fond of Margaret. She would like to have her for a sister-in-law. 'And Alice and the children? How are they? I miss them so much.'

'Alice works hard, but they are all well.' He glanced around the room, as if expecting Arabella's husband to appear out of the shadows at any moment. 'Where is he?'

Her face fell. 'John? He is out just now. I don't know where he goes, only that he's gambling heavily—and drinking.'

'Gambling?'

She nodded. 'It's nothing new—which you must remember, having known him a good deal

longer than me. He has an obsession for it. In the
past he used to win a little, but more often than
not lose heavily. Now his luck seems to have
changed. He believes gambling to be an effortless way of making money. At least it means we
are able to live well.'

'It must have come as a shock to you when
you realised he was still alive. I lost track of
him after the two of you wed. Edward has told
me how he feigned his death—although why
he should is a mystery to me. Is he treating
you well?'

She nodded. 'Yes—I am alone for most of the
time, but I am not complaining. Have—have
you seen Edward?'

'Of course I have,' he replied, his expression
grave. 'He's furious that you chose to return to
John. He won't admit it, but I know he misses
you. What on earth possessed you to go back to
him, after the way he deceived you?'

He turned from her in frustration. On seeing
her cloak flung over a chair he picked it up and
draped it over her shoulders. 'Come, let us get
out of here and go somewhere we can talk—
where there's no danger of your husband coming home and overhearing. The last thing I want
at this moment is to confront him until I know
what's going on.'

* * *

Neither of them spoke until they reached the small park where Arabella sometimes walked when she felt the need to be away from the rooms she lived in. Even though John left her alone his presence was like some evil spectre always looking over her shoulder. It had rained heavily the day before, but today the skies were clear and the park smelt fresh and fragrant. There were few people about. Taking her arm and hooking it through his own, Stephen strolled at a leisurely pace, deeply concerned for his sister and meaning to get to the bottom of it.

'Now tell me, Arabella. All of it. Has John some kind of hold over you? Is that it? Are you afraid of him?'

Arabella stopped suddenly and faced him. The strain and the tension she had been under since returning to live with John was sapping her strength and she began to tremble. Seeing her distress, Stephen gathered her to him, stroking her head gently.

'Tell me. Surely it cannot be that bad.'

'But it is,' she whispered, and she began to spill out her tale, relieved to unburden her heart, but omitting to tell him about the child she was carrying and John's terrible affliction.

But she was afraid of the consequences when John found out that she had betrayed him.

'So you see, if I were to disobey him, John has sworn to me that he will kidnap Dickon and have him sent to England—to Malcolm Lister.'

Stephen held her at arm's length and looked at her stricken face in horror. 'Edward's brother-in-law?'

She nodded. 'The same.'

'But I seem to recall Edward telling me he wants to seize Dickon to make him his heir.'

'Yes. When he captured Edward in Bristol, he hoped he would be executed for his support of the King. That would have left the way clear for him to take Dickon and raise him as he would had he been his own son.'

'So that is why you went back to John.'

'Yes,' she whispered wretchedly. 'To keep Dickon safe. John will not forgive me for telling you. I have learned to my cost not to cross him. He is evil and manipulative and I know he will carry out his threat if I leave him. What will you do, Stephen? Will you tell Edward?'

'How can I not? Edward has a right to know, to do everything within his power to ensure Dickon's safety.'

Before Stephen left Arabella, he promised to meet her in the park the following day. He had tried to persuade her to leave John and return to Verity, but she had adamantly refused, which led him to believe there might be more behind the hold John had over her than she was admitting.

Deeply concerned by what Arabella had told him, he lost no time in seeking Edward out at St Germain. As he had expected, on learning the truth, a fury the like of which he had never felt before erupted inside his friend. In a few seconds Edward's face expressed first stupefaction, then fury, then a look of implacable hatred which transformed his features.

Fairburn! Edward had seen Fairburn just once. For his part he did not merely dislike him, he regarded him with active hatred and a corroding resentment.

'So, he will take my son! He will make him part of his evil scheme to keep his wife! Arabella will leave him. She cannot stay with him now. The devil help Fairburn when I get my hands on him. I shall see he is made to pay in every possible sense of the word. Beginning with the gambling he is so fond of. He can't go on winning for ever. I intend to destroy him.'

Wrapped in her warm woollen cloak against the day's chill, the wide hood drawn over her head so that only her face was exposed, Arabella walked the short distance to the park to meet Stephen. The afternoon was pale and cool, the sun visible but remote. Overhead, birds wheeled before they dipped and vanished among the treetops. A cloaked figure stood some distance ahead, his plumed hat shading his face. With the cool air caressing her cheeks she moved towards him.

Not until she drew closer did the man remove his hat—and she recognised Edward. In her delight at seeing him again, she forgot everything else and was drawn to him irresistibly. When he saw her he strode towards her. Their eyes locked for a moment and time stood still. She saw a faint tremor pass over his hard, handsome face and she smiled at him with all the concentrated warmth and radiance of the love she bore him. His glance met hers. For only a moment his eyes were not contemptuous or cold. The blue depths held a warmth of feeling such as Arabella had despaired of finding. But suddenly the precious moment was gone and his face became hard, suspicious, his eyes cold and accusing.

They stood facing each other. There was something intangible between them which had developed when John had appeared and caused so much antagonism. She had wanted to see

Edward so much, longed to be alone with him, that now the moment had arrived she was suddenly shy of him and didn't know what to say. She stood gazing up at him with eyes shining with an unearthly brilliance. She slipped the hood from her head, her magnificent mane of hair tumbling about her shoulders.

Edward reached out and tilted her face a little further up to his, scrutinising her features as if she had changed somehow during their parting.

'How are you?' he asked suddenly, the question abrupt, although he was concerned to see that the lustre had gone from her eyes. Her face was like a delicate piece of carved ivory, so pale, but he thought it only served to emphasise the purity of its lines.

She gave him a faltering little smile. 'I am well.'

'You are very lovely, Arabella, and you have the most beautiful eyes I have ever seen. You are also exceedingly desirable—worthy of someone who is not a cheat and a liar—which your husband has proved to be,' he added bitterly. As he said this his face hardened and a fierceness entered his eyes.

Arabella's power of speech returned and with it her courage. 'Perhaps you are right. Who am I to say? Stephen has told you my reason for returning to John? Is that why you have come instead of my brother?'

'How could I not? Did you expect me to ignore it when someone threatens to harm my son?'

'No, of course not.'

'How could you keep it from me? Why did you not tell me this when last we met—when you had decided to go back to him?'

Confronted with his wrath, Arabella lowered her eyes with regret and remorse that she had allowed John to manipulate her so easily. 'Listen to me, Edward, and do not condemn me without hearing me first. You have no idea how I felt on that dreadful day when John came back from the dead. I went back to him because I was afraid—afraid that he would carry out his threat. I, too, love Dickon as if he were my very own. I could not bear to think of anything harmful happening to him.'

'I made a grave mistake in letting you go back to that man. I should have stopped you.'

'There was nothing you could have done. I am John's wife. He had right on his side. Please don't confront him with this, Edward. You don't know him—what he's like. He will kill you.'

Edward observed her with a faint, crooked

smile. 'What a poor creature you must think me if you think I will let this pass, or that I am so weak that I will let him overpower me. Your husband is in much greater danger from me, for I will do everything in my power to kill him. How dare he threaten my son! And you, Arabella. You intended to keep this from me!'

Arabella stood there, stunned and uncomprehending, as his bitterness engulfed her. She stared at him in disbelief, numbed at the unexpected reaction, at the unfairness of his failure to understand all that she had been through. Despite her intentions of keeping her temper, she found herself provoked almost beyond endurance.

'Please have the good sense to consider what I have done and why I did it. Can you not see that it has all been for you and Dickon, that I have risked everything for you? That everything I have done I have agonised over? Do you think it was easy for me? Do you understand nothing at all?'

'I understand very well. Bearing in mind that you have returned to your husband, how do you expect me to feel? Ever since you went back to him I have died a thousand deaths imagining you with him—of him touching you. I thought

I was stronger than that and I hate myself for my weakness.'

She averted her eyes and a small sigh escaped her lips. 'I'm sorry, Edward. At the time I did what I thought was right—the only thing I could do. Everything Stephen has told you is true. John threatened to kidnap Dickon and take him to Malcolm Lister if I did not go back to him. He—he has many friends who would be willing to help him. It wouldn't have been difficult for him to carry out his threat. Once Dickon arrived in England—with the threat of arrest and execution hanging over you—he knew there was nothing you could do. If you don't believe me, then there is nothing more I can say to convince you.'

'Then tell me this. Why did you decide to disclose this now? Forgive me, Arabella, but that is what I can't understand. Has he had a change of heart?'

'No. I have. I was not expecting Stephen to call. He found me at a weak moment. I did wrong not telling you why I went back to John. I do know that. But—I—I didn't know what else to do. My concern was not just for Dickon—but for you also.'

She moved closer and he was enveloped in the sweet fragrance of her perfume. Despite his anger towards her there was still an affinity between them which Arabella felt with every fibre of her being. Whatever Edward would say to what she was about to disclose, she had to let him know how she felt. Very softly and with a slight hesitation, she said, 'You see—I love you, Edward—and I knew that if anything should happen to your son, it would break your heart.'

As soon as she had uttered the words she felt surprisingly at ease and carefree. Edward merely stared at her. He didn't protest or contradict her, he merely stepped back.

At length, he said, 'Do you forget that you have a husband—a husband who is so ruthless he would harm a child to make you stay with him? He has created a chasm between us which cannot be overcome and which I would not cross without feeling repugnance and shame if I let my need and desire for you triumph over my will.'

'I do not lie. I do love you, Edward—very much. I think I have loved you since I was a mere girl and I thought you would be my—'

'Stop it, Arabella,' he uttered fiercely. 'Don't do this.'

'I have to. I have to let you know how I feel. When I gave myself to you I did so gladly—

without shame or remorse. I wanted you from the bottom of my heart.'

'And I will assume you have said the same words to the man you are living with—the man whose bed you share. How many times have you given yourself to him since you went back to him? How many times, Arabella?'

She glared at him, her temper rising. To have her declaration of love thrown back at her in so flippant a manner was intolerable. 'How dare you say that to me? You know nothing about what happens between—between—me and...' Unable to go on, with tears of misery almost blinding her, she bit her lip to keep it from trembling and turned from him.

Hearing the catch in her voice and seeing her obvious distress, Edward was irresistibly drawn to her. Her delicate scent proved potent and had him remembering how it had felt to hold her in his arms.

Standing close behind her, on a softer note he said, 'Tell me, Arabella. Does he hurt you? Is that what you are trying to say?'

Without turning, she swallowed audibly and nodded. 'Yes,' she whispered. 'But be assured that he—has not touched me since I went back to him.'

Not having expected her to say that, he

looked at her carefully for a moment before saying, 'What proof do I have that you are speaking the truth?'

'Because he—he can't.'

Edward studied the back of her head closely. 'Can't? What are you saying?'

'He—he was wounded at St Fagans—very badly as a matter of fact. He—he is in constant pain. As a result of his injury he—he is impotent,' she told him quietly.

Edward stared at the back of her head. Whatever she had been about to say he had not expected that. His self-control cracked and at almost the same moment Arabella turned round to face him, her lovely eyes moist with tears. Suddenly they were alone in the world. Edward drew her to him and wrapped his arms round her, burying his face in her wealth of sweet scented hair.

'Thank God,' he murmured hoarsely, his voice holding so much anguish that Arabella's tears overflowed. 'I have been tortured by images of you with him...'

Taking her face between his strong hands and wiping away her tears with his thumbs, he looked into her eyes with such intensity that she trembled beneath it. The hunger and the need that had been consuming him, unappeased for the time they had been apart, came to the fore. His mouth descended on hers, greedily devouring the soft, moist, inviting lips greedily. His arms were so tight around her that Arabella, almost swooning with joy, could feel his heart beating wildly against her. His kiss was fierce and hungry.

As the passion within them was rekindled and deepened, Edward tore his mouth from hers and, with his lips close to her cheek, he whispered, in a hoarse, almost inaudible voice, passionate endearments, only stopping to cover her eyes, her cheeks and her lips with kisses.

When the wave of passion lessened, remembering where they were, Arabella pulled back in his arms and gazed up at him, her eyes wide and soft, her lips swollen and rosy pink from his kiss.

'Night and day I have relived that day we spent together,' he murmured, his eyes warm with love.

'I have thought of it, too,' she murmured. Thinking back to that wonderful day when they had laid down on the forest floor, the smell and the sound of the rustling leaves mingled with the taste of Edward and the sound and feel of her own pleasure, looking up at the treetops afterwards, thinking she had never been so happy.

She looked at Edward now, met his eyes and knew he was reliving it, too.

When he would have kissed her again, she placed two fingers on his lips and shook her head slowly.

'Please, Edward, stop now. There is something else I have to tell you and if you continue to kiss me I will be so weakened I will not be able to.'

'What is it?'

'Something that will make the hatred you already feel for John deepen.' A different quality had crept into her voice. Her face suddenly looked drawn, a mask of profound sadness settling on her features.

Edward eyed her with concern. 'I doubt that is possible.'

'I think it is.' Taking his hand, she drew him down on to a wooden bench. She sat facing him, still holding his hand, apprehensive. He was silent, watching her, waiting for her to continue, his eyes holding hers with an enquiring glance. 'I—I am with child, Edward—your child.' Lowering her eyes, she heard his quick intake of breath. Looking at him through half-closed lashes, she saw shock register on his face.

'A child? Dear Lord, Arabella! Did you know this when you went back to him?'

'Yes.'

'Then—if this is the truth, why did you not tell me before?'

'Everything was against it. John knew—he could tell. He—he used it against me and to his own advantage. Since he is no longer able to father a child of his own, he...'

'Wanted mine,' Edward finished for her coldly, unable to believe the evil of the man Arabella was married to. 'It would appear that both my children are desired as other men's heirs. And you have suffered all this alone.'

Arabella heard the concern in his voice. 'John was determined. You already know what he would do if I refused to be a part of the charade. Ours has always been an unhappy, tortured marriage,' she whispered, and once again there were tears in her eyes. 'What will you do?'

A preoccupied expression drew over his face, showing that his mind was working swiftly.

It was very quiet in the park and the silence bit more keenly into Arabella's nerves more than ever. 'I have been honest with you, Edward. I have told you everything. It is now your decision entirely what you do. I have wronged you, I know, and for that I beg your forgiveness.'

Edward was horrified—horrified at what John Fairburn must have put her through to make her agree to his terms—which made him wonder at his own reaction. Where there should have been rage that she had been prepared to sacrifice one of his children to save the other, there was tenderness and sorrow, and he felt a surge of deep compassion as he saw how distraught she was. His love for her was deep and eternal, and all at once the jealousy and rancour he had experienced when she had returned to her husband seemed to dissolve.

Thinking back to the day she told him she was returning to her husband, he had spoken the truth when he had told her that he feared for her. Behind Arabella's determination to make him believe that what she was doing was right, he had seen fear in her eyes and the strain on her ashen face, and at one point he was sure he had seen tears glittering behind her lashes. But he had been so eaten up with his own sense of loss that he'd cast it from his mind.

Now he saw the pain, the hollow, biting misery on her face. Drawing her to him once more, he put his arms around her to comfort her, to staunch her tears.

'I am so sorry,' she mumbled against his chest. She looked up at him. Her lovely face was ravaged. 'I'm so sorry. Truly. I didn't know what to do. Please don't be angry with me. When I saw Stephen I knew I couldn't go through with it—keeping it from you. It wasn't right.'

'No, Arabella, it wasn't. Does Stephen know this?'

'No. I wanted to tell you myself.'

'You will not go back to Fairburn,' he said quietly.

'But—his threat…'

'Means nothing. I intend to deal with him. The man has attacked me in the heart of my family. I cannot let it pass.'

When John returned home to find his wife had left him, he was beside himself with rage. If she thought she could leave him, she was mistaken. He had known he was playing a dangerous game when he had forced her to go back to him. It had required deviousness, arrogance and absolute determination to carry it out—whatever the consequences—and John possessed all those things, and more, to see it through. He had been smug over his triumph, believing her affair with Edward Grey was well and truly over.

And now this.

He seethed with anger. Arabella had behaved badly and deserved to be punished. She thought she could have it all, did she—her lover and her child? If she thought he would simply allow her to walk away, then she was mistaken. He spent a while savouring his anger and pondering the revenge he would take, the kind of revenge that helped him get through the days, thinking hard about Arabella and Edward Grey losing everything. It made his own pain feel much better.

With John's threat to Dickon uppermost in Edward's mind, he asked Arabella and Verity when he himself was absent not to let him out of their sight. They were careful at all times, entertaining the children indoors and not allowing them outside unless they were attended by one of them. It was unfortunate that when the sun came out the children managed to slip their guard and went out into the garden.

Failing to locate the children in the house, looking out of the window and seeing they had disobeyed them, Arabella lost no time in hurrying outside. On reaching the garden she paused to take in the scene. Verity's children had their backs to her and were staring at a stationary carriage in the road. She saw someone push the door open. A man standing at the side of the carriage reached down and lifted a small boy up and shoved him inside before getting in himself and closing the door.

Arabella watched, her mind refusing to engage immediately with what was happening, unable to believe what she was seeing. 'Dickon,' she whispered, and louder, 'Dickon.'

Then she was shouting his name and, raising her skirts, went hurrying across the garden and out through the gate. She saw the carriage ahead of her. Again she frantically called Dickon's name, running forward to try to stop the carriage, but it was useless, for it immediately sped off along the road and disappeared.

She stopped, her face white and her whole body trembling. She had the awful sense that she was experiencing a nightmare. Gradually the fact became the horrible truth—Dickon had been abducted by her husband. She must get word to Edward.

She hurried back to the house to find Verity at that moment receiving Edward and Stephen, and the children, terrified by what they had witnessed, were trying to tell them with breathless excitement that Dickon had been kidnapped. They all looked at her when she came rushing into the house. Seeing how distraught she was, Edward immediately strode towards her.

'Arabella! Is it true? Has Dickon been abducted?'

White and shaken and breathing hard, she reached out and gripped his arm. With raw terror in her voice, she said, 'Edward, he's gone. It's John. It has to be. You must stop them. Go after them—before it's too late.'

Every muscle in Edward's body went rigid and his face became hard in that particular way Arabella knew so well. His eyes were filled with a mixture of rage and apprehension and dread—dread that John's abduction of Dickon had been well planned and that that by the time he caught up with them Dickon would be on a boat bound for England and Malcolm Lister.

'So—at last he shows his hand,' he uttered, his temper igniting fiercely. John Fairburn's clear intention to abduct his son for reasons of nothing but personal revenge infuriated him. 'How dare he make Dickon the instrument of his vengeance? I'll go after them. Time is of the essence,' he said, striding towards the door.

'I'll go with you,' said Stephen, hurrying after him.

'And me,' Gregory said. 'I have to saddle my horse so you go ahead.'

Arabella stood in the road and watched them ride off. Verity came to stand beside her.

'They will find him, Arabella. If it is indeed your husband who has taken him, he can't be

too far ahead. If they are taking the road to Calais they will stop him.'

Fear instilled itself into Arabella's heart, fear
and desperation. 'What if they have taken a different road and they aren't going to Calais at all?
Knowing Edward would be sure to follow them,
they might be taking him somewhere else. Oh,
Verity,' she cried, ready to weep with the uncertainty of it all, 'they have to find him. It's
my fault he's gone. I will never forgive myself
if anything happens to him.'

'That is not so,' Verity said. 'How can you
conclude that? John Fairburn is the guilty one—
not you. He is the one who ought to suffer—and
he will, you can be sure of that, when Edward
finds him.'

Not until Edward had disappeared from sight
did Arabella go back into the house, knowing
she would know no peace until they brought
Dickon home.

Chapter Ten

That had been almost two days ago. Accompanied by Stephen and Gregory, Edward had begun the hunt at once. Having made a wide sweep of the roads leading out of Paris and finding nothing, Edward's grief and fury over his failure to locate his son had not abated when he returned to the house.

His thunderous frown drew his thick black eyebrows into a single line as he battled with his dilemma. Now it was dark and the trail was cold.

Arabella went to him. 'Have you found anything?'

Edward reached out and took her in his arms. 'Nothing. Who knows what that devil has done with him, or into whose hands he has placed him.'

'I pray he does not reach England—and Malcolm Lister. If you value your life, you will be unable to go after him.'

'It will do him no good if that is what he intends.'

She tilted her head and looked at him. 'Why do you say that?'

'Because, my love, what John Fairburn does not know—what I only found out myself yesterday when I received a letter from a close friend in England—is that Malcolm Lister is dead.'

Arabella stared at him in disbelief. 'Dead? But—how…?'

'It happened when he was trying to find me after I escaped—a fall from his horse, apparently. He lived only long enough to be taken to his home. So you see, my love, there is no need for you to worry.'

'But John doesn't know that—and when he does find out he will do something else to hurt you. He is evil and I think he would do anything to take revenge for my leaving him.'

Stephen returned from making his own enquiries with one vital piece of information. His expression was positive and he spoke sharply.

'Fairburn is still in Paris.'

Edward straightened his shoulders and came to savage, frightening life. 'How do you know?'

'He's a gambler. He was seen by an acquaintance of mine—also a gambler—playing at the Three Moons Tavern.'

Edward stared at him in confusion. 'What is the blackguard playing at? And where is this tavern, pray?'

'Towards the river.'

The expression on Edward's face was so menacing Arabella stepped out of his way as he went striding to the door, watching in appalled silence as his hand went to his sword hilt.

'Edward,' Arabella cried, quickly going to him with a beseeching expression on her face. 'Please—I beg you to have a care. John is dangerous. I couldn't bear it if anything happened to you.'

He paused and looked down at her. Through all the pain of losing his son, he was beginning to understand fully the wonderful thing that had happened to him on finding Arabella. He touched her face with his lips, as though trying to convince himself that she was real. To lose her again would be an appalling devastation too dreadful to contemplate. Arabella stirred his heart, his body and his blood to passion, to a love he could not have envisaged. He could not face a world without her in it, without her humour and fearless courage and angry defiance, that passion he had experienced in her arms, her lips smiling at him, her amber eyes challenging him, the compassion, love and understanding she had for his son.

'Never fear, my love. I'll take care. The thought that something dreadful has happened to my son is torturing me. If it's the last thing I do I shall punish the man responsible.' He turned to Stephen. Edward was a man with a mission, knowing he needed to keep in complete control for what lay ahead. 'If he thinks he can escape me, I'll run him through. In fact, I may do that anyway—although to die by the sword is too good for him.'

In an agony of torment, Arabella watched him go for the second time. He was filled with rage, but no matter how distraught he was over Dickon's abduction, she knew he was in command of his actions.

When Gregory arrived at the house shortly after Edward's departure, she donned her cloak in a state of agitation.

'Edward and Stephen have gone to the Three Moons Tavern,' she told Gregory when he asked.

'I know where it is.'

'Good, then you can take me with you.'

He stared at her as if she had taken leave of her senses. 'No, Arabella, I will not. You have no idea what awaits you in the Paris streets after dark. It is too dangerous and Edward will be furious.'

She lifted her head, her chin set at a mutinous angle. 'I do insist, Gregory. If you don't take me, then I shall make my own way there. I am sure someone will tell me where it is.'

The hour was late. At this time of night gaming houses flourished all over Paris and the Three Moons Tavern, an odious establishment, was no exception. Ignoring the vagabonds and beggars and cripples that lurked in the recesses and dark alleyways close to the Seine, rolling its way along with its endless traffic of boats and barges, Edward stood in the darkness, peering through the window's thick glass, indifferent to the rain water dripping down on him from the roof. He could see it was a busy night. The men who made up the patronage of the tavern—gentlemen, clerics, ordinary citizens and monks, French and English—came here for the drink and above all for the dice and cards. When in drink some became rowdy and were thrown out into the street.

His eyes casually yet thoroughly swept the

dimly lit, low-ceilinged room for John Fairburn.
At the sight of him he felt ice-cold anger settle
in his chest, then spread to every part of his
body. He sat at a table with three other men
across the dimly lit room. They were engrossed
in a game of cards. Others leaned against the
wall, watching the play. Women in provocative
dress flitted among the tables. They were hired
to serve and entertain the patrons and encour-
age them to spend money on food and drink,
but most of all to gamble, for it was true that
the more the patrons spent on liquor, the more
recklessly they gambled.

Waiting for Stephen, who was taking care of
the horses, Edward continued to gaze attentively
at his prey for several minutes.

'Any sign of him?'

Edward turned round to see Stephen, then
gestured with his head. Stephen peered inside.
'That's him. Shall we go in?'

Pushing the door open, they stood on the
threshold. The fog of smoke from the badly
drawing fire caught in their throats. It was the
kind of establishment Edward would never have
entered had it not been forced on him by cir-
cumstance.

The room was crowded with patrons sitting
at tables. Some conversed in low tones as they

gambled away their money, while others sat drinking in silence. Entering the room and closing the door behind them, they mingled easily with those standing, pausing and pretending to watch the games in progress so as not to draw attention to themselves, whilst scrutinising John Fairburn and the game of cards he was playing.

Eventually they came to where John Fairburn sat. He had his back to them so he did not see them approach, and everyone else was so taken up with the play that they paid them no attention. The more John Fairburn drank the more risks he took and, unlike others who lost heavily when their heads were fogged with liquor, the more he won.

Edward shook his head to a woman with a proffered ale, all his attention on John Fairburn. He seemed well satisfied with his successful night with the cards. If his winnings were anything to go by the stakes had run high and heavy and the odds had been in his favour. His partners stood up to leave. One of them turned away, but the other, a surly-looking individual with his face set in grim lines, paused to look down at John Fairburn. He had lost a great deal of coin tonight, most of it going into Fairburn's pocket. Suspecting Fairburn of cheating, but reluctant to confront him in case he made a fool of himself, with a murderous glint in his eyes he turned away and followed his companion.

John Fairburn was about to rise from the table when he became aware of someone standing behind him. He half-turned, probably expecting it to be someone wanting a game, but instead he met the level gaze of Stephen Charman. His gaze went past him to his companion. Not a muscle moved in his thin face, but his eyes narrowed and became brittle.

'Stephen! I am surprised to see you here. I do not recall you being a gambling man. And Sir Edward Grey. To what do I owe the pleasure? Are you here to play? If you are, I would be happy to accommodate you.' He picked his winnings from his last game off the table and shoved the notes inside his jacket.

'I think you know why we are here,' Edward said coldly, fighting to keep his anger under control.

John's eyes narrowed and began to glitter dangerously. His smile was unpleasant. 'So, you have run me to earth, Sir Edward. I applaud your work.'

Edward looked at him, his face grim, his eyes glittering like steel flints in the dim light. 'It wasn't difficult. Your habits are well known,' he

said with bitter sarcasm. 'Because of the crime
you have committed against me, Fairburn, and
because Arabella has suffered and learned a
harsh lesson of what to expect from a black-
hearted villain like yourself—I have every reason in the world to kill you. But since my son is
still missing, I will let you live until you have
told me what you have done with him.'

Edward's words were savage and taunting,
causing John Fairburn's eyes to glitter with unconcealed hatred. 'Damn you, Grey,' he rasped.
'You take my wife and impregnate her with
your seed and expect me to ignore it.'

'You were dead, Fairburn. Or has it slipped
your mind how you deceived her into believing
that? She has left you—and who would blame
her after the misery you have inflicted on her?
And how dare you strike at me through my son?
To retaliate by inflicting fear on an innocent
who has done you no harm is a coward's way.'
Placing his hands palm down on the table, he
thrust his face forwards. 'Now I will ask you
one more time, Fairburn. What have you done
with my son?'

'I may be many things, Grey, but I am no
coward,' John seethed, his voice trembling with
anger.

'Then prove it. Either you tell me where he

is or I shall call you out. What is it to be?' Edward asked, with ominous coolness.

His deep loathing of John Fairburn was profound and after what he had done he would gladly kill him, but not until he had told him what he had done with Dickon. Knowing of his passion for gambling and his lack of expertise with a sword due to his battle injuries, he knew he would not be a worthy opponent. So perhaps he should opt for a different method to bring him down. He himself was more than a match for any man when it came to a game of cards—whether he was as proficient as Fairburn was to be determined, but he was willing to take the risk. Besides, Fairburn had been consuming liquor through the evening, which might very well have weakened his judgement.

'Perhaps you would prefer that we settle our differences with a game of cards,' Edward suggested calmly. 'If I win, you will give me back my son.'

John Fairburn smiled thinly, his eyes gleaming. 'And if I should win, my wife will return to me.'

'So you can take my unborn child and raise it as your own? I think not, Fairburn.'

'Then what do I stand to win?'

'Your life.'

Fired up by the prospect of subjecting Edward Grey to the same humiliation he had suffered at his hands when he had taken his wife, John Fairburn agreed to his suggestion, unaware that not one but two men were out for his blood tonight.

'You will play?'

'Yes,' Fairburn hissed through his teeth. 'I will play and make you regret ever stealing my wife. And if I win, I swear you will never see your son again.'

Refusing to contemplate defeat, Edward took his place at the table. All the patrons were aware that something unusual was about to take place and had ceased playing their own games to bear witness to the one about to begin. It was clear that it was no ordinary game of cards, for the atmosphere between the two players could be cut with a knife.

With her heart thumping in her breast and drawing a long, steadying breath, Arabella drew her cloak about her and pulled the hood over her head before nervously entering the tavern behind Gregory. Her eyes swept the room before coming to light on a game in progress that seemed to be attracting everyone's attention.

Conversation was muted so as not to distract the players.

Stephen turned when he felt someone press against him, his face registering shocked surprise when he recognised his sister accompanied by Gregory. He immediately took her arm and drew her away, but not before she had seen her husband sitting at the table across from Edward, his body taut, and a wild, concentrated gleam in his eyes which only gamblers had when, intent on winning, they saw nothing except the cards in front of them.

'What are you doing here, Arabella?' Stephen whispered harshly, throwing an accusing glance at Gregory. 'Why did you not stay with Verity? Edward will be outraged if he sees you. It is hardly the kind of establishment ladies attend.'

'I do not care, Stephen—and please don't blame Gregory. I made him bring me. I had to come. I know what Edward is doing. He must be made to stop. There has to be another way of getting Dickon back. Perhaps if I were to speak to John—'

'No, Arabella,' Stephen said, putting a restraining hand gently on her arm. 'Leave him. Edward is determined. Play has begun and it may surprise you to know that he is winning. He will not thank you for interfering.'

Relief flooded Arabella. Having no wish to distract Edward and taking Stephen's advice, she remained well back from the play. She watched Edward's long, flexible fingers shuffle and deal again and again, flicking over card after card, producing from his hand all the right cards. The flickering flames from the candles played on his chiselled features as he watched his opponent closely, quietly confident.

It became clear that his mastery of the game was equal to or surpassed even John's. A pulse beat at the side of John's temple, his play becoming erratic and desperate as Edward won time and again.

When play was over and people began to lose interest and move away, Edward rose from his chair and looked down at his defeated opponent with cynical disdain, holding him in absolute contempt.

'My son, Fairburn. Where is he? And do not think of double-crossing me by giving me false information. Is he here—in Paris?' John nodded. 'You will take me to him yourself. After that you deserve to live in wretchedness till your life's end for what you have done,' he said as he glared at him.

Despite the heat of the room and the liquor he had consumed, John's face was waxen—white

against the black of his clothes as he tried to ab-
sorb what had just happened to him. Stunned
and dazed by losing to a superior force, fear
wiped away his arrogance. He glanced around
as if seeking help, but there was no one. His
nostrils were pinched and he seemed to have
difficulty in breathing as he shoved his chair
back and rose, resting his hands on the table
for support. He looked what he was—a beaten
man. It was as if all the life had been drained
out of him.

'I will take you.'

When Edward turned to leave, he became
aware of Arabella standing with Gregory for
the first time. His jaw was as rigid as granite.
He looked at her for several seconds, his face
preoccupied and stony.

'Arabella? What are you doing here?' He
shifted his gaze to Gregory. 'You should never
have brought her.'

'Had I not brought her she would have found
her own way here.'

'I had to come,' she explained quietly, looking at his proud, lean face. 'When you find
Dickon you may need me. I want to help.'

Edward looked down at her, knowing exactly
what she was saying, for her thoughts were akin
to his own. The thought that somewhere his son

might be at the mercy of some evil people was almost more than he could bear. She was right. When he found Dickon he was going to need her. Her face was rosy and lovely and her eyes glowed into his. 'You have helped me already, Arabella, more than you will ever know.'

'So, Arabella,' John said coldly. 'At last you have what you have always wanted.'

'I sincerely hope so, John. For your sake I hope Dickon is unharmed. What you have done is pure wickedness.'

He shrugged. 'It matters not to me,' he replied, turning from her and heading for the door.

Arabella watched him go. 'He really does not care,' she said to Edward. 'I could never fathom what makes him as cruel as he is.'

Edward and Stephen, accompanied by Arabella and Gregory, followed close in John's footsteps. He led them towards the river. Torches had been lit and the light flickered over the buildings with their overhanging eaves and gilded and painted signs. They entered a labyrinth of streets and alleyways that twisted and turned, punctuated here and there with stone stairways. The stench was sickening. Here the darkness was intense and Arabella tripped over unseen objects, but Edward's hand was always there to steady her.

Gradually their eyes became accustomed to the dark. There was an eerie stillness about the alleyways, with sinister figures and shapes melting into the shadows. They came out into a small square surrounded by tottering, shapeless buildings which looked as if they would collapse at any moment.

John strode towards a door and knocked sharply. It was opened and he stepped inside. Edward was just behind him followed by Arabella. Stephen and Gregory waited outside. A tall, thin, lantern-jawed drab of a woman of middle age eyed them suspiciously.

Arabella glanced about her. A fire burned in the hearth, reeking its smoke into the room, which got into their eyes and throat. Herbs hung from the ceiling and phials and bottles of medicaments were lined up on shelves. Arabella realised that this was the woman John came to, to relieve his pain. The woman drew her shawl tightly about her thin frame and shrank from them, muttering something in French Arabella did not understand. But she saw fear and apprehension in her eyes.

John spoke in low tones to her. Without a word she gestured with her head to a corner where a child with curly black hair and a dirty face streaked with tears was sleeping on a pile of rags.

John turned and looked at Edward. 'Take him. You will find he has come to no harm.'

Arabella immediately crossed the room and gathered Dickon to her. He stirred, opening his eyes. On seeing Arabella he whimpered, his arms going around her neck, and he clung to her.

She kissed his cheek and murmured soft, soothing words of comfort. 'Everything will be all right now, my darling. We've come to take you home.'

'And you won't let me be taken away again,' he mumbled. 'I don't like it here. I was frightened and it made me cry.'

'I know and I'm sorry I wasn't there, but no one is going to take you away ever again. I promise.'

'I want to go home now,' he murmured tiredly.

Arabella looked beseechingly at Edward's stoic features. His face was ashen and she thought he was trembling. He was a strong man, but what he had been through these past days had burdened him. She looked past him to see John going slowly towards the door, his head hung low.

'John, wait.' He hesitated and after a moment

turned and looked at her. 'What did you intend doing with him? You told me you would take him to England—to Malcolm Lister.'

'That is what I intended—but I knew your lover would be close on my heels so I decided to wait a few days before heading for the Channel.'

'Then you would have been wasting your time. Malcolm Lister is dead, John.'

John shrugged. 'So be it. I failed. You have what you want so I will leave you now. Do not try to apprehend me.'

'You can't just leave…'

His expression became impatient. 'What do you want of me, Arabella?'

'Whatever wickedness you are guilty of these past days, you are still my husband.'

He gave a bitter smile. 'No. I have not been a proper husband to you for three years. And you—you are my wife, yet forbidden—inaccessible to me.'

His voice was low and hoarse and he turned his head away, but in the dim light Arabella saw his torment and for the first time there was no longer any anger in her, only sympathy which welled up in her heart towards this man she had been unable to love and had never fully understood.

A heavy silence replaced his strangely calm,

slow voice, broken only by the sound of Dickon's whimpering.

'What will you do?' Arabella asked.

He shrugged. 'Does it matter?'

'Yes—of course it matters.'

He smiled, his face giving an impression to Arabella of extraordinary resignation. 'What can I do? While ever I suffer this infernal torture—which is akin to the temptation of Tantalus—a prisoner of my own impotence that is eating me alive and will give me no respite.' He looked at Edward Grey. 'We agreed that if you won, if I returned your son to you, I would live.'

He nodded. 'You have my word.'

With that John turned and went out, disappearing into the labyrinth of dark alleyways that wrapped itself about him—as the cold, dark waters of the River Seine would do before dawn after the sharp blade of the man he had cheated at cards penetrated his heart.

When he had gone a sudden chill descended on the room.

After a moment, Arabella turned to Edward. 'Please, let us go.'

Without a word he took her elbow and led her outside where Stephen was waiting.

Clutching Dickon to her, eager to leave this awful place behind, they hurried back the way they had come. They emerged from the alley-way to find Gregory had managed to hire a coach to take them home. Not until they were within the safety of the house did they breathe a sigh of relief.

The house was in chaos. The children had refused to go to sleep until Dickon had come home and Verity was beside herself with worry. The minute they all walked through the door she was demanding to know what had happened, while Pauline fussed around, giving them all warm drinks. Arabella had worried that Dickon would not want to be parted from her, but Verity was there, taking him and shushing him as she made her way to the nursery for him to be bathed and put to bed.

When Arabella found herself alone with Edward, she walked into his outstretched arms and he held her firmly, murmuring words of comfort. She leaned into him, glad that their ordeal was over at last and that Dickon was safe. They had all been through hell these past days. When Edward would have mentioned John, she placed her fingers over his lips, silencing the words.

'Not now,' she murmured. 'Not tonight. Let it be.'

He nodded, understanding, tightening his

arms about her, content to hold her to him, knowing Arabella and his son were where they belonged.

Arabella clung to him, caring only that he was there with her and she could hold him again. Their bodies remembered each other as if they had been made to fit together, from top to toe.

Suddenly she turned in his arms and clung to him, for only in his arms could she find the peace she needed so badly.

'Will you take me to bed, Edward?' she whispered. 'I need you so much.'

'What, here?' He smiled down at her. 'My darling Bella, I can't think of anything I would like to do more than to take you to bed, but I fear my sister will not approve of such wanton behaviour beneath her roof.'

'Then hold me.'

Cradling her face between his hands, he tilted her face to his and kissed her lips softly. She had asked him not to speak of John, but he felt compelled to. 'I should never have let you go back to him. I should have stopped you somehow, despite you being his wife. He caused you pain.'

'Yes, yes, he did and the memory of the pain has not gone away yet, I fear. Every time he came near me I cringed. He would watch me like a cat toying with a mouse, knowing I was thinking of you. Even though I am here with you now, I am still not free. I am still his wife,' she said simply.

Edward held her away from him to look into her face, the deep-blue eyes serious. 'No matter what happens now, I will not let him take you back. I swear it.'

'And I will never leave you again. We are here now—together,' she said, closing her mind to her marriage. 'That is all that matters.'

The following morning John's body was pulled from the River Seine by two boatmen.

When Edward came to give Arabella the news she was alone in the garden, her thoughts still troubled over the previous night's events. Learning of John's death, she was unable to speak for she was overcome by the turmoil of her emotions, made up of a combination of shock and horror and at the same time a kind of relief that the man who had nearly destroyed her own life, and that of Edward when he had abducted his son, no longer had the power to hurt them.

When she had recovered herself she looked

at Edward. 'How can you be sure it was John?' she asked.

He nodded. 'I am sure,' he said, drawing her down on to a bench. He sat facing her, clasping her hands in his own. 'When he left us I had him followed. Apparently someone else was also in pursuit—more than likely someone who had a grievance against him—someone who had lost to him at cards. After a brief struggle your husband collapsed and his assailant was seen to throw his body into the river off the Pont Neuf, the bridge at the tip of the Île de la Cité. This time he is quite dead, Arabella. Are you surprised?'

Shaking her head slowly, she sighed. 'I am shocked that his end should be so tragic, but, no, I am not surprised—I half-expected it. At least his torment is at an end. It was a terrible thing that was done to him, which caused him a wealth of terrible suffering.'

Edward thought John Fairburn had got no less than he deserved for his treatment of his wife, but he kept his thoughts to himself. 'It's over, Arabella. You must not let your hatred for John Fairburn fester and destroy the future as it has done in the past. It is over. It is done. You must put the past behind you—along with all the misery he caused you.'

Arabella sighed. 'Sadly, the past has a habit of reasserting itself.'

'I know. But we are together now—you, me and Dickon and soon our own child. Nothing can ever change that or come between us.'

Raising her hand, he placed his lips on her fingers, holding on to it as if reluctant to let it go. Idly his thumb stroked her palm, gently, and she was sure he was aware of the waves of desire uncurling from it, moving slowly, insidiously, into her, stirring, disturbing her—making her remember the times they had made love.

Hearing her sharp intake of breath, he raised his eyes and looked at her, studying her for a moment, seeing a face of such exquisite loveliness and sweetness, understanding and love. He searched her eyes with a mixture of gentleness and gravity, a stirring of emotion swelling in his chest as he drew her close, the intensity of the love he felt for her making him ache. Placing his hands on either side of her face, he kissed her with hungry violence. A shudder shook his tall frame as she arched into him and returned his kiss.

When he released her lips, with her cheek resting against his chest, Arabella smiled. Her suffering really had been worth it, to be here in his arms, she told herself, feeling the rapid beat of his heart beneath her cheek and the rise and fall of his chest as he breathed. Her own heart began to beat with such joy it quite alarmed her, that she could feel so elated after their terrible ordeal. It was just too incredible for words.

Raising her head, she gazed at him, loving him.

Edward cupped her face between his hands. 'I love you, Arabella, so very much.'

She smiled serenely. 'I have already told you that I love you—and I do. But—what now, Edward? Where do we go from this point?'

'You know I cannot return to England now. I know you are carrying my child, but I do not expect you to share my exile and the hardships if you wish to return to Alice at Bircot Hall. Whatever you decide, I will abide by that.'

For a long time Arabella stared at him and Edward was suddenly gripped by fear that she might indeed prefer to return to England.

At length, she said, 'It depends.'

A coldness went through him. 'On what?'

'If you make me your wife.'

Edward stared at her, doubting he had heard her correctly, and then he saw she was quite serious. 'Of course I will. I thought you knew.'

She tilted her head to one side, her eyes sparkling with a teasing light. 'I don't recall you asking me. If you did, I don't remember.'

He drew her to him once more. 'You little fool. Do you really think that I would allow a child of mine to be born out of wedlock? To make you my wife is my dearest wish. Will you be my wife, Arabella?'

Arabella remembered that other time when she had thought they were to be married, but for the life of her, she could not remember her heart beating quite so erratically in her chest as it did now at his simple proposal. She considered what it would mean being married to him and sharing his life as an exile. She yearned to go back to England and to see Alice again, but nothing on earth could persuade her to part from this man who had first awakened passion within her when she had been nothing more than a girl.

Slowly she responded with a consenting nod and a lovely smile curving her soft lips. 'Then I will be happy to remain in France with you and Dickon—and our soon-to-be-born son or daughter. I want to be with you wherever that happens to be.'

They embraced passionately and their lips met, almost as if for the first time, and deep within her, Arabella felt joy spreading deeply and responded fervently to his kiss. When they finally drew apart, Edward smiled tenderly at her.

'We will be married as soon as it can be arranged.'

Since the outbreak of war there had been no cause for celebration in either family, but the wedding of Edward and Arabella, held at the palace at St Germain, was a truly joyous occasion, the guest of honour being King Charles himself. Stephen, in a state of supreme happiness, would be the next to marry, for Margaret had journeyed from England to be with him.

The room where the wedding celebrations were taking place was awash with flowers. The scent hung heavy in the air, intoxicating Arabella, or maybe it was sheer happiness that did that.

As the bride and groom embraced after saying the words that joined them together for all time, dazed, Edward looked down at his bride with pride. Her lovely face upturned to his was aglow with happiness and her amber eyes were fixed on his. Loving him.

The King, resplendent in a red-velvet suit with gold trimmings, had been watching the proceedings closely. Not one to stand on cer-

emony, he stepped forward and drew the bride
to himself.

'Allow me to be the first to congratulate you
both,' he said, his wide, full, sensual mouth
stretched in a smile. 'And permit me to kiss
the bride.'

Edward laughed, beside himself with happiness, for had he not married his own true love,
the only woman he had ever truly loved? She
was so breathtakingly beautiful, she looked like
a queen.

'Who am I to refuse a request from the King?'

Charles Stuart smiled down at Arabella, a vision in cream-and-gold satin and lace. Her hair,
a rich abundance of autumn hues, fell in soft
waves about her back and shoulders.

Arabella looked up at him, fascinated.

A chuckle accompanied his kiss when his
lips brushed her mouth, his black curling hair
caressing her cheek, and when he released her
a sudden roguish gleam twinkled in his dark
eyes, which had far too much eloquence when
he was close to a beautiful woman.

'Your wife is very lovely, Edward. You are
indeed fortunate to have found such a beauty
after so much strife. When I am restored to my
throne you must bring her to court. In fact, I
shall insist on it.'

'It will be an honour, Sire, but I am not a man who will wear a pair of horns gracefully.' Edward spoke lightly, but a well-defined eyebrow jutted sharply upward and there was subtle meaning behind his words, for it was well known that husbands were no obstacles when Charles Stuart was attracted by a beautiful woman.

Unoffended by Edward's remark—for his habits were well known—the King gave him a wink and laughed good-humouredly. 'You know me too well, Edward, but I hope you will permit me to dance with her later.'

'Of course, Sire. I have no objection.'

'Is it your intention to remain here in France, Sir Edward?' the King asked on a more serious note.

'It is. I will not return to England until you are restored to your throne, Sire. You have my absolute loyalty. I wish I could offer more.'

The King nodded slowly, his features marred by disillusion and cynicism. 'Your loyalty is quite good enough. I would present you with a gift on this your wedding day, but, alas, as everyone knows I am a pauper. However, I will make you a promise. Having fought by my side at Worcester, you have more claim on my gratitude than most. I assure you of a promise of my favour. When happier times return and I am restored to my throne, your estate and all your properties will be restored to you.'

'You are most gracious,' Edward said, bowing his head.

Later, when the celebrations were over and Arabella was alone with her husband in their bedroom at St Germain, she couldn't resist teasing him about the interest King Charles had shown in her.

Edward came to stand behind her where she sat at the dressing table. Leaning forward, he drew her hair aside and placed his lips on the warm, inviting flesh of her neck.

'It is obvious to me that he finds you pleasing, my love,' he breathed, 'but I will not share you—not even with the King of England. I love you so much that I would kill any man who tried to take you from me.'

'You need have no worries, Edward. I love you. There will never be anyone else for me. You have given meaning to my life—to everything I do. I am not complete without you. I am yours now and always.'

'I'm glad to hear it,' he murmured, meeting her eyes in the mirror, which were large and bright.

There was the faintest hint of a smile on his lips and his eyes blazed suddenly with their old vivid light. Arabella breathed deeply, then smiled at him as feelings rushed to her in a flood. He was her destiny, her future, and she would spend the night making that absolutely clear to him.

He seemed to read her mind, for they smiled at one another in perfect understanding of how things would be.

Towards the end of February fifty-two Parliament took the first step to a unified government when it passed an Act of General Pardon and Oblivion, that unilaterally forgave all of King Charles's dead father's supporters and removed them from threat of prosecution. Oliver Cromwell viewed such conciliatory policy necessary.

'It's something, at least,' Edward said to Arabella. 'Although should any of the exiles return, then they must swear an oath not to take up their swords to any future Royalist cause.'

'That should be no hardship, surely.'

'Some may think not. Robert is to return to Alice and their children. He has been away from his family too long and he is eager to be with them.' Frowning, he looked at his wife. 'I will not go back until the King comes into his own, Arabella.'

'*If* he comes into his own. There is no guarantee that will happen.'

'Then we will have to make the best of what we have right here. There will be new challenges to face and we will face them together.'

'And then we can go home?'

'That is my hope.'

Epilogue

During the following eight years, accompanied by Stephen and Margaret, Edward and Arabella followed other exiles to live in Holland. Here they raised their children and Edward gave his services to Charles Stuart in exile. They never gave up hope that one day the King would come into his own, and that day came at last.

Long oppressed beneath the mighty heel of Cromwell, the people of England began to think with longing of a restored monarchy and happier times after his death.

And so it was that in the month of May 1660, on the day of his thirtieth birthday, King Charles was restored to his throne. His ship, the *Royal Charles*, arrived at Dover, where he was received with obeisance and honour. Gripped by restoration fever, London was beginning to wake as if from a deep sleep.

The King set out with the highest intentions. All those who had remained loyal during his exile he remembered with gratitude, and he rewarded them well.

Not least Sir Edward Grey, whose estates in Oxfordshire were restored to him.

The sun was warm and shining with a brilliance that gave Edward's noble house a special glow as he strolled along the garden paths, remembering the past. With thoughts and memories drifting through his mind he smiled down at the woman whose arm was looped through his own. Words unspoken, she was occupied with similar thoughts.

At thirty-three years of age Arabella was beautiful. She had all the tenderness and happiness that brought contentment and he vowed that every day of his life, he was going to find a way to make her smile. At long last their dreams had been fulfilled.

As he gazed beyond the gardens to the undulating park, a handsome youth cantered into view on a splendid chestnut horse, a giggling Louisa, his six-year-old sister with a mop of bouncing dark curls, her little round face illuminated by a pair of huge blue eyes, tucked securely in front of him. Seeing Charles, his younger brother, riding towards them, the youth, Dickon, raised his feathered hat to his adoring parents before cantering off with his happy burden to join him.

Edward chuckled low in his throat, covering his wife's hand with his own. 'I cannot believe we have been so blessed in our children.' Arabella's amber eyes smiled up at him and there was a light in her eyes he had never seen before.

'Believe it, my love, because it is true. Everything I love most in the world is right here. I never want to leave it.'

A tremor of pleasure ran through Edward at the gladness in her lovely eyes. The vision of a future stretching endlessly before them was golden and he was certain that what they had now would flourish and blossom even more in the years ahead.

* * * * *

If you enjoyed this story, you won't want to miss these other great reads from Helen Dickson

MILLS & BOON®

& HISTORICAL

AWAKEN THE ROMANCE OF THE PAST

MILLS & BOON®

The Regency Collection – Part 1

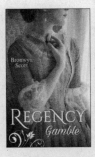

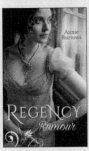

Let these roguish rakes sweep you off to the Regency period in part 1 of our collection!

Order yours at **www.millsandboon.co.uk/regency1**

MILLS & BOON®
The Regency Collection – Part 2

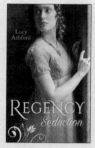

Join the London ton for a Regency
season in part 2 of our collection!

Order yours at **www.millsandboon.co.uk/regency2**

MILLS & BOON®

The Sara Craven Collection!